Enjoy The sho. V

Regards,

Dave Faulkner

davidfaulknerauthor
.com

DEAD ONES

A novel by David Faulkner

Published by BookLocker.com, Inc., Bradenton, Florida, U.S.A.

Printed on acid-free paper.

BookLocker.com, Inc.
2016

First Edition

Other Novels by David Faulkner

The Oyster Wars

The Oyster Navy

Street People

Acknowledgements

As always thanks to my family for their support

My thanks to Al DeRenzis for his friendship and counsel.

A special thanks to Paul Bendel-Simso for "being brutal" with his red pen.

Edited by Paul Bendel-Simso.

Cover art by Todd Engel.

FAHEEM

Saturday, April 10, 2010
Tarin Kowt, Afghanistan

Faheem appeared again at the front window, glanced up and down the road, and hurried back to the kitchen.

"I still don't see them, Mother."

Kamili, Faheem's Mother, smiled. "Perhaps if you waited at the window until you *do* see them, it will be easier on both you and the carpet."

Kamili's smile was radiant, and it frightened Faheem to think that, if the Taliban should return, that smile would disappear. Not merely concealed again beneath a *burqa,* but cease to exist amid the terror and dread.

The NATO military base at the edge of town gave some comfort to Faheem's family and their neighbors. However, the town fretted that when the Americans left Afghanistan the base would close, allowing the Taliban to once again inflict terror across the entire valley.

Faheem resumed her vigil at the window and was soon agonizing over her father's tardiness. Certainly the town housed informers for the Taliban, who would gleefully report that Doctor Muhammad El Safi had displayed the American flag on the living room wall of his home.

When Kamili questioned her husband about the flag, he responded that displaying the American flag was intended as a gesture of welcome to their guests and not meant to anger the Taliban.

Tarin Kowt, a dusty town of about 10,000, is situated in a mostly desolate valley of Southern Afghanistan. For the five years leading up to 2001 the area was ruled by the dreaded Taliban. By then the town had its fill of the radical Islamists, and Faheem's father joined with other town leaders to oust the Taliban's regional governor from their valley.

That November, tribesmen led by future Afghan president Hamid Karzai, aided by U.S. air strikes, successfully defended the town from an attack by 500 Taliban fighters. The Islamists were repulsed and had not returned.

In the following year, the town's tribal leaders elected Doctor El Safi to the post of district chief, which he accepted with resolve and humility. At the swearing-in, the elders begged his forgiveness that the only official vehicle the town could afford was an ancient Vespa moped freshly painted fire-engine red. It was indeed humble, but Muhammad El Safi accepted it gratefully. Thereafter, Faheem's father could be seen putt-putting about the town, proud of not missing a day of work, never failing those who counted on him.

Faheem and Kamili often wondered aloud at how El Safi managed to keep the ancient bike running.

Today, Tarin Kowt prepared to honor the arrival of Ms. Cerise Bevard, an honorary co-chair of the U.S.-Afghan Women's Council. Bevard's visit was sanctioned by the U.S. State Department, which provided her with a security detail while she was in-country.

Kamili and her children had barely slept for four days since learning that this honored American woman would spend an entire day in their humble home.

Cerise Bevard was an importer of the beautiful Afghan carpets handmade by women and girls in their homes across Afghanistan. Weaving the carpets is a cottage industry requiring talent and skill, and relying on an organized system to get the raw materials to the artisans, and their finished creations to the world market.

On behalf of the U.S.- Afghan Women's Council, Bevard sought to expand the industry into Tarin Kowt. Kamili, and the other women, were excited at the prospect of meaningful work for them and steady income for their families.

While Faheem fidgeted, her older sisters Amina Din and Diiva Khanon scoured their home, cleaning it inside and out. A third sister, Tor Pikai, worked alongside Kamili to prepare today's feast for their guests. Tor Pikai washed the vegetables for the baunjaun, a dish of eggplant, tomatoes and potatoes, and the salaata, a fresh vegetable salad of tomatoes and cucumber.

Kamili finished kneading the sweetened dough for the naan, a native flatbread, and left it covered, in a bowl, to rise. Next, she wrapped the potato filling in the fried eggroll wrappers for the bolanee.

In addition to the traditional supply of hot tea for the guests, Kamili was serving dogh, a refreshing drink of homemade yogurt stirred into a glass of cold water, along with cucumber, salt and dried mint. For dessert, rote, an Afghan sweetbread, accompanied by a bowl of firnee, a pudding made of cornstarch boiled with milk, sugar, cardamom seeds and ground pistachio. Kamili was determined to honor the Afghan tradition that no guest could leave her home hungry.

Faheem raised a hand and began to wave vigorously at Tabana Maaki who peered between the filmy curtains from a window across the street. Their homes were identical along with all of the others in the area. Two-story walls of sun-dried mud and straw supported a flat roof of wooden poles coated with the same mixture. A neighborhood of these whitewashed structures evidenced a housing project implemented by some past government.

The curtains moved in a window of the house on Tabana's right, and Faheem made out the form of Hafez Khan, a slow-witted twenty-year-old boy who never left the safety of his house. He was easily identified by the galvanized water pail which he wore over his head as protection against missile and drone attacks.

Faheem's neighbors, equally excited by news of the American woman's visit, began to line the street in anticipation of her arrival.

Doctor El Safi's red moped turned the corner and Faheem stifled a shriek of joy. During the Taliban years, there were no joyous outbursts, only screams of fear and pain. Even today a scream would freeze Kamili's heart.

Instead of screaming, Faheem clapped her hands. "They're coming, Mother", she called.. "They're finally coming!"

Muhammad El Safi waved to those lining the street before him as a Humvee and two heavily reinforced Land Rovers, each painted in camouflage, paused at the corner some yards behind.

Bobby Heavens, team leader of the security detail, rode shotgun in the first Humvee. He gripped an AK-47 in his left hand and held up the other hand in warning. "Hold up, Rich," he said. "Let's put a little more room between him and us."

As the moped slowed in front of Faheem's house, a bearded figure, clad in black, burst from the front door of the house of Hafez Kahn. Faheem, frozen with terror, watched as the hooded specter shoved his way through the onlookers.

Instinctively, Faheem began screaming as the menacing shape dashed into the street, wrapped Muhammad El Safi in a bear hug and shouted, "*Allahu Akbar*"!

The explosion shattered the windows of every house for two blocks.

2

Friday, April 23, 2010
Bethesda, Maryland, USA

Cerise Bevard stared out of a third-floor window as she waited for the surgeon to give her a status report on Faheem's surgery.

"Ms. Bevard?"

She turned and nodded at the man in blue scrubs who approached her. He spoke over the surgical mask which dangled at his throat. "I understand the Afghan child, Faheem, is in your charge?"

She nodded again.

"As for the surgery, the child came through just fine. But there is something that needs to be clarified with hospital admin."

"Yes?"

"I am told that the little paperwork we received from the hospital in Kabul identifies Faheem as a male. One of the nurses brought it to my attention that this is not the case. I conducted the appropriate exam. The patient is indeed a female."

Cerise stared a moment before saying, "I don't know what to say."

"You didn't know?"

"Of course not."

The surgeon eyed her, "Surely the doctors who treated her in Kabul must have noticed."

She shook her head. "If they did, they didn't say anything. Afghani doctors would consider that to be none of their business. In any case, no male doctor over there is going to discuss this with me, a women. I'll take care of it with your admin."

Faheem was awake and toying with the bed controls when Cerise came into the room. She walked to the bedside, trying to figure out what to say to the figure whose face and forehead were swathed in bandages.

The fatal blast that killed Faheem's father had embedded jagged shards of window glass into the child's face and upper torso as it flung her into the back wall of the living room shattering her right shoulder. Her Mother's and two of her sisters' rush to greet Doctor El Safi was delayed by their duties in the kitchen for mere seconds. It was enough time to save their lives.

Faheem had spent several days in the National Naval Medical Center at Bethesda before learning that her youngest sister, Saba, anxious to be part of the excitement, had flung open the front door just as the first blast wave reached the house. Mercifully, the child's death was instantaneous.

Cerise smiled down at Faheem. "How are you feeling?"

Faheem, speaking broken English, replied, "Not too bad," and touched her own face lightly with her useful hand. "The doctor said I could expect some pain here soon."

Cerise stepped away and dragged a small plastic chair to the bedside.

"Do you feel like talking a little?"

Faheem nodded.

Cerise sat her purse at her feet and positioned herself on the edge of the chair seat. "Faheem, forgive me, but the hospital says we must talk about this."

The child waited.

"Your Mother told me your name is Faheem. In your country that is the name for a male child; a female child would be called. Faheema." Cerise paused, waiting to see if she had been understood.

"I am a *bacha posh*," Faheem cried. "Do you know it?"

Cerise shook her head.

"It means 'dressed up as a boy.' It is an ancient custom in Afghanistan, though it is not much spoken about."

Cerise squeezed the girl's hand. "I would like to know how such a thing came about, if you feel up to talking about it."

Faheem nodded. "I will tell all that I know from my Mother and father. I was the fourth child, all girls, and the only one born during the reign of the Taliban. My Mother became very sad. All my father's family was angry with her for not giving my father a son to pass on the family name. They blamed her, and my father was saddened by the way she was treated by them. Also, an Afghanistan family must produce a male child to have a good name. The women in our town were also mean to my Mother."

Faheem's voice had become dry and scratchy. She licked her lips and tried to swallow. "Could I please have that glass of water with the straw that bends?"

The girl took the glass and sipped some water.

"Thank you. I will go on-—there were other reasons for me to become a *bacha posh*. First, I should tell you that my girl name was Faheema so it was quite easy to become Faheem."

It occurred to Cerise that the child was not offering excuses for her family's action, merely trying her best to explain it in terms that Cerise would understand.

"Under the Taliban, girls were not allowed to get an education. My family had no way to know that the Islamists would be driven away in a few years. As a boy I was able to go to school. Also, girls were forbidden to go out of the house without a male relative along. When I got older my duty was to serve as the male relative to walk with my Mother and sisters when they went to the market."

Cerise stood. "That's enough for now. You should rest."

"Please, just this. After the Taliban was driven out, as a *bacha posh* I could work for the American soldiers during the day. I shined boots and fetched things they needed."

Cerise smiled. "Fetched?"

A faint smile appeared on Faheem's face. "Fetched. It means—"

"I know what it means. It sounds odd coming from an Afghani."

"Being among the soldiers, I learned their language. I know many bad words, do you want to hear some?"

Cerise touched Faheem's hand. "No, thank you. That's enough for today. We will talk more next time I visit."

On Monday morning, Cerise was in her carpet showroom, the Magic Carpet, on M Street in Georgetown, by 7:30. This gave her time to check her email, and make some phone calls before the shop opened at 10 o'clock. She scrolled through her email, scanning and readily discarding most of the messages until she found the one she was expecting.

> Good Morning.
> I am redecorating my office and am interested in the latest selection of handmade carpets. I understand you have some new items from Afghanistan. Please let me know when I might stop in to see them.
> Regards,
> SW

Cerise provided the required response and then deleted both messages from her tablet.

At 8:45 she left her desk and hurried out of the store, locking the front door behind her. With a nonchalant turn of the head, her trained eyes swept the vehicles on M Street and the few pedestrians in her midst, before she turned to saunter east toward Thomas Jefferson Street.

Satisfied that she had attracted no following, she rounded the corner and continued toward Baked & Wired, a trendy neighborhood coffee shop and bakery. She felt a little silly taking such caution— this was Washington, D.C., after all, not Moscow or Vienna. Still, she was comforted by the knowledge that no interloper would evade the watchful eyes of Bobby Heavens, trailing a block behind her across M Street.

There were only two ahead of her in the bakery line. She added a steaming cup of dirty chai to the breakfast biscuit on her tray and proceeded to a table for two in the back room. She was not surprised that the man already seated at the table was the only other occupant of the small space. She was confident that it would remain so as long as Simon Wedge wished.

Baked & Wired is popular with students and faculty at nearby Georgetown University, and the man at the table appeared to have strolled over from the campus, perhaps having just given a philosophy lecture. Today, he wore a lumpy tweed smoking jacket with leather elbow patches over a maroon Henley-style shirt, with the top button open. He shifted in his chair, revealing baggy mustard-colored corduroys and crossed bare ankles above tasseled loafers.

His blond hair was unkempt. Seemingly, the most attention he gave it was to quickly run his fingers through it before leaving the house.

He smiled and raised a steaming cup of latte in greeting.

Prior to Cerise leaving government service a few years before, she and Simon had served together in several countries around the globe. Cerise had judged him to be about her age then, mid-thirties, and she had seen a vague resemblance to the actor Robert Redford; maybe just around the eyes.

She had wondered if this man found her attractive as well, and, if so, would there be more between them? One afternoon, in Sudan, she thought the circumstances might be right for more, but he was all business. Just the same as every other time.

Where did he go at night?

Lately he was using the name Simon Wedge. She was certain that name was no closer to being his true identity than the other names he had used over the years.

Several months ago, Cerise opened her boutique rug shop, and began frequent buying trips to the Middle East. Her travels always included Afghanistan and Pakistan, with an occasional side trip to Iran. A few days after returning from her initial overseas trip, she received a phone call at the store from a man inquiring about a particular Afghan carpet that had caught his eye on the internet. She knew the voice at once.

"I don't think I have that particular pattern, but you should stop in and look at my inventory. I'm certain you'll see something that appeals to you", she said.

In lieu of coming to the store, he suggested they meet for an after-work cocktail at the L2 Longue in Cady's Alley.

L2 is a late-evening membership club catering to Washington's elite and boasting secluded alcoves for greater privacy. Fortunately, this was a Wednesday, the only day the longue opened for happy hour or "Apres Work Wednesday," as it was billed.

After a few minutes catching up, Simon asked several detailed questions about who she met and what she saw while abroad. He stuck to the standard procedure for debriefing a private citizen, though he knew full well Cerise had conducted hundreds of such interviews during her own career.

They repeated this routine each time she returned from such a trip. Other than these debriefings, she did not see or hear from the man she knew as Simon Wedge.

Now she sat her tray on the table. "Good morning," she said and seated herself across from him. "I assume you want to hear about the attack in Tarin Kowt."

Simon nodded. "Naturally. I was copied on the after-action report from Kabul, but they always omit something."

Cerise nibbled on her breakfast biscuit as she struggled with memories of that horrible morning. She shook her head and began. "As you know, I was there under the auspices of the State Department to encourage Afghani women in the art and science of producing carpets in their homes. That day we were in Tarin Kowt, at the invitation of Doctor Muhammad El Safi, the town's district chief, 'mayor,' if you will. El Safi had helped Karzai eject the Taliban from the town in '01 and was a big supporter of his.

"Because of El Safi's close ties to the country's president, he was elected—probably not the right word—'chosen,' to be the town's chief. His official vehicle was an ancient bright-red Vespa and I'm told he spent long days on that bike, darting about the town as he worked to get children educated—especially girls—and secure a better life for women—the carpet cottage industry is a good example of that. All of this made him a target for the Taliban; I suspect his assassination was inevitable."

Simon waited until Cerise had sipped some coffee and nibbled some more biscuit before saying, "According to the report, the assassin was wired with C4 so it would appear that you and your team were lucky to have survived."

Cerise shook her head. "Luck wasn't involved. Bobby Heavens, the leader of the State Department security team, told the driver of the lead vehicle to hold up at the corner, a long city block behind Doctor El Safi. We were just beginning to move forward when the blast erupted."

Simon drank his coffee without comment, and she added, "The report must have listed the dead and wounded, so I don't need to repeat that."

Simon nodded and watched her closely. "What else?"

Matching his gaze she asked, "Are you familiar with the term *bacha posh* ?"

Simon shook his head.

"It means 'dressed up as a boy.' Doctor El Safi's youngest child is a girl who, for several years, has lived her life as the family's male child."

Simon's shrug meant *I don't get it.*

"That child, who I knew as Faheem, was severely wounded in the suicide bombing at El Safi's home. Believing Faheem to be a boy, and knowing how important a son is in the Afghani culture, I took responsibility for Faheem's recovery. I thought it was the least I could do to honor Doctor El Safi's sacrifice.

"I wheedled the State Department into paying most of the cost and got Faheem flown over here and admitted to the military hospital at Bethesda."

Simon sat his empty cup on the table and glowered at a student who appeared in the doorway, looking for a place to set his tray. The boy hesitated for a second before deciding not to challenge the man who might very well be a professor from his school.

"The fine points of the Afghani culture is not my forte, so I'm uncertain about the significance of being a *bacha posh.* Please enlighten me."

Cerise dabbed at her lips with a paper napkin. "This is new to me as well," she explained. "I asked Faheem about it, after the surgeon inquired why his patient was listed as a male when that was obviously not the case. Faheem spoke briefly about her own situation and I filled in most of the cultural blanks from the internet."

Simon's brief nod signaled impatience for her to continue.

"With rare exceptions, women have lived deplorable lives in Afghanistan for generations. They are forbidden to appear outside of their homes unless fully concealed from head to toe, and must be in the company of a male family member. They are subject to being stoned or beaten for speaking to a male who is not a relative. In many families, girls are openly abused by their fathers and brothers merely for being alive. Often, their own Mothers are abusive, being embarrassed for failing to bear a male child."

Cerise paused to sip some water, ignoring her coffee, which had grown cold.

"Men are often ashamed," she continued, "of being married to a woman who has only borne them daughters.

"I could go on ad infinitum, but you add what I just said, to the benefits to the family of having a *bacha posh*—a boy can hold a job outside the home; he can fulfill the requirement for a male companion to his Mother and sisters; the father and Mother are spared the humiliation of not producing a son, the list goes on. By the time Faheema was born her parents had given up all hope of having a male child. They agreed that Faheema should become Faheem."

Simon interrupted with a raised hand. "I have a couple of questions."

Cerise laughed. "Only a couple?"

"For the time being. How old is it?"

"It?"

"This he-she."

Cerise scowled her displeasure. "I am told that *Faheem* is fourteen."

"How long do you plan to keep it?"

"Please stop referring to Faheem as *it*. And that question can't be answered—yet. Faheem has to undergo at least one more surgery. There has been no discussion about if, or when, she might return to Afghanistan."

"At her age, she won't be able to conceal her real sex for much longer, and this *bacha posh* thing will be history."

Cerise shook her head. "Not necessarily. It depends on the person. Many women have remained *bacha posh* into their twenties and thirties before marrying and having children. In some cases, they have lived this lie for their entire lives. I ran across an old Afghani proverb about the *bacha posh* which speaks volumes: "Sex is determined at birth, gender is not."

Simon Wedge glanced at his watch and stood. "You have given me a lot to think about. I'll be in touch," he said and left the room.

3

Wednesday, April 28, 2010
Washington, D.C.

It was just after 2p.m. when Cerise received her next summons from Simon Wedge. She smiled as she unscrambled the location he had chosen for their meeting. She deleted all of her emails, walked to the front of her empty shop and placed a "Back in 1 hour" sign in the lower-left corner of the display window.

Today, she walked west on M Street for two blocks, to a quiet dessert cafe operated by three sisters simply known as, the Pie Sisters. The short distance offered little opportunity to identify anyone tracking her. Apparently, Simon was more concerned with pie than tradecraft.

Cerise found Simon Wedge seated at a table for two in a rear corner of an otherwise empty room. She set a cup of black coffee on the table and slid into the other chair.

"What, no pie?" He asked and took in a healthy portion of his favorite, bourbon chocolate pecan.

She shook her head. "If I dared to, I would succumb to the Key lime with a graham cracker crust."

Cerise drank some coffee and waited quietly while Simon savored his treat.

Eventually she asked, "Did you call this meeting just so you could have pie? Or do we have business to discuss?"

Simon, his mouth full, held up one finger before retrieving a package from the floor beside his chair. He placed the bag beside Cerise's cup, motioned for her to open it and returned to meticulously scraping the crumbs from his plate.

From the bag, Cerise removed a gift wrapped box and placed it beside her cup. "What is this?"

Simon, appearing pleased with himself, dabbed at his mouth with a paper napkin. "It is a gift for your visitor. A Dell laptop, with Microsoft Office and Skype, among other software."

She paused, looked at him over the cup rim and returned it to the table without taking a drink. "What's going on?" She asked.

Simon shrugged. "From what you said, it sounds like your guest will be recuperating for some time. We—I thought it would be more pleasant if it could stay in contact with its family and chat over the internet. It must have some friends over there."

Cerise's face colored at Simon's repeated use of the impersonal pronoun when referring to Faheem. Through clenched teeth she hissed, "Has it occurred to you that I am no longer required to put up with your bullshit? I agreed to be debriefed after my trips overseas because it is the right thing to do. I know that a couple of items I disclosed to you turned out to be gems. Both were single-source and were obtained at some personal risk. You wouldn't have gotten that information anywhere else. It's likely you received a financial attaboy from on high for those treasures."

She raised her cup to drink, but her hands shook so that she carefully returned it to the table. "So cut the crap. What's *really* going on?"

Simon, stunned by her response, carefully considered his next words. "We need eyes and ears in-country, regardless of how innocent those ears may appear. We would be derelict in our duty if we didn't monitor any lines of communication inside Afghanistan that come to our attention."

"Surely that can be done more impersonally. What about our friends at Fort Meade? Aren't they listening anymore?"

"They can't sweep up everything. As it is, they can't find enough analysts with the language skills to keep up with the current workload. Unless your guest is contacted by a flagged source it is unlikely that anyone at Fort Meade would hear a word of it."

Simon waited and, receiving no response, added, "Are you are convinced that this person is no threat to homeland security?"

Cerise snorted her reply, clearly disgusted by the suggestion.

Simon smiled. "Then we shouldn't hear anything scary. In today's world, anyone with any sense has to expect that communications involving Afghanistan are being monitored. If you denied to someone that anyone was listening in, they wouldn't believe you.

"Given this Faheem's background, she has got to be ultra-naive ..."

Cerise did not bother to deny it.

"... In our digital world, youngsters are often victimized by scheming online predators. Consider this an early-warning-system for Faheem's protection."

She stood and plucked the package from the table.

"I still don't like it."

4

Monday, May 3, 2010
Bethesda, Maryland

The Lincoln stopped at the front steps of a columned veranda that spanned the front of the house. Bobby Heavens got out, dutifully scanning the grounds as he mounted the steps and disappeared through the front entrance.

Cerise smiled. "I hope you like it here."

Faheem shifted in the back seat, careful to minimize the pain probing her scalp. She gaped through the sedan's windows. "How many families live in this vast *kor*?"

"Just me, alone, and now you and I."

Bobby appeared at the top of the front step, nodded to Cerise and came to the passenger-side rear door.

"What about him—Mister Bobby. Is he your *kiawand*?"

"My husband? No." Cerise gave a low chortle. "Bobby is almost young enough to be my son, if I had one. He works for our State Department and has an apartment there."

She pointed to a three-car garage close to the house.

Faheem was puzzled. "Mister Bobby lives with your motor cars?"

"No, no dear. He has a very comfortable apartment above the garage. Come now let's get you inside."

Bobby Heavens had placed the girl's few belongings in a second-floor bedroom and was gone.

The procedure of leaving the hospital and the subsequent trek home had exhausted Faheem.

Cerise steered her to a heavily cushioned chaise longue on a screened-in patio and helped her get comfortably situated.

"Just rest while I find us some lunch," Cerise said and disappeared into the dark coolness of the house.

Though unusually warm for May in Maryland, the sheltering trees made it quite comfortable. Faheem found it a welcome change from the stagnant heat of her home in the Uruzgan Province of Afghanistan.

The child ate a slow and visibly painful lunch. It was the first food she had been required to chew since being airlifted from Tarin Kowt to Kabul.

Now she lifted her head and sipped iced tea through a straw as she admired the lush grounds beyond the screened windows.

"You have such a lovely *kor*, Miss Cerise. And my sandwich is quite well. The meat is unknown to me. May I ask what it is?"

"If you are concerned that it might be pork, not to worry I am acquainted with the Muslim religion. It is pastrami, which is cured beef. I'm glad you like it."

Neither of them spoke for several minutes. Faheem lay motionless, her eyes closed.

Cerise was considering how she might leave the patio without disturbing Faheem's nap when the girl stirred.

"I am sorry to speak of this again but I worry about what is to become of me. What should I to do about being a *bacha posh* in America?"

Cerise had not expected such a question and she needed time to consider an answer.

The girl's head was swathed in surgical dressing, making it impossible to read her facial expressions.

"Have you been comfortable—happy—in your role, pretending to be a boy?"

Faheem sighed. "Our word for "happy" is *kosha'la*. I am very sad to say but that is a word that has had no meaning in my country for many years. It is not much spoken in Afghanistan. So, the best I can say to you is that I do not hate being a *bacha posh*. It lets me help my Mother and sisters. Also, I can wander to many places that are forbidden to me as a girl."

Gingerly, she moved her head to face Cerise. "Who would you like me to be while I am in America?"

Cerise's instinct was to respond— *be yourself.* But in her own life, Cerise had often been required to assume the persona of someone else, in order to survive in a temporary environment. Wasn't that, after all, what Faheem was doing?

Instead, Cerise said, "You may have no choice by the time you return home."

"I don't know what you are saying?"

Cerise, with no experience discussing a teen girl's changing body with the girl, was hesitant. "What I meant was that it won't be many months and you will not be able to conceal your woman's body beneath the clothing of a boy."

Faheem felt the heat of her own embarrassment reach the bandages covering her skin. With no response to give, she said nothing.

Cerise asked, "Do you know any fully developed women who have remained a *bacha posh*?"

Faheem shook her head. "No," she whispered.

An edgy silence followed before Faheem gathered the courage to say, "We have not said of this, but I have wonder: Am I to be going home to Tarin Kowt when I am healed?"

Cerise had not spoken directly to Kamili, the girl's Mother, since leaving Afghanistan. Would her wish be that her daughter remain safely in America until the fighting stopped at home, or would she insist that Faheem return home as soon as she was able?

Arrangements had been made for Kamili to receive periodic updates on her daughter's condition through the U.S.-Afghan Woman's Council. For Cerise, the girl's future had been weighed in terms of her next treatment, thus she had no answer prepared about Faheem's future beyond that.

"The doctor said that you need to recover your strength to ready yourself for the next operation. In the meantime, I will be able to talk to Kamili and we can figure out what's best for you after you have fully recovered."

"Oh, *Mor*. When may I soon talk with her?"

"Close your eyes and I'll have a surprise for you when you wake-up."

Faheem opened her eyes to find Cerise seated across the room thumbing through a back issue of *Cosmopolitan* magazine.

"Feeling better?"

Faheem patted very gently at the gauze dressing of her wounds. "They feel not to hurt so much."

"Good. Come with me. I have a surprise for you."

"What is a surprise?"

"Sorry. A nice gift for you."

Faheem closely trailed Cerise through the formal dining room, down a carpeted hallway decorated with a bronze and red textured wallpaper, into a small den. Cerise had converted the room into a home office with an array of glass cabinets and table tops of dark-gray steel from Ikea.

Faheem was shown to a table-top desk fitted into a three-window bay looking out over the spacious back yard. Situated in the center of the desk was a laptop computer, and tears stung the girl's face when she realized the *burqa*-clad form filling the screen was her Mother, Kamili.

"Oh, Mother," Faheem cried as Cerise guided her into the swivel chair in front of the screen. "Why are you all covered up? Did the Taliban return?"

"Praise to Allah. When your aunt Adila learned that I was to be exposed on this machine, she warned me to remain modest. Males can spy on a woman who shows herself on such a machine. They are perverts and some of them have machines that can see beneath a woman's dress. It is better for you, our —son—you don't have to be concerned about such things. Don't let the Christians change you back to Faheema, you are Faheem, the head of our family, now that your father has gone to Allah."

Did her Mother not see that Faheem's head was still covered in bandages? *How can she not ask about my own pain*? Faheem wanted to scream, *Am I required to cry out, before you—my own Mother— Feel my pain?*

Disheartened, Faheem swiveled her chair in search of support from Cerise, only to find herself alone in the room.

She faced around to the screen and replied," Oh, Mother, I am Faheem!"

Gently, Faheem touched the dressing covering her scars. "Soon, I will return to the hospital for more pain. Praise Allah, I will come to you as soon as I am healed."

"I don't like talking into this evil machine. My son, do not forget *Jumu'ah*. You will attend Friday service with the other men."

Kamili raised a hand and pointed at her own head. "Remember, it is important for you to be a *bacha posh* up here."

Before Faheem could respond she was staring at a blank screen.

5

Wednesday, May 12, 2010
Bethesda, Maryland

Cerise had spent most of the day in the hospital at Faheem's bedside, after the child's latest and, hopefully, final surgery.

In the back seat of the Lincoln, with Bobby Heavens driving, she took a call from Simon Wedge, who was insistent that they meet for dinner. She was firm that she would not travel into the District at this time of day, even with a driver.

Simon grumbled an agreement to meet at La Panetteria, off Wisconsin Avenue in Bethesda.

Cerise arrived at the restaurant to find Simon ensconced at a table for two in front of a massive fresco of a canal in Venice. He welcomed her by waving a piece of fried calamari on its way to be dipped in a dish of marinara sauce. "Dig in. This is as good as that *ristorante* in Tuscany."

Simon poured some chianti into her wineglass as Cerise took the seat across from him.

"Please forgive me if I don't join in your salute to 'the good old days.' What was so urgent that I just *had* to meet you *tonight*? Right now, I'm thinking you invited me so that you could charge this lavish meal to Uncle Sam."

Simon finished pouring her wine and set the bottle down before holding his own glass up in salute.

"I was lonesome. Relax. If this operation is a success, the taxpayers will look on this dinner for two as chump change."

Cerise sipped her wine while she tried to read his face. Was he being sincere, or merely softening her up for what was coming? Simon Wedge was, by trade, a polished liar, which required that there be a nugget of truth in every statement he made. For her, the question

28

remained: Was it worth the struggle required of her to search out the nugget that would be buried in tonight's conversation?

She selected a crisp piece of calamari and touched it gently to the marinara sauce. "Simon, you can be very charming if the need arises, and, you can be a world-class bullshit artist when it serves you. It's been a long day and I'm too tired to sort it all out tonight, so I'll eat the food and drink the wine and leave the moral considerations up to you."

She picked up a menu. "Let's order."

Simon Wedge reached for the menu beside his plate. "The *frutti di mare* is highly recommended."

As their server left with the menus, Simon topped off both glasses and laid the empty bottle on its side, as notice that he required a replacement.

"I'm going to make every effort to be Charming Simon tonight. I'll start off by inquiring about the condition of our guest."

"The operation went well and Faheem should be home in two or three days."

Reading the look on Simon's face she added, "By that I mean my house in Bethesda. You should know that before Faheem went into the hospital she said that she had chosen to return to Afghanistan as a male child, and begged me not to tell anyone in the U.S. any differently. I trust that you will abide by this wish and will cease referring to Faheem in derogatory terms."

Simon showed both palms in surrender.

"The doctor said that the post-op recovery would be six to eight weeks requiring regular follow-up visits to his office. That doesn't leave much time for whatever you are cooking up."

"We can be very flexible, when required."

They both reached for their wineglasses as the wait staff arrived to deliver their dinners. With their plates in front of them, Cerise returned her glass to the table and picked up a fork. "Let's hear what you have dreamed up."

Simon had ordered the *agnello alla griglia* and now smiled with satisfaction as he tasted his entree. "This leg of lamb is seasoned to perfection. Your salmon?"

"It's fine. It would taste even better if it was not for the side order of your crap."

"Has Faheem talked about attending *Jumu'ah* services, and which mosque she might use?"

"She's too concerned about getting well to think about anything like that."

Simon washed down a piece of lamb with a swallow of chianti before saying, "When she does consider services, we would like you to point her toward a mosque that is of particular interest to us."

"How can you be so sure that she will want to attend services here in the U.S.?"

"Apparently you weren't in the room when she spoke to Kamili in Afghanistan."

Cerise paused as she forked a wedge of salmon. "I was not," she said, "But clearly, you were."

Simon ignored her look and carved off another slice of the *agnello*. "Do you know the Islamic Center on Mass Avenue?"

"I've driven passed it."

Simon paused his fork for emphasis.

"Kamili did not bother to ask Faheem about her wounds, which made the girl very unhappy. She was too afraid the machine was looking up her dress. She told Faheem to remember that she was the *man* of the family, to attend *Jumu'ah,* Friday prayer, *with the other men,* and disappeared from the screen."

Simon glanced around the bustling restaurant. "That is my answer to the question about the urgency of our meeting. I needed to get that message to you before the child committed to a mosque. Why it was so urgent, we can discuss at another time."

"Of course, we will. You have no choice but to fill me in, if you expect me to lead Faheem where you want her to go."

6

Tuesday, May 18, 2010
Bethesda, Maryland

"Mister Wedge's office."
"Cerise Bevard for Mister Wedge."
"I'm sorry, but he is unavailable. Is there a message?"
"Please remind him that it is *imperative* I speak with him before Friday."
"I will see that he gets the message."
"Thank you."

Cerise chuckled over her use of Wedge's own word to mock the urgent nature of her message. Would he get it? Probably. Very little got past him. She hung up the telephone and walked out to the sun porch where Faheem was stretched out on a chaise longue.

From time to time, since Faheem's return from the hospital, Cerise purposely cast herself as someone seeing the child for the first time. Would such a person readily accept her as a male?

She took a seat by the window and re-examined the napping form. The gauze encasing her head had been replaced by a few localized dressings revealing the youthful texture of her face. Dark tresses, shorn pre-op, had reappeared as a dark fuzz covering her scalp, advancing the notion that this person was a teenage boy.

Cerise cast her eyes over Faheem's clothing. Baggy fleece pants and an oversize grey sweatshirt, purchased from J.C. Penny, served to perpetuate the *bacha posh* myth. The absence of any bumps on the girl's chest confirmed the notion that Faheema could remain Faheem, at least for the ensuing months. Probably enough time to suit the government's needs.

When Faheem opened her eyes, she was alone. She yawned and reached for the hand mirror on the floor beside her longuer. With the mirror, she considered the area around each surgical scar as she pressed on it with a gentle fingertip. Faheem was pleased to find that there was no inflammation and a minimum amount of soreness at each site.

Cerise appeared and placed a tray, with two china cups of tea and a plate of cookies, on the glass table between them.

"Oh, Miss Cerise, I am happy to be much healed." Faheem touched her face in various spots. "See. Such little hurting. Not like before."

"That is wonderful," Cerise replied as she poured two steaming cups of tea. "Do you feel like talking about your future while we have some tea.?"

"Yes. Please. Before we say that, I am so sorry that you have to be away from your rug store to watch me. Has it been closed all of these days?"

Cerise laughed. "You give me a good reason to be away from the shop. And no, it is not closed. I have a part-time person who does a good job for me."

"I am pleased. I was afraid that you would lose business for me."

Cerise smiled and saucered her tea cup. "This is Tuesday. If you think you will feel like attending *Jumu'ah* prayer on Friday, we should talk about it."

"Yes, please. We can talk now. *Mor* said I should go to Friday prayers with the other men. Suddenly the child's face and scalp were flooded with a scarlet tinge.

Alarmed, Cerise cried, "Why are you so red? Are you sick?"

Faheem lowered her gaze to the carpet. "So sorry. It is caused by my evil thoughts."

"Please tell me."

She turned her back on Cerise before saying, "I cannot say it at your face."

"Go on."

"The men's group are always at the front of the mosque, with the women's group in the back. That was not always so. I was told that the Prophet made it so, because the men were tempted by the sight of the women's bodies laying on a prayer rug in front of them. Do you think it is so?"

Cerise waited until Faheem turned to face her before replying, "I don't know, but it could be."

"If it is so, that makes me very ashamed to be a Muslim man."

"Don't be. It sounds like men everywhere."

"Even here? In America?"

Cerise nodded and rose to clear away the tea service. "Most especially here," she said.

Cerise returned to the sun porch to find Faheem gone. Knowing the girl's fascination with the computer, she went directly to the den.

In the few days she was in the house between hospital visits, Faheem spent hours exploring the vast expanse of the internet. Occasionally, when Cerise was busy in another room, the child would shout, summoning her to share a wondrous discovery.

Cerise, though well aware of the perils lurking along the information superhighway, had neither the time, nor felt it necessary, to monitor Faheem's internet travel. That was being taken care of elsewhere.

The girl seemed engrossed in educating herself about the world. Besides, she had no friends with whom to discuss mischief on social sites. Cerise would never admit it to Simon Wedge, but she was comforted knowing that he would alert her to any internet threat encountered by Faheem.

"There you are," Cerise called as she entered the den. "Have you found something interesting?"

"Oh, yes. On Google I have discovered that there are many *masjids* around us. Google, what a funny name."

Cerise leaned closer to the screen and followed as Faheem scrolled down the page listing the mosques in the Washington, D.C., area.

After a moment's silence, Faheem ceased scrolling with a sigh. "With so many, but I cannot walk to any of them from this house."

Cerise patted the girl's shoulder. "Do not worry about that. Mister Bobby will be pleased to drive you."

"And wait outside while I am praying?"

"If necessary."

"But—"

"We'll talk about that after you decide which *masjid* you would like to attend."

Faheem pulled up a Google Map page displaying clusters of Islamic mosques and Islamic culture centers in the District of Columbia and its environs.

"Please point to me, where is this house on the map?"

Cerise pinpointed the Bethesda neighborhood where they were, then moved her finger to cover a cluster of three green markers, saying, "These three look to be the nearest to us. Find their names."

Faheem quickly identified them as The Islamic Center on Massachusetts Avenue, a community center on Georgia Avenue and another center on 4th Street N.W. She lingered at each site, pulling up street pictures of the building and the surrounding area.

Cerise hesitated before saying, "Which one seems right to you?"

"Of these, which is closest to us?"

"It's hard to tell precisely, however, it seems this one is closer than the others. She pointed to the Islamic Center, 2551 Mass Ave. N.W., on Embassy Row. "The others are not much farther. You pick the one you feel good about."

Faheem looked up at her. She was smiling. "I'm very glad that one is close. The buildings of the Islamic Center are most beautiful."

Cerise smiled with relief. She had not been required to compel the child to attend the Islamic Center. It had been Faheem's own wish. That may seem a small matter today, but when whatever Simon Wedge had planned was over, this seemingly insignificant fact might be all that she had to cling to.

7

Friday, May 21, 2010
2551 Mass Avenue N.W. Washington, D.C.

Today they were in the blue Audi. It was several years old and
seldom driven, but Cerise knew that Bobby Heavens preferred it to
maneuvering the boxy Lincoln in D.C. traffic.

Faheem was seated alongside Cerise in the back seat, relishing the
passing scene as they turned off of Rock Creek Parkway and climbed
up Waterside Drive. As they rounded a curve and slowed for the red
light at Mass Ave. Faheem gasped, "Praise Allah! It is even more
beautiful in real life!"

Despite her feelings of hostility toward radical Islamists, Cerise
was taken by the brilliance of the massive white mosque agleam in the
mid-morning sunshine. If not for the slender minaret scaling the sky
above the otherwise flat roof, a visitor to the city could mistake this
temple for the White House, several blocks to the east.

Previously, when being chauffeured along Embassy Row, Cerise
had been engrossed in correspondence or social media, purposely
ignoring the splendid structure as she sped past.

"It is awe-inspiring," she admitted. "I envy you the emotion you
will experience when you walk through the entryway."

Faheem glanced at her with tears in her eyes. "If you wear a scarf,
you could come in with me."

Cerise shook her head. "Do you know what it means to be a
hypocrite?"

Faheem shook her head.

"It is not a good thing but that is what I would be if I walked in
there."

For Cerise, the pain in her chest was as close as she would come to
experiencing the anguish a Mother must feel as she leaves her only
child at the curb on the first day of school. What Simon Wedge had in

mind for Faheem was still a mystery which made this day much harder to bear.

She took a breath. "Bobby," she said, "Please pull to the curb."

To Faheem, she said, "We will return to this same spot to pick you up." Smiling, she added, "Remember to kneel with the men."

Faheem passed through the wrought-iron gate, the colorful hand-woven prayer rug Cerise had given her folded neatly under her right arm.

She had spent hours browsing the internet sites dedicated to the Center, intrigued by the color photos of the imposing structure.

Faheem had read of the Center's origin during the Eisenhower administration, the famed Italian architect who had used tiles from Turkey, Persian rugs from Iran and a glittering bronze chandelier from Egypt to create this opulent Islamic Center.

Faheem entered the *musalla,* a vast carpeted prayer room. It was hard for her to make out the far wall in the dim light, but the room would need to be vast, for she had read that thousands attend *Jumu'ah* prayers here each Friday. The flow of supplicants pressing around her attested to the truth of that number.

There could be no room in all of Heaven more beautiful than this room, she marveled.

Surely, God would heed prayers chanted from such a temple before he would listen to those spoken in a humble mud building in Tarin Kowt. That must be why God did not hear our prayers asking Him to protect my father during his daily rounds.

After prayers were recited, Faheem stood and very deliberately folded her prayer rug to allow the crowd around her to disperse. Though she craved to engage in a conversation with another Pashto speaker, she hesitated for fear that to do so might somehow reveal her as a *bacha posh.*

Instead, Faheem harkened to the rich babble of dialects and Middle East languages which burst forth all around her. As she observed the men in her midst, a gust of cold fear flashed along her spine.

Online, Cerise had bought her several sets of clothing identical to those worn by the Afghani men around her. Today, Faheem wore a maroon *kurta,* the popular collarless men's shirt, and a navy-blue *shalwar,* loose pajama-like trousers. Her hair was returning as a black fuzz which she covered with a *pakol,* a flat cap of black wool.

The men around her appeared as did she: dark skin, slender builds, clad in dark colored *kurtas* and baggy *shalwar* or *tunban* lower garments. She had believed they all looked alike until she realized the others were bearded; some wore bushy black full facial hair, others were neatly trimmed along the jaw and chin. She was not bearded. Not now, not later.

How much time did she have before her deception would become obvious? Certainly more than one year, but very likely less than two. When she reached sixteen with no evidence of facial hair, others would become suspicious. By then, she would be back in Afghanistan where, unlike here in America, someone would certainly report their suspicions to the religious police.

"*Assalami alaykum.*"

It was a moment before Faheem realized the throng had thinned and the traditional Islamic greeting, "Peace be upon you," was directed at her from behind. She turned to see a man in Muslim attire staring at her. He stood with his arms folded inside the baggy sleeves of his *kameez.* It was the black abyss of his eyes that fascinated her. She started to respond in English. which she knew would be a terrible insult, for she recognized that he was the imam who had led the prayer service. Never had she been so near to a holy man, and to have one speak directly to her was unthinkable.

Frightened, she was barely able to give the response expected of a true believer.

"*Wa alaykumus salaam*" —"And upon you."

Her wish of conversing with another in her native tongue had come true. But, it was frightening.

The imam continued speaking in Pashto. "I am the imam. I do not believe I have seen you kneeling with the other men before."

Is he saying I should not be with the men because I am a girl? But how can he know?

Faheem willed herself to keep looking into those eyes and shook her head.

"I have only just come to America and have not been to this center before."

The imam inclined his head, slightly and passed a bare hand over her face. "I would have recalled a lad with such a beautiful face. What are the circumstances of your presence in this country?"

Faheem had prepared herself for this question; someone would ask it. "I am a student here on an international grant."

"And may I ask your age?"

She had decided to give herself an extra year before the absence of facial hair would become a problem. "I am thirteen,"

I am becoming a good liar.

He must have noticed the fading scars on her face. *What will I say if he asks about them?*

Faheem shrank away as he reached out and very gently touched her cheek. "I can see you have suffered pain. Do not be alarmed, my child, such features are to be admired. Like chiseled ivory."

He took her hand. "Allow me to show you where to store your prayer rug, so it will be here on your next visit."

8

Monday, May 24, 2010
Tyson's Corner, Virginia

Cerise sat in the front passenger's seat as Bobby Heavens weaved the Audi through the I-495 traffic crossing the American Legion Bridge into Northern Virginia. Though just after 7 p.m., it was still rush hour around the nation's capital.

Within minutes, he was letting her out at the front entrance to Tyson's Galleria, a tony three-level shopping mall in Tyson's Corner.

Cerise rode an elevator to the third level confident that Bobbie Heavens had retained the evasion skills he learned during his training. She paused in front of a shop window to smooth her gray knit dress and check the reflected walkway behind her.

Satisfied that she was not followed, she entered Wildfire, a Chicago-style steakhouse billed as a 1940s supper-club.

After giving a name to the *maitre d'* she was led to The Wine Room, one of the restaurant's six rooms reserved for small private parties. Simon Wedge was seated at a table for two next to a back-lit glass-encased wall of wines. She was certain they would be the sole occupants of the room, for as long as they chose to stay.

In lieu of rising, Simon Wedge saluted her arrival with his glass. To the *maitre d'* he said, "Bring her one of these."

Cerise stopped the staffer with a raised hand. "Let me look at the cocktail list first."

Earlier, Cerise had found herself dressing for the evening with greater than usual care, paying attention to small details. Some time ago, Simon had complimented her hair style and she was careful to replicate that look tonight. Finally, she had applied a mere trace of makeup and lipstick. At her age, any more might make her appear slutty.

"You really ought to try this. It's one of the house special drinks, a Bomb Diggity."

Here I am dressed to the nines and he is too intrigued by a damn cocktail to notice.

"It has Bombay gin, extra-dry vermouth and passionfruit. You need to sip it. It has quite a kick."

Cerise ignored his offer and glanced over the cocktail menu, quickly finding a drink that suited her mood. With the waiter poised to write, she ordered a Meloncholy Chill.

"You don't know what you are missing," he said.

Neither do you, she thought. Aloud she commented, "I'm a fan of Grey Goose Le Melon vodka and I don't stock the St-Germain Elderflower liqueur at home."

She had more to say but hesitated until the server sat a drink in front of her and departed. After taking a welcome taste of the icy drink, Cerise returned her glass to the table and looked at Simon.

"If you had returned my call on Monday, you would know that Faheem planned to attend services Friday at the location you requested. She went, as planned."

Simon beamed. "That's great news. Sorry I couldn't call, I was out of town until yesterday. Tell me everything."

Cerise, feeling neglected, stifled an impulse to further berate him. He might not be lying, but she could not be certain. Besides, it was not in her best interest to reveal just how much he was getting to her.

She peered across the shadowy room, just able to identify the waiter rigidly waiting to be summoned. "Let's order first, before we begin our discussion. I'm afraid the waiter might topple over, while I told you 'everything.'"

"You haven't looked at the menu."

"This is 2010. I made my selection from their website before I left home."

Simon gave a slight nod and the waiter materialized at the table, pen poised to record their wishes. "For you, madam."

"The broiled crab cake dinner with a side house salad."

"No appetizer?" Simon asked without looking away from the menu.

"No. Thank you."

The server swiveled his attention to Simon, pen again poised.

"I'll start with the mussels roasted in your Wildfire Aviator beer. For the entree, horseradish-crusted filet mignon. A Caesar side and a cheddar double-stuffed potato."

"Very good, sir. Have you had a chance to peruse our wine menu?"

"Yes, thank you. From the cellar selection, a bottle of Goldeneye Pinot '12. And, if my memory serves, a split of the La Marca prosecco for the lady."

The server nodded and scurried away to submit their order.

Cerise felt her face tinge with the notion that Simon had recalled her fondness for prosecco.

"Rome was a long time ago. I'm surprised you remembered."

"Rome is a very romantic city. Maybe you recall that *trattoria* near the Spanish Steps."

What does this mean? That he thinks about me? Or has cared about me? More likely, he recalls their wine list.

Cerise was forming what she hoped would be a suitable response when the wine steward appeared with their wine and Simon proceeded into the arcane uncorking ritual of sniffing and tasting, practiced by wine aficionados everywhere.

The *moment*, if, indeed it was a *moment*, had evaporated.

Across the table, Simon was immersed in paying homage to the wine varietal. Cerise watched, expecting to see his lips moving in silent prayer.

His communion with Simon finished, the steward turned to Cerise splashed some prosecco in the bottom of her glass, bowed slightly and left the table.

Simon swished the wine around in his mouth before swallowing. "My favorite pinots are grown in New Zealand, but this Golden Eye is very nice."

She smiled benignly. "I just assumed you ordered it because it sounds like something from a James Bond movie."

"That would make me an exceedingly shallow person."

Cerise sipped her wine and, anxious to change the tone, said, "Keep a watchful eye for eavesdroppers, while I begin my report. On Friday, our friend spent some time at the place we had discussed. She was afraid she would be discovered as a *bacha posh*, but all seemed to go well. She commented that there were several hundred worshippers, mostly men."

Simon saluted her with a raised glass and moved his arms to make way while the wait staff distributed their meals. They waited in silence until their servers had retreated from the room.

"Did she indicate any trouble passing as a male?"

"None. Only one person paid any attention to her."

"Oh?"

"An imam. He welcomed her to the *Jumu'ah* prayer."

"Did she mention this imam's name?"

Cerise shook her head. "In most ways, she is naive, as you would expect of someone of her age and upbringing, but she had an interesting observation about him. She said that where most Afghani men have 'dead eyes,' the eyes of this imam 'burned' all the way through her."

"Was she evasive when you questioned her about him?"

"I had no reason to question her about him, or any other part of her day. Why? Is this imam a person of interest?"

When Simon said nothing, she added, "Just for the record, questioning her is exactly the wrong way to learn anything. She will confide in me as long as I don't seem to be interrogating her."

"Like butter," he muttered as he cut into his steak.

Cerise shrugged off his comment and continued, "She said he scared her a little. The way he stood very close while he spoke softly to her. She used the Afghan word for 'creepy' to describe the way he made her feel. He took her hand and led her to a spot where she could store her prayer rug until she returned."

"Isn't it possible he saw through her disguise and was feeling lustful?"

"Anything is possible. But highly doubtful."

"Or, it could be that he does believe she is a teenage boy, and still felt lustful."

They both fell silent, and Cerise took advantage of the quiet to sample her food.

Eventually he asked, "How is your crab cake?"

"Quite tasty." She paused to appraise a forkful. "Very little filler, with a lush golden crust."

When Cerise had finished her meal, Simon had already abandoned his plate and was staring at the floor. After drinking deeply of the Golden Eye, he sat absently twirling his glass on the tablecloth.

Cerise said, "Sorry, but that's all I have to report. It seems like Uncle Sam didn't get much bang for his buck. Even less if you order dessert. I don't think I've ever seen an unfinished plate in front of you."

Simon ceased twirling his wine glass and faced her. "I'm trying to sort out how what you told me fits in with what we know. Or at least suspect. Have any plans been made concerning her return home to Afghanistan?'

Cerise shook her head. "It's going to be at least a few more weeks until she is released by the doctor."

"Will she go back to that mosque, or did that imam scare her off?"

"You said Kamila asked that she attend *Jumu'ah* prayers. She gave no indication that she would stop."

Simon lapsed back into silence, Cerise waved away their waiter intent on securing a dessert order.

When Simon spoke, it was barely above a whisper. "Here's what we need to do—"

Cerise flung her right hand, palm up, in a sudden *stop* motion. "Not another word. You were going to discuss an operational plan involving our guest and I can't be a party to that."

"I'm not ready to bring our cousins in. "

"The law requires it. There's no way that you and your friends can legally run an operation in the U.S."

"It's premature—"

"I'm not a lawyer, but I know that just discussing it would set us up for a conspiracy charge. I hate the idea of either one of us going to prison."

Simon was quiet as Cerise eyed the room and leaned closer.

"Another thing. I am responsible for the girl's welfare, and I am unaware of a threat dire enough to make me consider involving her in an active counter-terrorism op. You need to do two things in order to move forward with anything involving her. Bring in the cousins, and read me in to the op."

9

Tuesday, May 25, 2010
Bethesda, Maryland

"I have discovered the Facebook!" cried Faheem, her eyes fixed on the computer screen.

Cerise, seated nearby in a leather wingback chair, marked her page in the historical novel she was reading and smiled.

"What do you know about Facebook?"

"I heard of it from the soldiers, while I cleaned their boots. They could talk to friends anywhere on Facebook. And," she nodded at the computer, "it tells me that it is *free* and 'always will be.'"

She turned to Cerise, "Such a thing cannot be bad, can it?"

"Would you like to sign up?"

Faheem appeared crestfallen. "I would be in love with it, if only I could."

"Why can't you?"

"It says I must have an email address and I do not. It says I must have a password and I have none. And, it says I must say whether I am a girl or boy."

"It will be easy enough to get an email account, and you make up your own password, so that only you will know it. And you have decided to remain a *bacha posh* so you just select 'male'."

"But that is a lie."

Cerise shrugged. "You have been living that lie for some years now."

"But, I only needed to say the words and then the lie was gone. If I leave a lie in their records, it will always be there—for everyone to see."

Cerise stood and crossed to the desk where Faheem was seated. "I will fix it so that you have an email address and password, but I will leave it for you to decide about the lie."

After accomplishing her tasks, Cerise walked to the darkened sun porch and picked up a decanter from which she splashed some Macallan single malt into a glass. The hand-blown glass decanter and matching set of initialed glasses were a parting gift from her work group.

At a farewell gathering in a small conference room, a woman who Cerise had worked with for almost five years and yet knew only as Cathy stepped forward to present her with a beautifully wrapped box.

"Think of us every time you pour one," Cathy said with a look that implied that those in the room would often be remembered.

Cerise felt the scotch burn its way into her stomach and immediately poured another. She instinctively knew that Faheem's desire to make friends on the internet would dovetail nicely with whatever Simon might be planning. Which could easily result in disaster for Faheem.

What am I doing? She alone chose the mosque and it is quite natural for a young girl to be fascinated by social networking. No one has pointed her in any direction—yet.

I never told anyone this, but I left them because I had trouble justifying some of the things required of us in defense of this nation. Every action seemed like the right one at the time. It was always afterward, when it was too late, that the questions came to haunt.

Cathy had it backwards. It's not every time I take a drink that I think of them, rather it is every time I think of them I need a drink.

Cerise emptied her glass a second time and left it sitting next to the decanter. She started toward the sun porch.

If there is a terrorist cell building, it is just possible that as a bacha posh *Faheem might insinuate herself into a position of trust with them.*

10

Thursday, May 27, 2010
Headquarters, Central Intelligence Agency
Langley, Va.

Cerise Bevard stood in the lobby of the CIA's Original Headquarters Building, her back to the Wall of Honor. This wall displays 113 stars as a memorial to those agency personnel "who gave their lives in the service of their country."

Below this inscription sits a glass encased Book of Honor which lists just 80 of those 113 names. Cerise never understood why the identities of the remaining 33 heroes should be forever secret.

"Cerise Bevard, I am Verona. Simon Wedge asked me to escort you to your meeting."

Cerise guessed the approaching girl was in her mid-twenties. Her blonde hair was pulled back in a tight bun and, coupled with the horn-rimmed glasses she sported, Verona could easily be mistaken for a librarian or homeroom teacher.

They crossed the massive CIA seal embedded in the lobby floor. Cerise, though well aware that thousands had trod across this majestic emblem, consciously avoided the seal's centerpiece, the head of the American eagle. To her, that would be akin to trodding on Old Glory.

Verona was saying, "I understand that you were once one of us."

"Yes."

"Personally, I can't imagine being anywhere else. This work is so important, and very exciting. All of it."

Cerise showed a quick tight smile. "Yes, it certainly is. If I may, where was your most recent field assignment?"

Verona colored. "Well, I...if I had been in the field I couldn't discuss it. You should know that."

Verona marched ahead, leading Cerise down a familiar hallway of tightly closed doors. During Cerise's final months, this hallway had been playfully code-named 'Starbucks'.

Behind one of these doors dwelt a group who specialized in matters related to Africa. This responsibility required frequent trips to that continent by assorted group members, trips which invariably included a stop in Addis Ababa, Ethiopia. There, the visitor would attend a conference with local officials and acquire as many pounds of that country's exquisite Harrar coffee as he could tote.

For days, following the visitor's return, this hallway would be filled with the intense aroma of blueberries and blackberries from the brewing coffee. Thus the code name.

Today, no inviting bouquet was present. Cerise had heard that, after she left, a department head had chanced into the hall. He quickly deemed the aroma a violation of the "need to know" doctrine of security.

His reasoning was "that the smell" allowed others to know that someone had recently been to the African continent, thus a potential violation of "need to know."

No one had the courage to point out that the coffee was available for purchase domestically, and, quickly, 'Starbucks' became history.

Verona tapped on one of the doors and pushed it open. "Ms. Bevard," she called out and stepped aside for Cerise to enter.

The girl had a way of announcing Cerise's name that made her feel old.

Cerise recognized the man seated at the head of a small gray, metal conference table as Ray who was, apparently, still Simon Wedge's superior.

Ray's physique was best described as compact, and he had short, wiry, salt-and-pepper hair and a scruffy beard.

Like Simon Wedge, he found his clothing in the best stores. The others present, a dark-skinned woman and two men in suits, were unknown to her.

Ray returned her nod, and Simon, sitting to his right, stood and began the introductions. "Cerise, say hello to Special Agent Martin Lemon. He is a counterterrorism section chief at FBI headquarters."

Cerise expected that someone holding such a title would be this distinguished looking, but so young?

The Bureau must give this meeting a high priority to send so much firepower.

"Next is Supervisory Special Agent Jason Stanley from the FBI's D.C. field office."

Cerise judged Agent Stanley to be near forty. He stood taller than she expected as he rose to shake her hand.

"Next to him," Wedge continued, "Delilah Bone."

Delilah Bone rose to shake hands and stood at least 4 inches taller than Cerise. Her dark features were made more striking by the contrast to the tan pants suit she wore.

Cerise was perplexed. *If Delilah Bone is a special agent, why wasn't she introduced as one? If she isn't, what the hell is she doing at a highly classified briefing in CIA headquarters?*

Ray spoke up. "Good to see you again, Cerise. Take the seat of honor next to Delilah. Please take a moment and look through the security documents in front of you. You'll find, as you would expect, a binding security agreement granting you need-to-know access for the duration of this project."

Cerise nodded. She rapidly scanned the familiar terminology, signing and dating the last page.

Ray nodded as she signed and retrieved the documents from her when she finished. Glancing at those seated around the table, he said, "By way of background, let me say that Cerise was with us for several years, during which she served very effectively in various overseas assignments. She is an experienced field agent and will be a valuable asset as this project progresses.

"Her present vocation, importing and retailing high-end hand-woven rugs produced in the Middle East, mandates that she travel frequently to that region of the world, with emphasis on Afghanistan and Pakistan.

"During a routine debriefing upon her return from her most recent travels to that area, Cerise alerted us to the identity of someone with the potential to be a double agent in the local Islamic community. I don't have to stress to anyone at this table how desperately we need reliable intelligence sources in the nation's capital."

Ray focused his gaze on Special Agent Lemon, the ranking FBI agent present. "After a brief assessment period, we agreed that a fully operational effort was needed, requiring the unique resources of the FBI."

Cerise read Agent Lemon's expression. This was not the first time he had been fed the CIA's line. No doubt he was aware that the agency would have clung to control of the case up to the point federal law forced them to share it, and beyond, if they thought that they could get away with it.

The reality was that an inter-agency rivalry between the CIA and FBI had persisted since the World War II discord between William "Wild Bill" Donovan, the first director of the CIA, and J. Edgar Hoover the longtime head of the FBI.

Much of the jealousy had to do with the fact that the FBI was able to trumpet successes in counter-espionage, or "spy" cases, to the media, while the CIA was mandated to remain silent in the face of both achievement and criticism.

During her days with the agency, Cerise had briefly known a co-worker, Sandy, who worked tirelessly, with others, to unmask, Aldrich Ames, the agency traitor directly responsible for the death of numerous Soviet KGB and GRU agents who had spied for the U.S. and then paid the supreme price.

Cerise was aware of the anguish Sandy and her co-workers had experienced when, after years of dogged persistence they finally had the evidence they needed to charge Ames with espionage and brand him as the traitor that he was, only to be required to step back while the FBI made the arrest of Ames and faced the media.

Now, Cerise was thinking, *they must understand what a mistake it would be to cut me out and try to deal direct with Faheem.*

"...So," Ray was saying, "I would ask Cerise to fill us in on how we have arrived at this point."

To hear him, one might think I've been holding out on both agencies. It would have been nice to get a heads-up that I was to be the guest speaker here today.

Cerise began. "The reason we are here today is an Afghani teenager named Faheem." She glanced at each of the visitors and went on, "Are you familiar with the term *bacha posh*?"

Agent Lemon spoke up. "I do not know it. But Delilah speaks fluent Pashto and understands the Dari tongue, so perhaps..."

Delilah Bone shook her head. "I know what the words mean, but not in the context Ms. Bevard is using them."

Cerise described the importance of the *bacha posh* concept in Afghani culture and then sketched in the circumstances of Faheem's wounds and her arrival in America for treatment.

"As long as she is in this country," Cerise concluded, her scrutiny of those at the table lingering on Ray and Simon Wedge, "Faheem is in my care and custody, a responsibility I take very seriously."

Ray hesitated, seemingly waiting for Simon to speak up. When Simon stayed silent, Ray made eye contact with Martin Lemon, and said, "I'm certain Cerise understands that everyone at this table is mindful of the child's welfare. She didn't mean to imply..."

Cerise bore in. "My intention was not to *imply* anything, it was to be explicit. It is customary in such matters, where one agency transfers an asset to another agency, that the initial handler hears nothing more.

"The asset is relocated, assigned a code name and is never spoken of again to the original handler. Is he/she dead or alive? Sorry, that's classified. It's need-to- know, and you don't. If that is what you have in mind for Faheem, it won't work."

Jason Stanley shifted in his chair and said. "If the agency expects to share this asset, I don't see how that will work, legally or practically."

Ray opened his mouth but Cerise spoke out. "Keep in mind that I don't speak for the CIA. In this case, I'm putting the welfare of Faheem on an equal basis with the welfare of this country."

Stanley muttered and shook his head.

Simon Wedge and Ray spoke at once, but Cerise cut them off with these words,

"You should also know that I won't let her be a party to being cast out like a fishing lure, trolling for terrorists, as it were. As an interest was expressed in which mosque she would attend, I assume that you have a target for this operation. I consider that I have "a need to know" regarding that as well."

Ray looked toward Cerise, saying, "Please give us a few minutes." He nodded to the door.

Cerise, used to compartmented meetings, rose without comment and left the room.

Out in the hallway, she headed down the corridor, turned right and located the lady's room. As she walked, it occurred to her that she should not be wandering about unescorted and wondered who would be in trouble if she was discovered. It would not be her—hopefully it would fall on her earlier escort, that snip Verona.

Cerise returned to the meeting room and dutifully took up a position by the door. Two women wearing employee badges, eyed her visitor's badge as they passed and continued down the hall without comment.

As she waited, Cerise had a pretty good idea of what was being said behind the closed door. The FBI had arrived expecting to be briefed on Faheem's background and then, following a quick introduction, Faheem would thereafter deal only with them regarding operational matters. That was SOP in these situations. What wasn't standard procedure is the fact that Faheem would continue to live with Cerise—what else could they do? Yet, they would be forbidden to discuss her activities. Any such conversation between Faheem and Cerise would violate the need-to-know doctrine of national security.

Ray and Simon Wedge were now trying to convince the FBI that, due to Cerise's unique relationship with Faheem—she had been there when the girl was wounded and her father killed—she had been with Faheem during her surgeries and ensuing recovery.

Cerise should remain the principal contact with Faheem, at least until the girl became comfortable with Delilah Bone.

Ray, as Cerise's former supervisor, would be going to great lengths to assure the agents that Cerise's experience in similar matters would be an asset that must not be ignored. And, above all, she could be trusted with sensitive information, such as the identity of their target.

Ray would understand that he was not presenting an argument merely to assuage the FBI agents present in the room, his words needed to be equally convincing to their higher-ups who would later hear them repeated in a secure room at FBI headquarters.

Cerise was absorbed in parsing her thoughts when Simon cracked the door and nodded her back into the room with a wink.

Everyone had a cardboard coffee cup sitting in front of them, and Cerise headed around the table toward the coffee station against the wall.

"I imagine your ears were burning," was Ray's feeble attempt to acknowledge that she had been the subject of their discussion.

Those at the table sat in a strained silence while Cerise fixed her coffee and returned to her chair.

Ray cleared his throat and spoke to Cerise.

"As you may expect, the FBI voiced some concerns about deviating from the usual tradecraft in this operation. Specifically, allowing a civilian without a valid security clearance to have active knowledge of an on-going operation. They have agreed that your relationship with Faheem, coupled with your recent experience in intelligence matters, makes this a unique situation.

"We have mutually agreed to operate, at least initially, as follows: You may continue to monitor Faheem's activities, but will not initiate any action by her unless that action has been authorized by the FBI."

While Cerise mulled that over, Ray emphasized, "Faheem is to take no action that has not been previously authorized by the FBI."

He paused for effect while he scanned the table. "The secret of Faheem's gender must be as closely guarded as her identity. "

Cerise nodded her understanding, as did the others.

Ray continued, "As soon as possible, you will arrange to introduce Delilah to Faheem."

Jason Stanley spoke up. "We were thinking a lunch on Saturday. You take Faheem with you to meet an old friend who speaks Pashto. You believe she would like an opportunity to speak her own language."

Cerise shrugged. "I don't see why not."

"Later, you and Delilah can discuss a short-range operational plan which, of course, will require approval from FBI HQ before being implemented."

"Any questions so far?" Ray asked.

"Only one I can think of," Cerise replied. "Who is the target?"

Simon Wedge opened a leather binder and read from a single sheet of paper stamped "TS/SCI", intelligence community shorthand for Top Secret/Sensitive Compartmented Information.

"A reliable source reported that a Pakistani citizen, living in Washington, D.C., is part of a terrorist group that is planning an attack on an unknown target in the near future. The citizen receives instructions and funds from visitors to the Islamic Center on Mass Ave., and his cover may be as an imam conducting prayer services there."

Ray turned to Special Agent Lemon, who said. "FBI Headquarters has assigned the code name 'Trapdoor' to this operation."

11

Saturday, May 29, 2010
Washington, D.C.

Cerise Bevard and Faheem were seated at a table for three in the Lebanese Taverna on Arlington Road in Bethesda. The restaurant was chosen because of its renowned menu of Middle Eastern food, coupled with a proximity to the Bethesda Metro station.

They were anticipating a late lunch with Cerise's "friend", Delilah Bone, who, according to Cerise, was a grad student at Georgetown University.

When Delilah Bone approached their table, Cerise forced a smile and stood to exchange a perfunctory hug with her "old friend, the grad student."

She said, "Faheem, greet my friend Delilah Bone."

Delilah smiled. In Pashto she said, "Hello, Faheem, I have heard a lot about you. You seem to have recovered nicely from your terrible wounds."

Faheem touched the side of her head and nodded. "Yes. Thank you. I am more well now."

Delilah sat in the chair next to Faheem and looked across the table to Cerise.

"Sorry I am late. I had a question for Professor Thorpe after my 11 o'clock class. I hope you aren't starving."

Cerise assured her that they were not starving and they proceeded to chatter at one another as old friends who need to catch up are wont to do.

As the two women loosely followed a rehearsed script, Cerise noticed Faheem studying Delilah and felt the girl was trying to ascertain the newcomer's ethnicity.

The olive complexion, sharp nose and dark brown eyes above high cheek bones were indicative of a Mideast heritage .

Cerise observed that by adopting a younger hair style and donning campus apparel, the woman had created an entirely new look for herself as Delilah Bone, grad student.

After the waitress interrupted them to take their lunch orders, Faheem spoke to Delilah. "You look like a Muslim, but you do not wear a *hijab,* so you are not a Muslim. What are you then?"

Cerise shook her head. "Faheem, in America it is rude to ask directly about a person's faith."

Delilah Bone, responding in Pashto said, "Miss Cerise is correct, however, I do not object to answering your question."

As Delilah spoke, Faheem became increasingly excited. She turned to Cerise, "She talks Pashto. She says she will answer my question."

Cerise nodded. "Yes, I understood what she said."

Faheem turned back to Delilah. "You talk my language very good. Please, we are in America, it would be better for me to learn if we talk only in American."

Delilah smiled. "As you wish. As to your question, my family is from Lebanon and belonged to the Maronite Catholic Church when they came to this country."

An anxious Faheem proclaimed, "I am a Muslim. Yesterday, I went to *Jumu'ah Mubarak*—that is Blessed Friday prayer—. I kneel with the other men, the women must pray while looking at our backsides."

It was apparent to both Cerise and Delilah Bone that Faheem had no interest in Delilah's religion but had used that question as a segue to share her excitement about the mosque.

Delilah replied, "Please, tell me more. As a student of sociology, I am curious about all religions."

Faheem was interrupted by the arrival of the wait staff with their lunch order. As soon as the staff retreated, she ignored her food and continued an animated commentary on her recent visits to the Islamic Center Mosque on Mass. Ave.

"It is the most beautiful mosque in the world. I'm certain of it. The inside is as very awesome as the outside. Thousands of Muslims come each Blessed Friday. I have not dreamed there would be that many of us in America."

Faheem looked at the two women and said, "That is why it is so wonderful that the imam again made me feel so welcome."

Glancing at Cerise, Delilah asked, "Please tell us, what the imam did to make you feel so welcome?"

Faheem pulled a morsel of lamb kabob from the skewer on her plate and chewed it before saying, "Last week he led me to a place where I can put my prayer rug until the next *Jumu'ah* prayer day.

"This time he again approached me, even though many older men wished to speak with him. Imam Wala*d*i spoke to me only, and then took my hand and we walked to a quiet corner so that I might greet another boy of my age. His name is, Qader."

Faheem's mind seemed to stray and she resumed eating her lunch in silence.

Cerise and Delilah exchanged looks. Cerise was about to pose a question when Faheem blurted, "Oh! I forget another wonderful thing that Imam Waladi did. When I told Qader he could talk to me on the Facebook, the imam was in delight and said he would talk to me also on that same book."

12

Thursday, June 3, 2010
FBI Headquarters
J. Edgar Hoover Building
Washington D.C.

Delilah Bone stepped from the grey Chevrolet with smoked windows into the dim light of the massive garage beneath the Hoover FBI building. She nodded her thanks to the driver and covered the few steps to the elevator marked "Restricted."

She had been an FBI special agent for nearly four years and had used the identity of Delilah Bone for almost eighteen months of that time.

By the time she graduated from the FBI Academy at Quantico, Virginia, she was destined for a career as a deep-cover agent working against Middle Eastern terrorists.

Her Lebanese ancestry and swarthy complexion initially intrigued her academy instructors. As her training progressed, she tested high in language proficiency, out-scored most of her classmates during firearms training and exhibited a unique combination of native intelligence and "street smarts" required of undercover agents for survival when facing an insidious enemy.

Upon graduation from the FBI Academy, her initial assignment was to the Defense Language Institute in Monterrey, California. There she studied Pashto, a national language of Afghanistan and a tongue widely spoken in Pakistan.

To satisfy an administrative requirement that all new agents serve in a field office, she was assigned to the FBI's Denver Division. In an unusual maneuver, FBIHQ instructed the field office that this new agent was to be transferred directly to the resident agency in Casper, Wyoming. There she was to be assigned only to the investigations of routine matters.

At FBIHQ, all matters related to Delilah Bone were classified need-to-know thus the rationale behind the unique instructions regarding the new agent, were not shared with anyone in the field office, even the special agent in charge of the Denver Division.

Casper, had been painstakingly chosen for her assignment, by the counter-terrorism section at FBIHQ to achieve the following ends: Being assigned routine investigations in such a remote area minimized the likelihood that she would be involved in a major case attracting media attention. She would not be exposed to Arab-American residents who might later confront her in her undercover identity.

Her assignment offered maximum flexibility to fully develop her undercover identity. This included travel, often for extended periods, on orders from HQ. Being assigned routine matters would make her absence less disruptive than if she were the case agent for a complex major case.

Delilah Bone began by following established protocol for building a false identity: Stay as close to the truth as possible—it is easier to remember and thus she would be less likely to be tripped up. She combined her aunt's given name with her Mother's maiden name to become "Delilah Bone."

Delilah's hometown would be a city with which she was intimately familiar, other details would be added as required by her current assignment.

The elevator sighed to a stop on the fourth floor, and Delilah Bone stepped across the hall to Martin Lemon's office.

Once inside, she received a smile from Connie, sitting behind her desk in the outer office. Typical of the FBI, it was more accurate to say that Connie was the secretary to the office rather than to its current occupant.

Lemon, like the others who had passed through that office on their way up or out, was temporary, two or three years at the outside. Connie had occupied her chair for 32 years, with the same smile for everyone who entered.

Connie pressed the intercom. "Mister Lemon, your 3 o'clock is here."

Delilah took one of the two visitors' chairs in front of Martin Lemon's desk. He said, "Jason is on his way up. Unlike yourself we don't care who sees his face in this building, so he to take a more circuitous route than yours. While we wait, why don't you bring me up to date on Delilah Bone."

"I'm still getting settled in. I have found a small apartment near the Georgetown campus and intend to audit a couple of courses during summer school. For now, I'm acquainting myself with the area, particularly interested in identifying gathering places for Middle Eastern students. Coffee houses, bars and restaurants. Hangouts. Places I can practice my language skills."

Martin Lemon nodded his agreement. "What courses do you plan to audit?"

"I'm looking at the school's Arabic and Islamic studies program. Eventually, I expect Faheem may ask me to attend Friday prayers and, if we are lucky, someone there might recognize me from a classroom or coffee shop around campus."

Connie cracked the office door and said, "Agent Stanley is here."

Lemon's voice boomed. "Stanley, get in here, there is much to discuss."

13

Friday, June 4, 2010
The Islamic Center
Northwest, Washington, DC

Faheem stood after prayers, stretched as best she could amid the crush of worshippers, and reverently began rolling her prayer rug. Next to her her new friend Qader performed the same task.

"Faheem, will you be joining us to study the Quran on Tuesday?"

"I'm unsure, Qader. If I cannot, I will be certain to read it on the computer."

Qader shook his head. "Imam Waladi wants his young men to show that they are true believers by joining him in this holy place, as he wishes."

Faheem, embarrassed by the idea that she would displease the imam, hurriedly finished rolling her prayer rug.

To Qader she said, "We will speak more about this on the Facebook," and hurried off to shelve her rug.

14

Monday, June 7, 2010
Washington, D.C.

Cerise hung up the phone following a lengthy discussion with a good customer regarding a 4'x6' carpet hand made in Afghanistan. She was thinking about stepping out for coffee and wondered when she might again see Simon Wedge when the phone rang.

"Magic Carpet. How may we help you?"

"Cerise. This is Delilah. As you know, I'm just up M Street at Georgetown. I have some time to kill this morning and wondered if I could stop in for a few minutes. I'll bring the coffee. There's a Starbucks on the way."

The two women sat at an elegant work table in a rear corner of the main showroom, their venti-size cups of foaming latte resting on thick ceramic coasters.

Delilah began by asking, "I presume it is secure to talk here?"

Cerise nodded. "Bobby sweeps the store every seven days. The back door is locked and we can see if anyone enters through the front door. My sitting with a customer, drinking coffee, is less suspicious than locking the front door so soon after opening."

Cerise sipped her coffee before raising it in a thank-you gesture. "Proceed," she said.

"As we have no way of knowing what is discussed between you and Faheem, I'll need you to fill in some of the blanks as I go along."

"The FBI has a way of knowing things. It is comforting to hear that they have chosen not to bug my house."

Delilah shrugged. "It was discussed, briefly, then disregarded."

"Because they know that Bobby also sweeps the house regularly."

Delilah, satisfied that Cerise had no more to say on the subject, began.

"Faheem has been on Facebook with several youths she met at Friday prayers. We haven't been able to come up with much on any of them, but two of them, Atal and Qader certainly are worthy of more digging."

"What about the imam, Waladi?"

Delilah shook her head. "But it's early. Does Faheem speak freely to you about the Islamic Center? "

"She chatters to me after each visit and has mentioned Atal and Qader, and someone she calls Bakht. If you mean, is she consciously hiding things from me? I don't believe Faheem knows how to be devious. But how can one be certain?"

Delilah asked, "Do you have Faheem's Facebook password?"

"No. I —"

"Has there been any discussion about you accessing her site?"

"No. But —"

"We have seen no indication that anything sub rosa is being discussed. Hopefully that will change, and when that time comes we want Faheem to feel confident that no one, including you—especially you—can see what is being discussed."

Delilah read the distaste in Cerise's eyes and added, "I know what you are feeling, you abhor the idea of abetting our intrusion into Faheem's private thoughts. But look at it this way once her thoughts are put into words and dispatched across the internet, they cease to be Faheem's personal property. And, if these words involve committing crimes against the U.S., we need to know it."

Cerise was defiant. "Faheem would never be involved in a terrorist act against us. Against me."

"Perhaps, unknowingly. Time will tell."

Cerise sat in thoughtful silence and drank her coffee.

Having no intention of debating the ethics of eavesdropping on Faheem's internet communications. Delilah said, "We were a little surprised to see that all of her communications are in English."

"Faheem says she already understands Pashto and wants every opportunity to improve her English."

Delilah nodded. "We saw that. Those that she has been in contact with offered no objection to English. Why not? They all love it in America.

"We have seen this before. The bad guys go along for a while in English and, as things heat up, all of their jabber suddenly appears encoded in their native tongue. What they don't seem to get is that when different cells across the world use identical codes, it identifies which terror group's flag they are flying. Of course, that lets us immediately fill in some of the blanks regarding organizational structure, financing, possible targets, etc."

Because of Cerise's previous experience in the clandestine service, she quickly digested what she was being told.

Delilah continued. "The immediate issue concerns Qader. He has implored Faheem to join him on Tuesday night to study the Quran with Imam Waladi, among others. I take it Faheem has said nothing to you about that."

Cerise shook her head.

"This is too good of an opportunity to miss. There were two exchanges over the weekend. Sunday evening, Qader insisted on an answer and Faheem put him off by saying that she would speak to you about it."

Cerise replied, "Faheem's recovery is just now getting to the stage where I feel she could travel out of the house on her own. As it happens, I was going to speak to her about that anyway. Why don't I bring it up tonight, giving her the opportunity to raise the subject of the study group."

Delilah nodded and changed the subject. "For planning purposes, we need to know what you two have discussed about Faheem's eventual return to Afghanistan."

Cerise was prepared for this topic. She would do her best to conceal the pain it caused her to think of the girl's leaving.

"Faheem has at least one more visit to the hospital. At the end of next month. A lot will depend on what the doctor says."

Delilah produced a small gift bag from her shoulder bag and presented it to Cerise.

"For Faheem."

15

Tuesday, June 8, 2010
Washington, D.C.

Faheem stood under the canopy of the Woodley Park-Zoo Metro Station watching the cars on 24th Street slowing for Connecticut Avenue. In about thirty minutes it would be dark, and most of the cars were already running with their headlights on. From her jacket pocket, she pulled the new smartphone Cerise had presented to her, and jabbed the speed-dial number for home.

"Mother Cerise, I am Faheem using the new telephone you gave to me. I want to tell you that I have came to the Metro place, okay. No attacks on myself, by anybody."

This was not Faheem's first visit to the Zoo Metro stop.

Monday, after her meeting with Delilah Bone, Cerise closed the store early and went home to talk with Faheem. Eventually, they agreed that, under certain conditions, she would be permitted to attend the Tuesday evening session at the Islamic Center. She followed this up by presenting the smartphone to an astonished Faheem.

Cerise then retreated to her office, leaving Bobby Heavens to explain the intricacies of the device to Faheem.

Next, the three of them gathered in the sun porch, where Cerise explained the conditions necessary for Faheem to be allowed to travel about the city alone.

"Tomorrow evening, Faheem will be traveling to the Islamic Center to join other young men in studying the Quran."

Bobby Heavens' face was impassive, giving no indication that he was already fully briefed on the situation. Had, in fact, been instrumental in the planning of what Cerise was about to disclose.

The fact that Faheem did not know her way around the area was critical. It meant that, at least for the near future, she would need to rely on Cerise and Bobby Heavens for her transit.

Cerise continued to explain. "Faheem's plans include traveling by Metro from Bethesda station to Woodley Park-Zoo, where she will be picked up by one of her friends and driven the short distance to the Islamic Center."

She directed her attention to Bobby Heavens. "Tonight we will have a practice run. You and Faheem will drive to Bethesda station, where she will take a Red Line train to Woodley Park, get off and come to street level to wait for you to drive up. Tomorrow night, she will be met there by Qader."

The test run had gone smoothly, and now Faheem stood waiting for Qader to arrive, unaware that three FBI surveillance vehicles lurked nearby in the gathering dusk.

Faheem ended her call to Cerise and stood, legs aquiver with anticipation for what lay ahead. As far as she knew, no one else at the center would be a *bacha posh*. They would be real boys. Would she be able to fool all of them?

And the imam. His mere presence was alarming. Those black eyes seemed to bore deep within as he spoke, allowing him to scour your soul. And when he spoke to her, he leaned so close that their bodies touched.

Faheem said nothing to anyone about this concern. Who was she, still a child really, to speak ill of a leader of the faith?

Qader worships the imam and would very much hate me if he knew that I held these thoughts.

A warm breeze stirred. Faheem checked the time on her new phone. it was 7:15. Qader was late.

What if he does not come? I should have to call Mother Cerise and be fetched home. Like a schoolchild. What will happen to me if they discover that I am a bacha posh? *As a female, I am good only to prepare men's food and to give them pleasure in the bed.*

Faheem began to tremble.

I have heard of bacha posh *who had terrible things done to them before being stoned to death by the same men who used them. That was not in America. Could that happen to me in this country?*

"Faheem!"

Someone was calling her name.

Speaking Pashto, the voice said, "Come. Get in the car. We are very late."

It was Qader, calling to her from the driver's window of a faded yellow Volkswagen minivan idling at the curb.

Faheem replied in English. "Hello to Qader and Bakht. Here I am."

As Faheem climbed into the seat behind Qader, a sport-bike gunned to life nearby on 24th Street.

"Thank you so very much for this asking of me to go with you," Faheem blurted, again in English.

Qader's voice was chilling. "True believers have no use for English. When we are together, we only speak in our own tongue."

Though barely sixteen, Qader's demeanor called for deference from those around him.

"*Bakhshel ze.*" Faheem muttered her apology and shrank into the seat back.

Faheem had little time to feel humiliated before the minivan was stopping in front of a well-kept two-story white frame house in a neighborhood of tightly spaced, similar dwellings. A grassy median, lined with a single row of flowering trees, split the street in front of the residence. A single-car garage, with the door pulled tight, was tucked under a wing of the house.

At first, Faheem thought someone would be leaving the house to join them and became alarmed when Qader moved to leave the car.

In Pashto, she blurted out, "Why do you stop here? We are already too late for the imam!"

Qader motioned toward the house. "Pay attention. The imam waits for us in the doorway. Leave your phone in the car and prepare to greet him as a true Muslim."

When Faheem balked at being separated from her new phone, Qader snapped, "The imam's home is considered a holy place. No devices are permitted inside."

As the three visitors reached the front door, each extended the required greeting, *"Asalam Alaykum"* (The peace be upon you) to the imam, who in turn replied, *"Wa Alaykum Asalam"* (And peace be upon you, also.)

The imam led them along a short entryway, then turned right and continued down three steps to a small paneled room, barren with the exception of a straight-back wooden chair located in the middle of a thickly carpeted floor.

Imam Waladi turned and smiled benignly as his guests removed their shoes before descending onto the carpet.

Two other young men, both strangers to Faheem. stood and exchanged the ritual greeting. The imam gave their names as Amir and Wazir.

Imam Waladi occupied the lone chair while the others sat clustered, cross-legged at his feet.

Faheem was squeezed between Qader and Amir, their legs touching through thin cotton pants.

Faheem had never before been situated among older males in a circumstance of sustained intimacy. The small places on her body which rested on the boys legs felt as if they were on fire. They seemed to transmit surges throughout her frame. It was a bewildering experience.

The imam was speaking Pashto."Welcome, all, to our Quran study group." He reached out and patted Faheem's head. "Especially to Faheem, our newest student."

Smiling directly upon her, he continued, "I notice that your face is now aglow with warmth. Do not be flustered—you will soon become at ease in my presence."

16

Wednesday, June 9, 2010
Washington, D.C.

Delilah Bone and Cerise Bevard were seated at the elegant work table at the rear of the Magic Carpet showroom. Venti-size containers of steaming lattes sat before them.

Looks like this is going to be a weekly thing, Cerise thought, and gave a mental shrug. *Fine by me, as long as she brings the coffee.*

Cerise selected a buttery croissant from the box Delilah had set between them.

And these delicious croissants.

Delilah sipped her coffee before asking, "Did Faheem say anything about her activities last night?"

Cerise shook her head. "She went straight to her room when she came home and was still asleep, or at least in bed, when I left this morning. Why? Was there a problem?"

"We don't know. Qader was adamant that they speak only Pashto and ordered her to leave her smartphone in the car because they were going inside the imam's house, which was a holy place. So we know where Waladi lives, but have no idea what was said inside the house.

"Strangely, back in the car not a word was spoken. Eventually Faheem says goodnight and the car door slams when she gets out at the Woodley Metro stop. Then, only ambient sounds until she speaks to Bobby Heavens when he picks her up at the Bethesda station."

"I thought they were going to the Islamic Center?"

Delilah selected a croissant before saying, "So did we. Fortunately, the surveillance team didn't wait for them at the center but picked them up as they left the Woodley stop."

Each woman took a bite of roll and a sip of latte before Delilah asked,

"Now that Faheem is recovering and becoming more active, have you given any thought to how she will occupy her days?"

"Her doctors say she can do whatever she feels up to, short of kick-boxing. I'll talk to her about it." Cerise waited for the other woman to offer suggestions, but when none were forthcoming, she continued, "The only thing that she has felt up to is sitting at the computer, so you would know better than I what she is doing."

Delilah nodded. "Besides visiting Facebook, she spends a lot of time in chat rooms for Afghani young people. She seems homesick.

"We ran a check on Waladi. All we have is from 2006, an obscure mention of a Haamid Waladi, who left the Pakistani military after he was openly sympathetic to the Taliban.

"Sounds promising."

"We're not certain he is the same Waladi. We're tracking that onel to see where he ended up."

After Delilah Bone left the Magic Carpet, Cerise dialed her home phone and, while waiting for Faheem to answer, she speculated about the odds that her phone was tapped.

"Yes?"

"Faheem, it's Cerise. I am coming home for lunch."

"Yes."

"Would you like me to bring you a lamb kabob?"

"Oh yes! Please and thank you."

" I will get some carryout."

They were seated at individual tray tables in the sun room. Cerise picked at her Lebanese salad and tried to figure out how to ask her questions without alerting Faheem. She was, after all, a trained interrogator. She should be able to frame her questions to determine if Faheem was withholding anything.

"How many were there at the center last night?"

Faheem chewed some lamb kabob and washed it down with a drink from the can of Coke Zero on the small table.

"Five of us students and the imam."

"Only five? Many hundreds attend Friday prayers, I would have expected more. Didn't it feel strange, only five in such a large building?"

Without looking up from her kabob, Faheem replied, "Oh we did not go to the center, we were welcomed into the imam's own house. We met in a small room, only five of us young men. There would have been room for one or two more only."

"Why do you think, of all the men at the Center on *Jumu'ah* Friday, the imam has selected the young men in your group?"

Faheem mulled the question briefly. "Because he has no room for more others in his house?" She shrugged and bit off more kabob.

Cerise returned to her salad while she considered her next question.

"How long has the imam been in America?"

"That has not been spoken of."

"What country is he from? Afghanistan? Pakistan?"

Faheem shook her head.

"What about your friend, Qader. Is he Afghani?"

"Please, why do you ask me these questions to which I do not know the answers?"

Cerise drank some tea as she formed a response. "You call me Mother Cerise, and while you are here I am to look after you, just as Kamili would do back home. But, in Tarin Kowt, you meet few strangers. Except for the soldiers, anyone you will see has, most likely, lived there all of their lives.

"America is so much bigger. People come here to Washington from all over the world—not all of them are good people. If you will be in cars with them and going into their homes, I must know about them. I am responsible to keep you safe."

Faheem paused and smiled across the small room. "Oh, Mother Cerise, you are not to worry about me. The imam is a man of God. Qader and the others are his disciples, as I am. These are not bad people, I will come to no harm from them."

17

Friday, June 11, 2010
Washington, D.C.

Imam Waladi closed the Quran from which he had been reading and turned to scan the worshippers as they began drifting toward the entrance to the Islamic Center. He was anxious to see if Faheem had returned for the *Jumu'ah*, Friday prayer.

Qader stood nearby, waiting to do Waladi's bidding. Earlier, he had gloated to the imam about forbidding Faheem to bring his cellphone into Quran study, claiming the building was sacred ground.

Faheem is the most beautiful boy I have seen, Waladi thought as he searched the worshippers. *Qader is very jealous. He hates it when I am attentive to any of the others. If he has frightened this beauty away from me ...*

"Qader." Waladi called the boy to him. "Have you seen Faheem among the worshippers?"

"No, Effendi. Do you want me to bring him to your presence?"

"You need to find him first. If he is not here, then you will contact him on that Facebook page in your computer and be certain that he agrees to attend our Quran studies on next Tuesday. You will meet him at the Metro station as you did this week and bring him to me."

Without comment, Qader turned and disappeared into the mass of worshippers moving slowly toward the center's entrance.

That night, just after supper, Faheem activated her laptop and read the Facebook message from Qader.

faheem
our imam is quite angry with you for not coming to Jumu'ah
prayers today. you must come to Quran study on tuesday night
or you will be punished. i will collect you from the same train
station as we did this week and at the same time.

if you do not come, it will be very bad for you.
Qader

Unknown to Faheem and Qader, Imam Waladi was simultaneously reading the message and muttering curses at Qader in Pashto.

Faheem was pained by the scolding Qader had given her, and feared offending the imam. Clearly he had ordered Qader to invite her to Tuesday studies, and that pleased her. She sent the following reply:

Qader, please tell the imam that I am was sorry to miss Jumu'ah *Friday prayers today. Miss Cerise took me to see the doctor. I am also sorry if I offended you on Tuesday when you were kind enough to give me a ride. I will be at the Metro station to meet you, as the imam wishes.*
Faheem

Imam Waladi smiled and logged off of Facebook, aroused by the expectation of again being close to Faheem. Touching him.

Next, Waladi accessed a subscription website, from Afghanistan. The site broadcast well-attended *bacha bazi* parties in various Afghan locales, principally the major cities of Kandahar and Mazar-i-Sharif.

Bacha bazi translates as "playing with kids." As Afghan women are forbidden to dance in public, attractive teen-age boys, known as *bacha bazis*, are dressed and made up as women, and forced to perform exotic dances before crowds of lusting men.

As Waladi beheld the dancers on the screen, he envisioned hosting similar live performances for a select few Muslim men, here in Satan's Capital city. He fancied the beautiful boy Faheem as his star attraction, eager to help his imam bring a touch of culture to this wretched land.

18

Monday, June 14, 2010
Bethesda, Maryland

Cerise Bevard had established a Facebook account for Faheem's Mother, Kamili.

Today, Faheem and Kamili were making their second Facebook contact. Delilah Bone eagerly awaited the report from the Bureau clerk monitoring Faheem's computer traffic. She was desperately in need of some insight into Faheem's thoughts about the imam and the girl's expectations for the future.

Was she anxious to return to Afghanistan, or was she hoping to stay in America?

There was little doubt that Faheem's presence in Tarin Kwot as the family's "male" child would make Kamili's life easier, but, so far she had not pushed for that.

Monitoring Faheem's computer provided the FBI with direct access to the girl's internet communications and, just as important, a way for them to determine if Cerise were disclosing to them everything she has learned about Faheem.

Faheem sat at her computer carefully composing her Facebook letter to Kamili in Pashto.

Mor
As Salaamu alackum
my news is not all good. i was needed not to go to Jumu'ah *Friday prayers, because of going to see the doctor. i have gone to Friday prayers, as you wished, on most Fridays and spread my rug with the other men. The doctor said I am a slow healer and need some more days to see him. After then i can tell you when I will be able to come to my home. Insallah.*

You will be glad to know imam waladi is happy with me. i went with my friends to his own house on tuesday to learn more about the Quran. i am asked to come back on tomorrow.

miss cerise has spoken that she likes me to be living here, so you are not to worry about that.

your respectful son
Faheem

19

Wednesday, June 16, 2010
Washington, D.C.

Delilah Bone was meeting with FBI surveillance specialists Will Kelly and Neal Brady of the Washington field office—known throughout the FBI as WFO—at an off-site location.

This off-site, popularly referred to as a safe-house, was a townhouse maintained by the Bureau in Northwest Washington. Such sites were covertly leased by the FBI and maintained for the exclusive use of undercover operatives and surveillance teams.

A box of donuts from Mama's Donut Bites sat on the table in the eat-in kitchen, and the aroma of fresh coffee drifted toward Kelly and Brady when they walked in. Kelly broke into a grin as he raced Brady to the table.

"You are definitely a class act, Bone."

Delilah Bone stood with her back to the sink and nibbled on a sugar donut.

"There's a dozen—well, eleven now. Enough to take back to your team, if you two aren't greedy."

Kelly carried his coffee mug to the other side of the table and took a seat in one of the three straight-back, painted wooden chairs. He dragged the donut box to his side of the table and nodded for Brady to begin updating Bone on the FBI's surveillance and technical coverage of Faheem, Imam Waladi and Qader.

Brady flipped open a notebook. "We'll start with Faheem's computer:

On Monday, she sent her Mother a Facebook message about missing Friday's *Jumua'h* prayer service because Bevard took her to see the doctor. And that the doctor said she is, quote, 'a slow healer' and he would need to see her at least once more, therefore she couldn't say when she might return to Afghanistan."

He turned a page and continued. "Faheem visits Facebook pages without much success at initiating any friendships. She seems wary of chatting up boys. Likely she's afraid she will give herself away in an extended conversation with real males. She has better luck chatting with girls until she mentions being a boy and they quickly sign off. She is awkward in her role as a boy, and, it seems, the girls figure they're wasting their time talking with some nerd.

"In either gender, Faheem is a lonely person."

Delilah Bone scribbled some notes. "Maybe we should create a friend for her. A girl who doesn't get scared off. Faheem might open up to her."

Bone looked up and nodded for Brady to continue.

"She spends a lot of time on Islamic websites, but rarely participates. Mostly she behaves like an eavesdropper, just watching."

He looked at Kelly, "Anything I missed?"

"The cellphone."

"Oh. Right." Brady leafed through his notes until he found the page. "We have no idea what this means, maybe you and Bevard can sort it out. The cell we provided her hasn't produced as much intel as we had hoped. You remember, Qader banned her phone from Waladi's house. We don't know if that is a routine counter-measure or he was just showing off his authority.

"In any event, we are only privy to conversations in the car. Last night, after they left Waladi's house, we can hear Qader angrily telling Faheem that he, refering to Waladi, 'will ask you to dance for him. Don't do it!' We can't tell if he is angry at Faheem or Waladi."

Bone nodded, and when she had finished her notes she looked from Brady to Kelly. "What's next?"

Kelly swallowed his last donut bite and opened his own notebook.

"This is a rundown on our physical surveillance of Waladi yesterday. He left his house about 11:00 a.m. and proceeded directly to Aspen Hill, Maryland, where he stopped at a little restaurant called, The Kabob House, in the Aspen Hill Shopping Center."

Kelly handed Bone a manila envelope. "We got snaps of Waladi and the man he met inside, as well as a couple of white guys who probably have no connection. But, just to be safe...You've never seen Waladi, have you?"

Bone shook her head and spread the envelope's contents on the table.

Kelly pointed to a photo of two men standing on the sidewalk under the Kabob House sign. "With their beards and Islamic garb they are hard to tell apart. The one on the left is Waladi, the other one is Adeeb Ali."

Delilah Bone gave him a questioning look.

"We know this because, since we were in Maryland, we sent these pictures to the Baltimore office."

Brady gave a low chuckle as Kelly explained. "Baltimore has an open case on Ali. It turns out they had him under surveillance on Sunday, but they had lost him, with no idea where he had gone, until we told them."

Brady laughed. "They owe us, big time, for that one."

Bone asked Kelly, "What kind of a case do they have on Adeeb Ali?"

He shrugged. "We're going to get together with them in the next couple of days for a data swap. If we are lucky, they have seen Waladi and Ali before."

Bone put down her pen. "At least it shows we're not wasting our time with Waladi. It seems to validate the agency's original source."

"Or it was merely a meeting between two lovers of lamb kabob," Neal added.

Bone said, "Waladi didn't drive to Aspen Hill only to have lamb kabob with another suspected terrorist. They are cooking up something, and I'm betting his Tuesday night students of the Quran are involved. Waladi is not going to surround himself with innocent waifs. They will try to recruit Faheem soon."

Kelly glanced at Brady and then addressed Delilah Bone. "Our supervisor," he began, and waved a hand between them indicating what he was about to say included the three of them. "Has directed that we are not to discuss anything about our investigation of Waladi with Bevard. She is not cleared for it and definitely has no need to know."

Bone returned his gaze and waved a finger between the two men.

"Since I'm the only one of us who has any contact with Bevard, that rule is obviously directed at me. And I believe that Cerise does have a need to know. After all, she has a responsibility toward the child, and we need her involved. If trouble erupts with this imam and we have kept her in the dark ... "

Kelly closed his notebook and signaled Brady. "I'm just the messenger. If you have a serious problem with this, take it up with Stanley." He stood and headed for the door with Brady close behind.

20

Thursday, June 17, 2010
Washington, D.C.

Delilah Bone arrived at the Magic Carpet carrying two grande lattes only.

"It's just as well," Cerise said as she led the way to the work table. "I, for one, don't need a diet of croissants."

"Nor do I."

Cerise faced these meetings with angst, wary that she would be told something dreadful concerning Faheem, while at the same time fearful that Delilah was withholding details which Cerise would find distressing.

Delilah began, "The techs tell us that Faheem spends equal amounts of time on Facebook and Islamic websites, in an effort to find a friend, with little to show for it."

Delilah paused for a reaction.

Cerise nodded. "She has told me that. Of course, she is lonely and gets very discouraged about it."

Delilah went on. "I think it's only a matter of time until she might be taken in by one of the many weirdos trolling the internet. My solution is to provide a friend, hopefully one she can confide in."

"You are going to be the friend?"

Delilah shook her head. "Not exactly. The Bureau has a cadre of people who surf the net to identify child predators. They use gender- and age-appropriate identities and are trained to chat up potential subjects. In this case, one of them will be using a script, which I will provide, to become Faheem's friend."

Cerise drank some coffee and considered Delilah's words before replying. "You are hoping that eventually Faheem will confide something material to our case to this on-line friend".

Delilah shrugged.

Cerise said, "I'm still opposed to invading Faheem's privacy, but this seems like a benign way of protecting her."

"Did she mention to you that she wrote to Kamili?"

"Just that. She wrote, but gave no details."

"She told her Mother that she didn't attend Friday prayers because you took her to the doctor."

Cerise nodded.

"And that she couldn't say when she would be coming home as the doctor called her a 'slow healer' and she would be required to see him some more."

Cerise jerked away from her coffee cup.

"What? It was just the contrary. He remarked how well she had healed and that she wouldn't need to see him again."

Cerise reflected for a moment before adding, "Faheem has declined to speak to her Mother on Skype. She says it's because her Mother is afraid of the machine, and there is some truth in that, but I don't think she wants Kamili to see how well she has healed. She must have decided she doesn't want to go back. If she stays in America she can live her life as Faheema and return to being a teenage girl."

Delilah riffled through her notes. "Here. She wrote this to Kamili, 'Miss Cerise has spoken that she likes for me to be living here, so you are not to worry about that.'"

Cerise was quiet for a moment. When she spoke, she said, "It sounds like I need to do some long-range planning. If the government needs her for Trapdoor, she will be allowed to stay as long as she is useful.

"That would only happen if she has penetrated a terrorist ring of concern to our national security and exposed herself to some degree of danger. If the ring is rounded up, and she survives the ordeal, she will likely be a hero and, as such, allowed to stay in this country.

"On the other hand, if Trapdoor proves fruitless, it is likely that she will be denied resident status and returned to Afghanistan. And, finally, if she should decide she would not knowingly be a party to this op, they would most assuredly send her home. Do you agree that is a fair appraisal of the situation?"

Delilah nodded. "It is, except for the fact that Faheem knows nothing about Trapdoor." She searched Cerise's face as she finished her thought. "Does she?"

Cerise was quick to reply, "Not from me. Which prompts me to ask: Am I being told everything?"

"None of us is told *everything*. Nor should we be. It is not necessary that you and I know everything at this level."

"I need to know what you have learned about this imam, Waladi. Is he the terrorist the CIA source reported on? Has NSA picked up anything about him?"

When Delilah failed to respond, Cerise added, "And don't bullshit me by saying that nothing has changed.

"The FBI is not going to invest this amount of time and resources pursuing Trapdoor, unless there have been some positive results."

Delilah responded."If there have been any 'positive results' they would very likely be unavailable under need-to-know."

Cerise stiffened. "In that case, you can tell this to the suits you work for: The longer this operation continues, the more danger an unwary Faheem is exposed to. I need to know what has developed, so that I can better decide at what point I will be informing Faheem what she is involved in.

"And I will tell her. I'm certainly not going to allow her to be sacrificed without ever knowing what it was that she was sacrificed for. She can decide for herself how badly she wants to stay in this country."

21

Friday, June 18, 2010
Chevy Chase, Maryland

Simon Wedge had surprised Cerise by insisting that she name the restaurant where they would meet.

She chose La Ferme, a replica French farmhouse on Brooklandville Road in nearby Chevy Chase.

Remarkably, he had not heard of it, and it pleased her to be able to introduce him to a restaurant of some note.

Her one visit to La Ferme, some months ago, was a vivid reminder of a French farmhouse off the A10 south of Paris where she and Simon had spent two nights while waiting for a contact, a Syrian national who never appeared.

It was as close as they ever came to being intimate, and now Cerise could not recall why that had not happened. At the time, she had very much wanted it to.

Now, as she sat in what La Ferme listed as 'porch seating,' sipping a champagne cocktail, she had misgivings about her choice.

Would Simon remember the Loire Valley the same way she did?

Not very likely.

Cerise had cajoled the *maitre d'* into showing her to an intimate table for two at the far end of the "porch", which spanned the entire back of the house. Due to its size, she thought it more aptly identified as a veranda than a porch.

She would soon know if this had been a mistake. Simon Wedge appeared at the door, a cocktail glass in one hand. He waved the *maitre d'* aside and threaded his way through the tables toward her.

Simon took the other chair and, as was his custom, greeted her by raising his cocktail glass in salute.

"Kudos! It's obvious that I don't know all of the better restaurants in the D.C. area."

He took a drink and repeated his raised glass salute. "I guessed you might be late, and I was thirsty, so I picked this up at the bar."

Cerise allowed a brief smile as she returned the gesture.

Simon smiled broadly as he took in the verdant grounds and nodded toward the front of the farmhouse. "Hard to believe that just out the front door is a noisy, congested thoroughfare."

Simon studied his glass, and Cerise was certain she detected his face coloring. She was about to ask if he had been spending time in the sun when he spoke.

"You probably don't remember, but this place brings to mind a farmhouse in the Loire where we spent a couple of wasted days...and nights."

He looked up and, after reading her face, added, "or maybe you do."

The waiter put in a perfectly timed appearance and Simon ordered another round.

Cerise was silent.

"What?" He asked. "Did I say something wrong?"

"No. Truthfully, I didn't expect you would remember that farmhouse."

"Just the opposite. I recall every day we were together." Simon shrugged. "But I'm a firm believer that workplace relationships are fraught with peril, especially in our business."

He pointed a finger straight up. "If the boys upstairs thought there was something between us, we would have been separated, and worked oceans apart."

"If you felt that way, why didn't you say something after I left?"

Simon shrugged. "I guess I didn't see much point in it. We were going in different directions, and I had the feeling that you didn't think much of me. Didn't agree with many of the decisions I made in the field."

The waiter appeared and distributed their drinks. Satisfied that they had no further interest in him, he glided away to another table.

Cerise nodded. "That might have been so at the time. But, in retrospect, I realized that many times I would have done it the same way. You spared me having to make some very tough choices."

She smiled and added, "Besides, it is hard to know exactly how you feel about someone when you are uncertain of their real name."

She continued. "Before this goes any further, I would like to know what it is that you were instructed to tell me."

"You make it sound like I am going to take you out behind the woodshed for a whuppin'." He glanced at their surroundings. "This hardly looks like a woodshed."

Cerise sipped from her fresh drink, offering no encouragement.

"Okay. No bullshit. The FBI has asked me to take your temperature. In other words, determine how imminent is the danger that you will reveal everything to Faheem. They are assuming that you have not yet taken that irrevocable step.

"Before you ask, I assured them that you would not have just blurted out the details of Trapdoor ... However, I did say that they need to plan for that contingency, because it is inevitable. And, I told them, 'Don't expect that I can just forbid her to do it.'"

"And yet here we are. What do they hope to accomplish by this meeting?"

"The suit from FBI headquarters started off our meeting by saying that if you don't swear not to reveal Trapdoor, I was to threaten you with federal prosecution. That didn't even get partway up the flagpole before it was shot down. I must say, Delilah Bone was 100 percent in your corner, saying at one point it made much more sense to read you into the entire op than risk having it come out in open court at a trial.

"There was a lot more back and forth before we settled on this: We all agreed that there will likely come a time when Faheem will need to be brought on board. Until then, you will be fully briefed on all phases of the op. In return you must agree not to reveal anything to her without prior discussion with *and* approval of, the FBI."

When Cerise failed to respond, Simon added, "That's it. It isn't going to get any better."

"This definitely requires further discussion."

Simon shrugged. "Okay, but..."

"Where do you live?"

Jolted by the question, Simon stammered, "Why, uh, I have a townhouse in Georgetown. What...?"

"Is there anyone there—waiting for you to come home?"

"Why...no. Who would...?"

Cerise smirked. "I've imagined many possibilities. A live-in girlfriend, an invalid Mother. Even a wife and kids..."

"Are you suggesting that we finish this discussion at my place?"

She glanced quickly around the porch. "It would be more secure."

He nodded his agreement. "It would, but what about your driver, Bobby Heavens?"

"I drove myself. tonight."

Simon smiled. "I agree that we should be in a more secure location. What about dinner? Aren't you hungry?"

Cerise finished her drink."Surely there must be a pizza joint along the way."

Simon Wedge signaled the waiter for the check.

22

Saturday, June 19, 2010
Aspen Hill, Maryland

Imam Waladi and Adeeb Ali sat in a small table in the Kabob House, sharing their midday meal. The only other diners were a couple who were there when Waladi arrived, and Ali was the only person to enter after Waladi.

The restaurant was run by a Greek couple and attracted few customers of Middle Eastern origin, still the two men spoke in Memoni, a minor Pakistani dialect. Waladi, confident that, if overheard, their words would not be understood, spoke freely.

"I trust that you are familiar with the famous Trango Towers cliffs in Pakistan's Karakoram Range,"

It would not do for Ali to admit he had never heard of these "famous" cliffs and he nodded accordingly.

"I have received word that some of our most capable airmen are in training there. And, when that is completed, some of them will join us so that, *insallah*, we may complete a joyous and successful mission in this land."

"This is a country of many targets. Are we to be satisfied with one?"

"This will be but the second of many."

"The second?"

"September 11th will the tenth anniversary of their Pearl Harbor. Merely the first one of this century."

"Of course, Sahib. A glorious day. When may I know which target, in all wisdom, has been selected?"

"Patience. All in good time. First there is much work to be done."

"I am at your service."

Waladi insisted that he have Adeeb Ali's undivided attention before continuing. "Listen to me with all of yourself. This is most important. You must not become so anxious to destroy the infidels that you become tempted to act alone."

Ali looked stricken."Oh no, Sahib. I..."

"Silence. You will hear me out. It is very possible that their FBI will send traitors who will seek you out, pretending to be your friends and lure you into joining them in an attack. They will give you some broken weapons, lead you to a target, like their Fort Meade, and then arrest you."

Ali knew about such things and grew fearful that Waladi might decide that he could not be trusted. He would never tell them anything.

"So," Waladi was saying, "You are not to discuss such business with anyone, except me or a brother I might send to you."

Ali nodded vigorously.

"Say to me that you swear it."

"I uh, I uh, I swear it unto Allah. May peace be upon him."

Waladi studied him quickly. "Yes. I believe you," he said. "Our people will soon be here. Once the Pilot arrives, things will happen very rapidly. For now, you will come to my home on Tuesday evening. I ask a few young Muslims to join me in study of the Quran. You know Qader."

"Yes, Sahib."

They spoke for several additional minutes during which time the other two diners paid their bill and left.

When he and Ali finished, Imam Waladi paid at the cash register and they left the restaurant together, Ali heading to Baltimore and the imam south, returning to the District.

The couple who had been seated in the Kabob House when Waladi arrived were part of a surveillance team from the Baltimore FBI office assigned to follow Ali.

When it was apparent to the team that he was heading for Aspen Hill the couple had sped on ahead. He wouldn't think they were following him, if they arrived ahead of him.

After leaving Aspen Hill, Waladi followed Connecticut Avenue to Military Road, where he turned east toward Rock Creek.

The four Washington field office surveillance units maintained a loose coverage until he approached the entrance to Rock Creek.

Driving vehicles Waladi had not seen allowed them to close the space between them, as it became necessary.

Waladi turned right on Oregon Road and unit C-2 continued east on Military Road passing the "eyeball" to C-3, who quickly reported that Waladi was turning left onto Glover Road.

"Somebody else needs to step up. What's back in there?"

"This is C-1. I'll make that turn with him. There's a planetarium and nature center in there. Spies have been meeting there for years."

"1 to 3, Glover Road winds back into Oregon up ahead. Watch for him to come out there."

"10-4."

When C-1 rolled into the planetarium parking lot, he spotted Waladi's car parked near the front entrance. He circled the parking area, noting that there were only five other cars in the lot.

"C-4."

"Go ahead."

"I need you and your partner in here, in position to take some family vacation pics to include the target and everyone who comes in or out until the target leaves. It's a beautiful day for a Kodak moment."

"We'll be there in 3."

"While you're strolling the grounds, take down the tags of the other vehicles. We might get lucky and identify who he is meeting."

When the C-4 team was positioned in the planetarium parking lot, C-1 radioed, "The eyeball is with you," and headed out onto Glover Road.

23

Tuesday, June 22, 2010
Washington, D.C.

As Faheem followed Qader and Bakht from the car to Imam Waladi's front door she cast furtive glances at people strolling the neighborhood clad in shorts and tight fitting-tops, enjoying a warm summer evening.

With the onset of summer, Faheem had found it all but impossible to heed the imam's rebuke—not to be tempted by the flesh on display around them.

Faheem was not stirred by the sight of bare skin, instead, she was envious of the comfort they were afforded in the steamy heat of a Washington, D.C., summer. She was pleased to see that the eyes of Qader and Bakht also wandered as they strolled up the walk to the imam's front door.

As they stood to leave, following an intense study session, Imam Waladi asked Qader and Bahkt to wait in the car.

When the others had gone, Waladi put an arm around Faheem's shoulders and spoke softly.

"Do not be alarmed my child. You have done nothing wrong. In fact I am prepared to award you with a great honor."

Faheem, too fearful to speak, trembled at the imam's touch.

"Faheem, I see in you a smart boy, who is of good character and takes his studies of the Quran very seriously. When I am satisfied that you possess the knowledge that is required to lead a prayer, that is when I will name you an imam. You will be a leader at the center."

Faheem was overwhelmed by the prospect of being a leader within the mosque. "But...but...I am too young."

"All that matters is that you be of good character, which you are, and have a great knowledge of the Quran, which you are gaining. In a *hadith* Muhammad himself —may the mercy and blessings of God be upon him— said, that the age of an imam is of no importance."

Waladi hugged Faheem tightly, releasing her only when she began to struggle.

"I'm sorry, Sahib, but I could not breathe." After another moment, she was able to continue. "I am honored by your faith in me at my early age. I will not fail you."

"Go now and say nothing of this to anyone."

24

Friday, June 25, 2010
Washington, D.C.

Cerise picked up the phone on the second ring. "Magic Carpet."
"Sorry, I'm late. I'll be there in about fifteen minutes."
"Hurry. I need my mid-morning pick-me-up."

Delilah Bone arrived to find Cerise running a woman's credit card in payment for a carpet she had ordered, and carried their containers of coffee to the work table. She fixed her own cup as she waited.

Once Cerise was seated beside her and had downed some coffee, Delilah began, "I understand we have reached an agreement."

Cerise responded with a nod.

"You are to be briefed fully. In return you will say nothing to Faheem about this operation without the concurrence of the Bureau."

Again, Cerise nodded.

Delilah unzipped a maroon leather folder she carried, but paused before beginning. "For my own comfort may I ask, when was the store swept?"

"Bobby was here earlier, this morning, in anticipation of your visit."

"Fine. Let's start with the imam, Waladi. On two occasions he drove to a tiny restaurant, the Kabob House, in Aspen Hill, Maryland. Both times he met with one Adeeb Ali. As it happens, Ali was already being investigated by our Baltimore office. At their second meeting we had agents inside. Waladi and Ali spoke softly, in a strange dialect and the only words our people could make out was FBI."

"Do you think they knew agents were watching?"

Delilah shook her head. "No. Because when they separated Waladi went straight to a nature center and planetarium in Rock Creek Park, where he made another contact.

"We had a couple, posing as vacationers from Delaware', strolling the grounds, snapping pictures. Waladi was in there for about fifteen minutes, and just before he reappeared, a man of Middle Eastern heritage emerged.

"From photos of him and the tag on the car he left in, he has been identified as Colonel Muhammad bin Hassani, the air attaché with the Pakistani Embassy. From there, Waladi went straight home."

Cerise's coffee had grown tepid. She rose and stepped to a small table along the wall where a microwave oven sat beside a tiny countertop refrigerator.

"You?" Cerise asked as her coffee heated.

"I'm good. One more thing re: Waladi. Last night, when Qader and Bakht got back in the car, Faheem wasn't with them. While they waited, her cellphone picked up what they said.

"Qader was very angry, he didn't like it that Waladi had asked Faheem to stay behind. It's pretty clear that Qader is jealous of the attention his imam is paying to Faheem.

"You can hear Faheem getting into the car and Qader demanding that Faheem tell him what Waladi said. Faheem mumbles something as they drive away.

At one point, Qader asks if Waladi had asked Faheem to dance for him.

"All Faheem will say is that Waladi told him how well he was doing with his Quran studies. It was evident that Qader didn't believe him and, frankly, neither do I."

Cerise had returned to her chair and now leaned forward to say, "If I didn't know better, I would tell you that you are wrong. That Faheem doesn't have what it takes to stand up to Qader's fury, that she is guileless and couldn't lie—not to anyone. However, I would be mistaken.

"Last night she was very proud to tell me what Waladi had spoken to her about. He said he will designate her an imam to assist him with the prayers when she finishes her study of the Quran."

"That is very significant—for two reasons. It means that they have no suspicion she is a *bacha posh*. Waladi would never entertain the idea of naming a female an imam. It also indicates that, if she is cornered, she might have the guts to lie her way out of it."

Cerise scowled at the thought of Faheem in such peril that her survival could depend on her own skill at deceiving bloodless terrorists.

Delilah, though troubled by the look that passed across the other woman's face, continued without comment.

"You may recall our conversation about Faheem's need for a Facebook friend. She now has one. Her name is..."

Cerise managed a smile. "Her name is Naz, which means 'timid' in Turkish."

"Good," Delilah replied. "She told you. What else did she say?"

"Faheem doesn't bother to hide behind a screen name, and is happy that Naz doesn't either. When I pointed out that Naz might not be a real name, she looked shocked, then said it didn't matter. She can get much closer to a person when they use the name of a real person, not a made-up one like some she has seen online. 'Badass 69,' 'Deathmask 187.' I can see her point."

Cerise looked away. "I don't have any idea how this will play out, I don't want her to get hurt, somehow, by this new 'friend.' "

"We can't know how long this will go on, or how Faheem is going to react to what her friend says to her, but there are safeguards built in. Turkey was chosen as the friend's country to provide the kinship of a Muslim nation, yet one unlikely to have any emotional pull for Faheem. It is far enough away from Afghanistan that there should be zero expectation they would try to meet."

Cerise was quiet, mulling over what she had just heard, searching for any oversight which might inadvertently expose Faheem to anguish. She was certain that if she left it up to the FBI, what was best for Trapdoor would outweigh what was best for Faheem.

After a moment, she said, "I want an unedited copy of every communication between Faheem and this Naz you have created."

25

Monday, June 28, 2010
Washington, D.C.

Delilah Bone sat at the kitchen table of the FBI townhouse on Prospect Street, awaiting a confrontation with Agent Jason Stanley. He had erupted on the telephone when Delilah reported Cerise Bevard's demand that she be provided with a verbatim transcript of every conversation between Faheem and her Facebook friend, Naz.

Cerise's sole concern was Faheem's welfare, the FBI's concern was the mission. Whatever their decision today, Delilah would wind up boxed into a corner.

While she waited, it occurred to Delilah that the mood of today's meeting would be poles apart from that of her last visit to the safehouse.

Jason Stanley was all business—no coffee, no donuts and no straying from Cerise Bevard: the issue of the day.

The supervisors of undercover operations she had worked for in other offices were flexible. They invariably attended safehouse meetings in casual attire. Khakis or cargo pants and sweaters or windbreakers.

Stanley bustled through the door and set a tan leather drop-handle briefcase on the table. "Sorry I'm late," he said and slid into the chair across the table from Delilah.

As she expected, he was dressed for success. A dark-blue business suit, long-sleeved dress shirt, a woven silk jacquard necktie and matching pocket square. She was certain that he maintained his blond hair in a buzz cut to accentuate the "hard Marine" look of his square jaw.

"I haven't been here long myself", she replied.

You'd think he would take off his jacket.

From his briefcase, Jason removed a lined, legal-size yellow tablet and Cross fountain pen.

"Let's be clear about this," he said. "There is no way that we are going to give in to her demand."

"What do I tell her when she brings up the fact that she is cleared for all aspects of this case?"

"She is not cleared to receive internal FBI documents. Once we turn them over, the FBI loses control of the content. We would have no recourse if we should find them floating around the world on Facebook or Twitter."

"But, it's..."

"I can't be any clearer. She is not getting a verbatim transcript of any FBI documents. We are here to come up with an alternative, one that she is likely to accept."

Delilah sat in silence, tapping her eyeteeth with a ballpoint pen.

Jason said, "Would she agree that you care about Faheem and have the girl's welfare at heart?"

"It's likely."

"Do you think that she would accept your word that you will read each transcript and tell her if you find anything objectionable?"

"Doubtful. I wouldn't accept it."

"What if that was your only choice?"

Delilah shrugged. "How about this," she said. "We give her phony transcripts."

Jason made a face. "I don't know..."

"They wouldn't be official FBI documents."

Jason shook his head. "In order to fool Cerise, they would have to look official. If they were circulated on the internet, they would do the same damage as the real thing."

He glanced at his watch and began packing up. "I have to get back inside for a supervisors conference. We'll talk again before you see Delilah. Absent anything better, were going with your promise to read and report to her. She has no choice but to accept it."

"She could tell Faheem what she has been really involved in."

26

Saturday, July 3, 2010
Bethesda, Maryland

In the morning, Faheem was ecstatic to find a Facebook message from Naz on her computer. It seemed like weeks since they had met on Facebook, and Faheem had grown anxious.

My friend Faheem.
How do you like America? The few pictures I have seen of it show me a beautiful country. Please send me pictures of the house where you are staying. And also ones of Miss Cerise and the imam, so that I can see them when you tell me more about your adventures over there. Oh, and of course pictures of yourself.
My country is also very beautiful. Soon my family will drive down to Antalya on the Mediterranean Sea, for our vacation of fourteen days. Each year we stay at the same hotel which is directly on a sandy beach.
I would very much like to hear all about your friends. Write soon.
Your Facebook friend, Naz

There are some who would wait before replying, lest they appear overly anxious, however, such an idea did not occur to Faheem. There was much she was eager to share with Naz, some things with Naz only.

Besides, it made sense to her that the quicker she replied, the quicker she would receive another letter to read.

Dear Friend Naz,
I have visited your country by Google and I too think it is quite beautiful. I have read some history of Turkey and was very surprised to learn of how one man, Mustafa Kemal Ataturk, united all of the tribes and made them change their ideas about how to be a good

Muslim. Every day we have bombings and killings in Afghanistan,   I have not heard of such things in Turkey.

Your country had Ataturk and America had George Washington, I wish Afhanistan had someone like that to save us from the Taliban.

By the way, tomorrow night the skies all across America will light up with fireworks to celebrate freedom day.

Anyway, I will send you many pictures by using my smartphone,   I have told you how good Miss Cerise has been to me and I love her dearly, but she is always afraid that something bad will happen to me. So, there are some things I am afraid to tell her. I'm sorry that you, Naz, are the only one I can trust to talk to about these matters. I hope that you understand.

There have been some things happen with Imam Waladi. At one of the Quran study sessions on Tuesdays, he told me, in private, that my studies are so well that he will soon name me to be one of the imams to help him with his duties in the Islamic Center. I must admit I was very proud. I told this to Miss Cerise and she tried to be happy for me but I think she saw something bad instead. See, that is what I was talking about. Yesterday, after Jumu'ah *Friday prayer, Imam Waladi spoke to me very quietly. He said that it would dishonor Allah to have an imam (he meant me) of such an important Islamic Center living in the house of a heretic. He told me that I must prepare to leave Miss Cerise's house to go and live with him. I do not know what to do. I must not dishonor Allah, but Miss Cerise will be very angry. I know she would cry. She has done so much for me.*

Oh, this must be a secret between the two of us.

Your dear friend, Faheem.

27

Monday, July 5, 2010
Washington, D.C.

Delilah called Cerise on her cellphone to confirm that they were both on their way to the Magic Carpet and Cerise, arriving first, would not bother to open for business before their meeting.

Delilah rushed into the store, somewhat breathless and empty-handed. This action, coupled with her anxious phone call, were designed to instill in Cerise the mindset that Delilah could be trusted to share news concerning Faheem without delay.

After locking the front door, behind Delilah, Cerise took her usual chair across the work table, her body rigid, her hands clenched tightly on the table.

"Well!"

"There was Facebook traffic between Faheem and Naz over the weekend. I called you as soon as I heard about it. Faheem told Naz that she loves you very much and is thankful for all you have done for her, still she feels she can't tell you everything."

"Did she say why she feels this way?"

"You're over-protective. You worry too much about her security."

Cerise looked bewildered.

"For example, when she told you that Waladi was going to name her an imam, though you sounded pleased, she read you as displeased. Sounds like she is good at reading people."

"There's more, isn't there? Something specific she has not told me."

"After Friday prayers, Waladi told her that it would dishonor Allah for her to be an imam and live in the house of a heretic—you. Faheem was told to make plans to move out."

`"And move in with him, right?"

Delilah nodded.

"That Muslim Motherfucker. I'm ..."

"You can't do anything! We'll figure something out. Trust us."

"The only other option is to castrate the bastard."

"He doesn't know she's a female," Delilah replied. "That can't be it."

"Ironically, that is exactly it. He thinks he's getting a boy and that's what he wants. A boy. Have you heard of the *bacha bazi*?"

Delilah shook her head.

"*Bacha bazi* translates to 'playing with kids', but it is much more depraved than it sounds. In Afghanistan and parts of Pakistan, where women are forbidden to dance in public, teenage boys, usually urchins, are taken off of the streets and forced to dress like women and dance like women for their patrons' pleasure. And, of course, it doesn't end there.

"No doubt Waladi turns the boys he entices to attend Tuesday Quran studies into *bacha bazi* and uses them to entertain himself and a few choice friends. Hypocrite sons of bitches."

Delilah was making notes. "In addition to being a terrorist, Waladi is a corruptible imam, and a sex pervert."

She looked across the table. "We must take this bastard down."

Cerise gave an emphatic nod. "Agreed. But I have no intention of sacrificing Faheem in the process."

28

Thursday, July 8, 2010
Chevy Chase, Maryland

At La Ferme's front door, Cerise shook the rain from her umbrella, collapsed it and proceeded into the dining room.

Until this morning, Cerise had not heard from Simon since the last time they were together, and she was determined to make him pay for that.

She followed the *maitre d'* to their table and ordered a vodka and tonic from the waiter trailing close behind.

Her drink arrived at the same time as Simon himself, who ordered a Beefeaters on the rocks with a twist. He took his seat and reached across the table for her hand. While she did not pull back, she was cool, almost hostile, leaving him bewildered.

His hand resting on hers, he said, "If you are pissed off because I have not called since our night, I was out of the country on something of an emergency."

He squeezed her hand. "If I could have called you, I would have. I hope you know that."

Cerise maintained her silence, without moving her hand.

Simon ignored his drink when it was set in front of him, which Cerise took as a hopeful sign.

She said, "I am protecting myself in the event that you came here as a messenger for the FBI."

"Cerise, our night together was not just a roll in the hay. Not for me. I regard it as the culmination of a long and sometimes arduous courtship. Albeit one without a speck of romance. I can't imagine two people who would know each other so intimately, without ever having been intimate. Until now."

Cerise squeezed his hand. "The ice in your glass is melting. Drink up and we'll finish this discussion on your carpet."

Simon nodded and glanced around the restaurant. "Someday I hope to find out if the food here is any good."

Simon Wedge's townhouse was on a shaded street of three-story buildings, each adorned with coach lights and fronted by a sidewalk of red brick. Every home was painted in a Colonial hue, and collectively they were reminiscent of a trip to Williamsburg, Virginia.

Simon's house had been painted a warm cream color, with shutters and front door a glossy black.

Years ago, when he bought the house, he had just returned from London and the street reminded him of a mews in London's Mayfair district, just a short walk from his office in the U.S. Embassy on Grosvenor Square.

Tonight Cerise, driving her Audi, trailed Simon into the alley behind his house.

As he turned into the paved driveway, Simon activated the garage door and pulled into the single bay. Cerise parked on the macadam and accompanied him through the garage and up a flight of stairs to the second floor.

At the top of the stairs they turned left, away from the spacious kitchen, skirted the maple dining table and entered the greatroom, which looked out on the street at the front of the house.

Simon squeezed her hand and said, "I'll open some wine. We have to talk."

Cerise hugged him and sat on the Italian sofa, of maroon leather, which faced the blackened fireplace in the corner. After kicking off her shoes, Cerise tucked her legs under her and looked fondly at the plush gray carpet stretching between the sofa and the fireplace.

She smiled at memories of a naked Simon crawling across the carpet for a drink of wine and then crawling back to snuggle up to her.

She was certain the carpet pile was still depressed in the spot they had used —each time.

They had not climbed the stairs to the third floor owner's suite until the fire had died and the greatroom was pale with the breaking dawn.

Simon returned with an open bottle of wine, a chilled Lambrusco from northern Italy, and two glasses. He poured Cerise a half-glass and kissed her tenderly on the forehead as he presented it to her.

With glass in hand, Cerise indicated the floor. "Here's to a return visit to the carpet."

Simon returned a brief nod, wondering if she would feel that way after their talk.

Cerise drank some wine and sat her glass on the end table next to her.

Simon had shed his suit jacket and tie in the other room. Now he kicked off his shoes and sat facing her on the sofa, wineglass in hand.

"I was not present during the meeting where this was discussed. Ray filled me in, and I think he intended for me to pass it on—to warn you. But I'm not certain of that. Knowing you, I don't expect it would do any good to say—*don't let them know that you know*—but I really don't care. Whatever happens, we are a team."

Cerise braced herself in anticipation of what was coming.

"The FBI is working on a way to separate you from Faheem. They're afraid that it's only a matter of time until you tell her what she is getting into. Everything they have seen leads them to believe that, when that happens, Faheem will run straight to Waladi, and Trapdoor will be blown."

"What does that mean, exactly—separate me from Faheem?"

"I don't know. And I'm not sure that they know. Maybe a plan to wedge Delilah Bone in between the two of you. They've mentioned that you are not her legal guardian, so maybe some sort of legal action. They've just started—"

Cerise was on her feet, searching for both shoes, "You bastard! They sent you to scare me off with this not-so veiled threat. And you agreed to it. What's phase two? You probably told them that you could get me naked on the carpet, again, and I would cave on Faheem while you were screwing my brains out. "

"What? No!"

Cerise had both shoes on and turned toward the door. She stopped and looked back. "You are a natural for this job. You do so love to bullshit people. And I, of all people, fell for it. Jesus, what a fool."

Simon pushed himself off of the sofa.

"Don't think about coming after me. I swear, one of us will get hurt."

Simon saw the tears on her face and for a minute expected that he would be sick. "Please, Cerise. Please, I really am on your side...I love you."

The door to the garage stairs closed on his pleas. He waited, with a desperate hope that he would not hear her car start. When the engine roared, he buried his head in a sofa pillow in an effort to shut out the terrible noise.

The Audi's tires shrieked on the macadam until they reached the alley, and then the smattering of gravel ricocheting off of metal trash cans as it careened down the alley.

29

Friday, July 9, 2010
Washington, D.C.

Following *Jumu' ah* Friday prayers, Imam Waladi sought out Faheem and led her to a secluded corner of the mosque. He placed a gentle hand on her shoulder.

"My young imam, why have you not spoken to me of the day when you will leave the infidel woman and come to live with me, as God wishes? I know you do not want to anger Muhammad."

Waladi's grip tightened on Faheem's tender shoulder as he spoke.

"Forgive me, Excellency, but Miss Cerise has been very busy and I have not been able to speak of this with her."

"If you wish to be an imam you must not anger God—you must please him."

Faheem stifled an anguished cry as Waladi's hand dug deeper into her wounded shoulder. Holding the child's gaze he said, "You will bring all of your possessions with you to my house for next Tuesday's Quran study night, and only then will you receive Muhammad's protection. Tell the infidel woman that she is not to interfere—the penalty is severe for those who defy the Prophet."

Waladi released his hold on Faheem and strode away.

The frightened girl swallowed her tears and tried to rub the pain from her shoulder.

After receiving a call from Bobby Heavens, Cerise left the Magic Carpet and rushed home. Heavens reported arriving at the mosque to find the girl waiting at the curb, pale and shaken. He questioned her, but she merely shook her head in response. During the drive home he glanced in the rear-view mirror to find her stoned-faced, eyes brimming with tears.

Cerise found Faheem at the laptop, pounding fiercely at the keyboard.

"Don't break it," she said, attempting a smile.

Faheem gasped and swiveled around to face her.

"Oh, Miss Cerise. I was shocked by you. I'm sorry about hitting the keys too hard. I would not want to break the beautiful machine you gave to me."

Cerise patted the girl's shoulder, pulling quickly away when Faheem cried out in pain. "I'm so sorry. How did you reinjure your shoulder?"

Faheem, head down, sat with her hands clasped tightly in her lap.

Cerise drew up a chair and sat, watching her for a moment, before saying, "I can't tell if you believe you are protecting me or yourself by being silent. But I can't help you unless I know what has happened."

Faheem unclenched her fists and pulled a handful of tissues from a box on the desk, jamming them into her face in an effort to stanch the flow of tears that began streaming down her cheeks.

"Oh, Miss Cerise. Faheem is very sorry to be bringing these troubles to your house when all you have done is be wonderful to Faheem and her family. I'm sorry. I'm sorry."

"If you are truly sorry, you will tell me what has happened."

"Yes. Yes, I must tell it." Faheem gulped in air, sighed heavily and began.

"I have told you that the imam has said he will name me to be an imam, very soon."

Cerise nodded.

"At our last Quran reading, he told me that to be an imam means that I could no longer live with you. To do so would anger God."

Faheem's voice fell as she continued, "He called you an infidel."

She searched Cerise's face. "I do not think that you are an infidel."

Cerise smiled. "I know."

"I did not tell you of this before, because I was feeling that I did not want to become an imam if it means I must leave here and"— she shuddered—"and go live with him. I was going to tell him my thoughts on that at next Tuesday.

"Today, after *Jumu'ah* prayers, Imam Waladi came to me, we were alone, and laid his hand on my shoulder. He was hurting me, and ordered that I bring all of my clothes with me to his house next Tuesday, and never return here again." Faheem reached for her shoulder as she spoke. "He was very angry and squeezed my shoulder most tightly as he said these things. It was much hurting me and just before he let me go, he looked at me with those terrible black eyes and said to tell you that ..."

Faheem hesitated to recall his exact words before saying, "'The penalty is severe for those who defy the Prophet.' What could that mean?"

"I'm certain it is nothing to worry about." Cerise stretched to view the computer screen behind Faheem. "What were you writing so furiously when I came in?"

Faheem swung back to the desk and before Cerise could object, hit the 'send' button. "There. I was just finished of a Facebook letter to my friend, Naz. I was still very upset about Imam Waladi. I feel not so angry now that I have told everything to you and Naz."

Cerise's anxiety remained hidden from Faheem.

Damn! Now the FBI will know about her pending split with Waladi. There's no doubt in my mind that they will do anything to convince her that she must move into his house.

Those bastards and the agency really are cousins. Nothing matters to either of them but the case. Whatever the cost..

Cerise immediately cast aside the anguish she felt at a fleeting memory of the plush carpet in front of Simon Wedge's fireplace.

Well, screw all of them. This is over now!

She faced Faheem and said, "I've been saving a surprise for you."

Faheem's head turned away from the computer and waited, a look of eagerness spreading across her face.

"Tuesday, I'm leaving on a business trip to Pakistan and Afghanistan. And you are going with me."

30

Monday, July 12, 2010
Washington, D.C.

Following Cerise's surprise announcement of their travel to Afghanistan on Friday, she and Faheem spoke excitedly for some time about their plans.

The discussion briefly involved the question of Faheem's possible return to America with Cerise. No decision could be made until they had spoken to Kamili, Faheem's Mother. Finally, Cerise insisted that Faheem not tell anyone about the trip, as it was to be a surprise for the girl's Mother and sisters.

The Magic Carpet was open from 9 to 3 on Saturdays, and after Cerise left the house that morning, a thrilled Faheem had to share the excitement with someone.

She would honor Cerise's request by not telling her Mother that they were coming. But what harm would it do to tell her friend, Naz? She was in Turkey and had told Faheem that she knew no one in Afghanistan.

Faheem had sat at her computer and composed a short note to Naz on her Facebook page, saying that by next Wednesday, she would be back home and was very anxious to see her Mother and sisters. She mentioned nothing about the likelihood of returning to America.

Monday morning, Cerise opened the Magic Carpet and was seated at the same work table where she met with Delilah Bone. There was much to be done today in preparation for tomorrow's hasty departure.

Occasionally, her thoughts were invaded by images of herself and Simon at his home. Together on the carpet, and the look, approaching panic, on his face as she leveled him with her parting words that last night.

Was I wrong? Was he really on my side? Maybe I was too hard on him.

I'll call and listen to what he has to say, when I get back.

Cerise's effort to focus on her work and the invasive thoughts of Simon were largely responsible for her failure to notice the man who entered quietly through the front door. Or that he was pulling on rubber gloves as he glided toward her.

She was unaware of his presence until he stood before her, with an automatic pistol pointed at her head.

Cerise's last thought was that the man looked awfully young to be an assassin.

The first shot echoed sharply off the heavy brick walls behind her. Cerise did not hear the second or third shot.

The assassin removed the cotton plugs from his ears. Next, as he had been instructed, he grabbed the few dollars from the cash drawer, pausing to glare at her twisted form, angry that there was so little cash.

He turned and headed toward the back door, surveying the area for anything worth stealing as he moved. Anyone responding to the sound of shots would likely be coming through the front; he would leave through the back.

He threw the deadbolt on the back door, paused to remove the gloves he wore, stuffing them in his pocket as he sauntered away down the alley.

Who wears gloves in Washington in July?

31

Monday, July 12, 2010
Bethesda, Maryland

Delilah Bone was driving as fast as she dared. She had just left an emergency meeting of Trapdoor officials at FBI HQ. They were assessing what effect Cerise Bevard's killing could have on their case.

Imam Waladi was the topic of discussion when headquarters supervisor Martin Lemon thundered, "Never mind that! Our biggest concern is our cousins across the river. They have a misplaced proprietary interest in that girl, Faheem.

"I know they are looking beyond Trapdoor. Those bastards figure that, after this is over, they'll send her back to Afghanistan and run her as a fully vetted operative. Screw that—we need her for anti-terrorism work right here."

Lemon's eyes darted to Delilah. "Get out to that house ASAP. Your sole mission, until you hear different, is to ensure that the girl does not end up in the clutches of the agency, or Waladi. Both are equally bad for us. Be especially alert for Simon Wedge."

She gave him a questioning look.

"Because that's who they will send. He and that woman had a thing going on. He probably sees himself as the rightful heir to the girl."

"How...?"

"I don't care how you do it. At gunpoint if necessary."

Delilah, still several blocks from the Bethesda address, was besieged by conflicting thoughts.

She was still trying to process the circumstances of Cerise's murder. When she left FBI HQ, they had already dismissed the idea of a robbery gone bad.

Jason Stanley had been very vocal with his own hypothesis: "D.C. Metro is saying the weapon was a .22-caliber pistol, probably a Ruger. A .22 is not a gang banger's weapon of choice, it's an assassin's."

No one had posed an argument, so Delilah had come away with one thought: Waladi is a very dangerous man.

With more pressing problems to be concerned about, she forced the murder from her mind.

Though Delilah was a federal agent, circumstances required that she obey the traffic laws. If stopped, she dared not break her cover by identifying herself as an agent. In any event, she had no ID to back up her claim.

She was well aware that D.C.-area police were not particularly impressed with federal lawmen, who were known to refer to themselves as "the big law," signifying a superiority over the "locals."

On the other hand, being forced to slow down afforded Delilah additional minutes to plan for what she might encounter upon reaching the house.

Has Faheem heard about Cerise's murder? If not, how should I break it to her?

What will I do if Simon Wedge is there? Will we be like divorced parents fighting over custody of a child?

Or Waladi? Could it be possible that I will have to deal with both Simon Wedge and Imam Waladi? If that happens and things turn bad, can I count on Wedge to back me against Waladi, or will he just sit back and wait to take on the winner for possession of Faheem?

Delilah reached the address and drove through the open gate. There were no other vehicles in sight, and the doors to both garage bays were down.

Her rental car was not equipped with a two-way radio, so she used her cellphone to contact Jason Stanley.

"It is very quiet here," she reported, "No other cars. Not certain whether anyone is home."

"Stay in touch."

She returned the cellphone to her handbag and emboldened herself by momentarily gripping the handle of the Beretta Nano automatic pistol she carried.

Delilah found it to be the perfect weapon for a woman working an undercover assignment. Its 9mm caliber supplied the necessary firepower, while the compact frame and 3-inch barrel fit snugly into the reinforced side pocket she'd had sewn into the lining of her handbag.

The pocket, crafted as it was into the bag's lining, was nearly invisible, while serving to holster the weapon, keeping it above the typical handbag clutter for easy access.

Delilah had an explanation ready if the pistol were inadvertently discovered while on an assignment. The Beretta Nano was not a weapon readily associated with any law enforcement agency, so that question was unlikely to be raised.

The reason for the gun? If confronted, she would say that she bought it after having fought off an attacker while walking across a dark campus one night. Everyone knows how dangerous a college campus can be.

Delilah got out of the car, slung the handbag over her shoulder and walked up the front steps, struggling to project a confidence she lacked.

Faheem opened the front door after the second ring of the doorbell.

"Hello, Faheem. I am Delilah. We met ..."

"I remember. I peeked among the curtains to see who was ringing the door. I am forbidden to open it up to any strange ones. But you are not that, so I'm happy that Mother Cerise did not mean you."

The girl did not seem upset and it did not appear that she had been crying.

Delilah took a step toward the door. "May I come in?"

Faheem glanced at Delilah's car. "I'm sorry that you have drove all this way, for she is gone to her carpet store."

Delilah's next step took her into the entryway. "Actually, I have come to see you."

"You must know that we are flying to my country on tomorrow," Faheem said as she shut the door behind them.

"Did you come to wish me a safe trip? I have been packing up. It will be very hot, but I remember how lucky I am to be a son and not be needing to wear a *jilbab* like a girl. I am very excited to be seeing my family in Tarin Kowt."

Faheem led the way to the sun porch, continuing to chatter excitedly about tomorrow's trip that would never come.

In the sun porch, they sat on adjacent longue chairs and Faheem, her back rigid and both feet on the floor, waited eagerly for Delilah to speak.

Delilah, having decided that there was nothing to be accomplished by beating about the bush, inhaled deeply and began.

Faheem's face paled, her features became set as if in stone. Though her eyes reddened, no tears fell.

I am not surprised, Delilah thought. *This is not a teenage American girl. She has already experienced more violent deaths in her young life than most people ever will. She watched her father blown up on the street in front of her home and suffered traumatic injuries of her own. She has had to deal with the angst of impersonating a boy in a society where she would undoubtedly be stoned to death if the truth were revealed.*

Faheem sat at the edge of her longue chair and beheld the lush lawn and vivid flowering plants arrayed before her. This she compared to her existence in the dusty and decrepit town of Tarin Kowt. Beyond the town stretched barren mountains, the lunar-like landscape of the Baluchi Valley.

Eventually, Faheem looked at Delilah. "I'm sorry to hear about what has happened to Mother Cerise. She was a good person who saved my life by bringing me to America. But I must ask, what will become of *me* now?"

Delilah Bone had prepared a story to address this question. If Faheem had not raised it, Delilah would have.

"Fortunately, Cerise called me yesterday and asked if I would like to stay here while you two were away—a nice break from campus life for me—so it will be no problem for me to move in here with you. At least for a few days."

Just then, the doorbell shrieked. Angrily. Impatiently. Repeatedly.

Delilah grabbed up her purse, reassured by the heft of the Beretta. Keeping Faheem behind her, she led the way to the front windows.

She peered between the closed drapes and recognized Simon Wedge, leaning relentlessly on the buzzer.

Motioning Faheem to wait there, Delilah walked into the vestibule and flung the door open.

The look of anger on Simon's face was puzzling. Was it because it was she who had answered the door, because the FBI had beaten the CIA to claim possession of Faheem, or was it evidence of his anguish over Cerise's death?

"What the hell are you doing here?" He snapped.

"I'm so sorry about Cerise. Please, come in."

Reluctantly Simon Wedge did her bidding, a move which, at least initially, gave Delilah the upper hand. Gambling that Wedge could not refute her story, Delilah stayed with her lie to Faheem.

"I assume you knew that Cerise was taking a somewhat unexpected trip to the Middle East."

A stunned Simon Wedge reacted as if he had been slapped across the face— clearly he had known nothing of Cerise's plans.

Faheem appeared from the hallway and stood beside Delilah, who placed an arm around the girl's waist. The gesture appeared comforting, while demonstrating to Simon Wedge the FBI's dominion over the girl.

"Do you know Mister Wedge?"

The girl's shake of the head affirmed Delilah's suspicion that Cerise had not exposed Faheem to Simon Wedge or, likely, anyone else from the Agency.

With Delilah leading the way as if the house were her own, they retreated to the sun porch. She showed Wedge to a longue chair and turned to Faheem.

"Would you mind making some tea for us?"

Faheem smiled briefly at Simon Wedge and left the room.

Delilah sat in a cushioned chair facing Wedge and leaned forward. "Now, why don't you tell *me* what the hell it is that *you* are doing here?"

Delilah immediately regretted mimicking Wedge's tone and words. His angry mien dissolved, in its place languished a shattered man, his pain visible to anyone who cared to see.

Simon's voice trembled. "I don't really know why I'm here ... or ... what I expected to find." He shrugged, his voice barely audible. "I guess I was praying that, somehow, it would be Cerise who would open that door."

Delilah laid a hand on his arm. "I'm sorry. I did not realize how close you were."

Simon hid his face in one hand, an obvious effort to mask his swollen eyes, the tears streaking his face.

"It's awful. The last time I saw her, we fought and she stormed off, as angry as I've ever seen her. And ..." His voice trailed away, chin quivering.

Faheem appeared in the doorway to announce that tea was ready, took a look at the scene and retreated back to the kitchen.

Delilah retrieved a box of Kleenex and passed it to Wedge, who used the tissues on his eyes and nose.

"Sorry. The last time I saw her, she left thinking that I had betrayed her."

His look implored Delilah to believe him. "I was always on her side. Even when I was carrying the FBI's water. I did it because I figured she needed somebody to look out for her. I believed that she understood I was running interference for her...and for Faheem, I guess. I knew how determined she was that nothing happen to the girl..."

Wedge looked up at Delilah. "...You don't want to hear this..."

"No. Please. I liked her, and what's more, I respected her. She had been put in a very bad place. Doing what she believed was right for Faheem, and for her country, was tearing her up. I don't know if she felt the same toward me, but I had come to consider Cerise Bevard my friend."

"Goddamned job!" He blurted.

"What?"

"The morning after our fight, I was sent out of the country and didn't get back until late last night. If I had been here, I know we could have worked it out...things would have been different."

"There is nothing you could have done. She would still have been in her shop today. The only difference is, maybe you wouldn't feel so angry because of the way you left it."

Delilah leaned closer to Simon. "Am I right that the Agency did not send you here to take charge of..." She nodded toward the kitchen.

"What? No! I've had no discussions with anybody about that. Ray knows better than to broach something like that...now."

His voice rising, Simon added, "What the hell is this about? Are you here as Cerise's friend, or to stake the FBI's claim to the girl?"

Delilah, alarmed that Faheem might overhear what was being said, lowered her voice, trusting that Simon would follow her lead.

"I'm sorry, I didn't know how close you and Cerise were. I am here to do whatever is needed. Anything to help. Particularly to make it easier for Faheem."

She glanced toward the door. "This is not the time nor place to discuss her future."

Delilah, satisfied that Simon had been calmed, stood up. "I'll help Faheem bring in the tea."

Simon slumped in the chair, ignoring his tea while the two women sipped from their cups. Delilah set her cup on the glass tray and broke the uncomfortable silence. Based largely on what Simon had told her about his final contact with Cerise, she felt confident in continuing the pretense of an invitation from Cerise. She said, "Faheem is quite rightly concerned about what will happen to her. When you drove up I was telling her that Cerise had invited me to house-sit while they were gone."

She nodded to Faheem. "Now I'll be happy to have her here. We can help each other get through the terrible days ahead."

Simon was silent, offering no challenge.

Delilah, unsure how much Simon had been told about Imam Waladi's demands on Faheem, had decided not to raise that issue unless it became imperative to convince him that Waladi posed an immediate threat to the girl.

Simon seemed oblivious to any movement as Delilah collected his untouched tea cup and followed Faheem to the kitchen.

After setting the dishes next to the sink, Faheem moved closer to Delilah and whispered. "Please, I do not wish to go back in there with Mister Wedge. He is very frightening to me."

Delilah smiled. "We'll give him a few minutes alone and then I will go back. You may stay here. I will explain that you are busy cleaning up."

"Yes. Thank you."

When Delilah finally returned to the sun porch, Simon Wedge was still slumped in his chair, staring straight ahead. She returned to her own chair and waited for him to stir.

Moments later, Wedge sat up and looked over at Delilah. He stood and mumbled something unintelligible before stumbling from the room. Delilah resisted an impulse to assist him, sitting still until the engine of his car roared. She listened as he drove away.

Delilah found Faheem seated at her laptop, logged on to Facebook.

`"Mister Wedge has left. I'm going to get my travel bag from the car. We can talk when I come back."

Faheem, engrossed in the message on her computer screen, nodded without looking up.

Delilah sat in the driver's seat and hit the speed-dial number for Jason Stanley's office phone. When he came on, she furnished a detailed scenario of the events since her arrival.

"It sounds like Wedge was serious about her. That's a real shame."

"He looks destroyed."

"Well played, Bone. That house-sitting ploy was a stroke of genius. If needed, we'll contact you on your cell. Unless Wedge volunteers, I guess you're stuck with making Bevard's funeral arrangements. You okay with that?"

"Do I have a choice? They didn't cover that at Quantico—but people seem to get through it every day."

"The difference is, you won't have access to her funds, and we're not paying for a funeral. I'll get legal on it, see if they can come up with anything."

"Faheem is a tough kid, as you might imagine, after all she has been through. There were no tears after I broke the news, and her only comment was, 'What's going to happen to me?' What can I tell her?"

Stanley was thoughtful, before saying, "We haven't had time to sort that out. You can stall her for a few days, at least until after the funeral. By then we will have decided how to handle this. For now, just keep her safe and on the team."

"Anything else?"

Stanley's tone hardened. "We're working a joint investigation with Metro on the murder. It's still early, but we believe we're looking at a contract killing. Waladi is still the only name on our screen."

"Oh, shit."

"Well said. Do you know Bobby Heavens?"

"No."

"Bobby is a special agent with State Department's Diplomatic Security. They don't come any tougher than Bobby Heavens. He's shot it out with drug lords in South America and warlords in Afghanistan.

"Anyhow, for the last few years when Bevard traveled overseas, she was sponsored by State, and he was always assigned to her protection detail. At home, when he was available, Bobby served as her driver and quasi-bodyguard. In return, she gave him a rent-free apartment over her garage. You've seen the grounds, I doubt that the apartment is a dump.

"Make it a priority to introduce yourself to Bobby so he doesn't shoot you, and keep him current on the Waladi threat. He doesn't need to know anything about our case."

Delilah was pondering another question when Stanley added, "I can't stress this enough: If you see or hear anything of Waladi or any of his minions, call me immediately. Day or night. In addition to Bobby, a Bureau surveillance team will be close, plus Montgomery County police will be patrolling. We told them there is a concern about armed burglars. Of course, you'll be told if we pick up anything on the intercepts."

"Not the usual day at the office."
"And, Bone, watch your 6 o'clock."
"We'll be ready."

32

Monday, July 12, 2010
Bethesda, Maryland

Delilah grew edgier as the evening progressed. Unable to sit still, she paced the floor in front of the window overlooking the drive, watchful for Bobby Heavens. He had called on the house landline while she and Faheem were eating Chinese carry-out.

Now, as they awaited Heavens' arrival, Faheem longued in front of the f lat-screen television engrossed in reruns of "Glee", her favorite American show.

After her talk with Jason Stanley, Delilah had dropped her travel bag in the spare bedroom.

Thereafter, she felt like an intruder peering into each room as she trailed Faheem on a tour of the house.

Delilah had shuddered involuntarily whenever they encountered a personal item casually discarded by Cerise Bevard mere hours before.

Delilah ceased pacing at the roar of a car's engine in the driveway. At the front window, she identified a blue Audi emerging through the dusk.

Delilah met Bobby Heavens at the front door. They quickly exchanged identification and condolences as he stepped into the entryway, visibly shaken by the day's events.

Faheem appeared, curious about their visitor. "Mister Bobby is here!" she cried out.

Cerise had told Faheem of how, while others stood by in shock from the blast that had killed her father, "Mister Bobby," hearing her screams, sprinted through the mangled doorway, scooped her up, then darted out to the Humvee.

He had stanched her bleeding while Rich Kelly floored the gas and, one hand working the horn, the other on the steering wheel, had sped to the military hospital at the edge of town.

Cerise had made it clear to Faheem that "Mister Bobby's" action had, very likely saved her life.

Faheem ran to embrace him.

Voice trembling, he asked, "How are you, kid?"

"It is so very awful, Mister Bobby. Miss Cerise was the most wonderful of people. Who could do such a terrible thing to her?"

Heavens held her away from him and looked into her eyes. "I promise that we will find out who did it, and they will be punished, most painfully."

She nodded. "I know that is God's wish."

Delilah's cellphone chimed "The Stars and Stripes Forever." As she dug it out of a pocket, Heavens motioned that he and Faheem would give her privacy.

Delilah's call, though brief, was troubling.

Later, when she located Bobby Heavens, he was at the wet bar in the sun porch, perched on a barstool. An open bottle of the Macallan single malt was next to him, a glass with scotch splashed over ice in his right hand.

"I hope you don't mind," he said, "I know Cerise wouldn't." He reached for the bottle to pour a drink for Delilah when he spotted the handle of a Beretta jammed into the waist band of her slacks. It had not been there earlier.

Bobby showed Delilah the bottle and she shook her head. "Another time. When things settle down."

His response was to push his own glass away. "Shame to waste. Are we expecting trouble?"

"I don't look for trouble, but I always expect it."

"Care to share?"

Earlier Delilah had studied Bobby Heavens. He was 2 to 3 inches taller than she, 5 foot 9 or 10. Solid, his polo shirt straining against unyielding muscles. She imagined him repeatedly curling massive barbells with ease.

She contrasted his tenderness, the emotion he had shared with Faheem, to Jason Stanley's comments. "Bobby has shot it out with drug lords in South America and warlords in Afghanistan."

Instinctively, Delilah trusted him and decided to include him in the intrigue being formulated to protect Faheem, while thwarting Waladi.

In response to Heaven's question about sharing, Delilah replied, "Jason Stanley, the FBI supervisor on this case, speaks very highly of you and has instructed that you be brought up to date. I am ready to send, if you are ready to receive."

Bobby reached out and retrieved his glass."I am now."

Delilah held out her right hand, thumb and forefinger about one inch apart, indicating the amount of scotch she would accept.

She welcomed the glass and quickly tossed back most of the drink.

Before beginning her account of the situation, Delilah shifted in her chair so that, as she talked, she would be alerted should Faheen appear in the doorway.

Aware that Bobby Heavens was thoroughly familiar with the roles played by both Cerise and Faheem, Delilah condensed the elements of Trapdoor as she brought him up to date.

"That brings us to today's tragedy."

"On that subject, it looks like you drew the short straw," he glanced around the room, "and got thrown right into the middle of it. Looking after our friend in the other room won't be a holiday."

"It's the job. And I really don't mind. Faheem needs caring for, and I want to see her through this, to the end."

"This may not be the time to bring it up, but I would like to drive the Audi for a while, if you have no objections."

Delilah, confused by the question, stammered, "I'm...why are ... it's not for me to say."

"Who then? As far as I know Cerise had no one close. Eventually, it will get sorted out, but I don't want some court-appointed lawyer accusing me of stealing her property. At the least, I told someone in authority what I was doing."

"Me?"

"You!"

"... Okay. I'll be your witness—on one condition."

"What?"

"Clearly, if there is to be a funeral, I'm the one who must make the arrangements." She shrugged. "I don't know where to start, I can use some help with that. Actually, a lot of help."

"I wondered about that. I don't see the agency getting involved, and Cerise had a contract with State. She was highly regarded there. I spoke to someone up the ladder, and I think they will agree to take care of it."

Delilah suppressed an urge to hug Heavens; instead, they clinked glasses in a gesture of mutual support.

Smiling, Delilah said, "If you keep riding to the rescue, we'll need to change that blue Audi for a white Charger."

Bobby grinned and reached for the scotch bottle.

"Cerise Bevard was a wonderful person and a good, good friend. I can't think of anyone's death that would affect me more. Including my own Mother. You probably thought it reckless of me to promise Faheem that Cerise's killer will be punished. I wasn't just blowing off steam in front of the kid. I really mean to see it happen."

Delilah declined his offer to top off her glass, checked the doorway with a glance and resumed her account. "As you might expect, the FBI has joined the Metro police in the investigation of her shooting. Did you know the weapon used was a .22 Ruger?"

Bobby nodded. "So it wasn't a botched robbery."

Delilah had to be careful here. Her orders were to bring Bobby Heavens up to date—on everything. And she expected to, but would such a man, one so close to Cerise, one who had shot it out with Afghani warlords, hesitate to execute a phony imam who was presented to him as a known terrorist and likely killer of his dear friend?

"Everything seems to point to an assassin. Who would hire someone to kill Cerise is still a very big mystery."

When Bobby offered no response, she added, "The call I received when you and Faheem left the entryway—thank you for that, by the way—was from my office, to let me know that Faheem had published the facts of Cerise's death on Facebook. She included the item that 'Aunt Delilah' had moved in and was caring for her."

Delilah saw nothing to be gained by mentioning that Faheem had included a message for Qader about missing Tuesday's Quran study but expected to be at *Jumua'h* prayer on Friday.

If Bobby had any questions about the FBI's source for this information, he was too much of a pro to ask. For this briefing, he would settle for absorbing everything she was willing to provide. Any additional answers he sought would be retrieved through other sources.

Purposely omitting any reference to Waladi, she added, "The significance of that is, if Faheem is the real treasure here the treasure seekers probably realize that they will now need to come through me to collect their prize."

Bobby glanced at the pistol butt jutting above her waistband. "Hence the recent addition of the weaponry to your wardrobe."

"As I said, I don 't look for it, but I do expect it."

33

Friday, July 16, 2010
Washington, D.C.

Cerise Bevard's funeral was held at 11:00 a.m. in a non-denominational chapel within the confines of the U.S. Department of State compound on C Street N.W.

The small room, tightly packed with mourners, was stifling. The front pew, traditionally reserved for family, held Bobby Heavens, Faheem, Simon Wedge and Delilah Bone.

Delilah wondered if others perceived that arrangement to be as odd as did Delilah herself. In her mind, Simon Wedge and Faheem deserved to be so honored. Possibly Bobby Heavens, but certainly not an FBI agent who feigned being an old family friend. At least 20 or 30 people lining the walls knew Cerise better than did Delilah.

It was very likely that Cerise had not even liked her, indeed may have seen Delilah as an enemy in her efforts to protect Faheem. Yet it was Delilah who had found herself deciding who would occupy these few seats. Undoubtedly, many of those crowded behind them speculated as to what role Delilah played in the family.

She hoped they believed the story that she was indeed an old friend. Perhaps a distant cousin. Anything but who she really was.

Delilah had called Simon to ask that he sit in the family pew. Initially, he declined, saying that there were others more worthy.

"Okay," Delilah replied, "Please let me have their names and phone numbers. I need to call them."

When his only response was a series of gasping sounds, she added, "You owe her that ..."

Oddly, he agreed to Delilah's request only after she had said, "I don't know what your beliefs are, but if there is any chance that she is watching us, she would be terribly hurt not to see you in that pew."

Now Simon sat beside Delilah, his head bowed, avoiding the nearly life-size picture of Cerise on display beside the bronze coffin.

Faheem sat at Delilah's right side, silently staring straight ahead. Delilah reflected on whether the girl was thinking of her friend, Cerise, or the fact that she was missing *Jumu'ah* Friday prayers being conducted a few blocks away.

It occurred to Delilah that knowing the answer to that question could go a long way to understanding where Faheem's loyalty would lie should she be forced to make a choice between Delilah and Imam Waladi.

The FBI's monitoring site had reported that, yesterday, Faheem had posted the time for Cerise's funeral, but not its location, on Facebook. Other than condolences from Naz, Delilah was unaware of any responses.

Bobby Heavens was located on the other side of Faheem. He had prevailed upon a senior State Department official to give the eulogy, saving Delilah, or perhaps himself, from being forced to prepare something to say. For this, Delilah was very grateful.

From time to time, as the woman spoke, Bobby patted Faheem's hand. Beyond that, Delilah observed no evidence of grief by either of them.

As for herself, she was appropriately solemn, nothing more.

34

Saturday, July 17, 2010
Washington, D.C.

Delilah sat drinking coffee in the FBI off-site on Prospect Street with Special Agent Monte Sheppard, the lead agent on Trapdoor, and Will Kelly, who headed up the surveillance team. They waited somewhat impatiently for their supervisor, Jason Stanley, who was habitually late for every meeting.

While they waited, Sheppard and Kelly sought, without success, to extract from Delilah Bone details of her Bureau career.

"What number was your new agents class at Quantico?"

"Where was your first office of assignment?"

"What type of undercover roles have you worked?"

"What 'real cases' have you worked?"

Her initial reply, to each query had been, "Sorry, but I'm not free to discuss that."

When the inquiries had persisted, her comments switched to questions about the Washington Redskins.

"I'm very excited about getting to go to some of the games. Are tickets hard to get?"

Sheppard was shaking his head in frustration when Jason Stanley rushed through the front door, mumbling his apologies for being late.

Everyone in the room was routinely on call weekends and holidays, so they would hear no regrets about being summoned into work on this particular Saturday.

The three agents glanced at one another, silently confirming their expectation that though it was a Saturday, and near 90 degrees outside, Stanley would arrive nattily dressed in a long-sleeve dress shirt with a blue necktie beneath a two-button searsucker suit jacket.

Stanley, as if conceding to their thoughts, removed his jacket and hung it over the back of his chair. He grabbed a bottle of water from the minifridge and joined them at the table.

The necessity for this gathering was obvious: Determine how to proceed with Trapdoor in the aftermath of Cerise Bevard's death.

Stanley nodded to Delilah. "You are the closest to the Bevard situation. Let's hear your thoughts."

Delilah said, "The way I see it our dilemma is this: How can we successfully conclude Trapdoor, while shielding Faheem from Waladi?

"On Monday, I moved into a dead woman's house, a house I had never even been in, and have essentially taken over. A real coup, when you consider Faheem is a minor, alien child who belonged to none of us."

Stanley asked, "What is your sense of how Faheem is reacting to your presence?"

"Faheem is a very tough kid and therefore hard to read. She has shown very little emotion following Cerise's death. How much her reactions are influenced by her culture, which would include the Muslim religion, and the rather unique relationship that she and Cerise shared is anybody's guess. Maybe she is being a typical teenager, if there is such a thing.

"It will eventually occur to her, if it hasn't already, that I have no business being in that house, let alone having any authority over her. I really can't tell how she felt about Cerise. Did she love her or hate her?"

Stanley began to speak. "I..."

Delilah interrupted. "...The only one I have seen her respond to is the State Department security guy, Bobby Heavens. I understand that he saved her life following the terrorist bombing that killed her father. How much he would be willing to interact with her on our behalf is anybody's guess."

Stanley looked across the small table at his case agent. "We'll talk to him, Monte," he said, and scratched a reminder in his folder.

Delilah added. "Heavens has been a blessing. Today he agreed to watch out for her while I came here." She shrugged. "Since she can't know that I'm an agent, I guess I would have had to dump her at a movie theater and hope she was still there when I got back."

Stanley made more notes. "We need to solve that problem. You can't stick with her 24/7."

Will Kelly spoke up. "There's been little movement by Waladi this week. Any idea how Faheem feels about going back to her routine with him?"

Another shake of her head. "Again, Faheem has spoken very little since Monday's tragedy."

Stanley laid down his pen. "You haven't spoken to her about any of this?"

Delilah shot a look across the table. "Cerise's funeral was yesterday. I really haven't found an opportune time for a such a discussion. And she knows me as Aunt Delilah, a college student," she pointed to Stanley. "I thought we should talk before I arbitrarily changed the game on her."

"That subject is on today's agenda."

"Anything new on the murder investigation?" Will Kelly asked.

"Sorry," Stanley said. "I wish I had more to report. HQ is keeping the heat on Metro. Each detective is teamed up with an FBI agent for the duration. The neighborhood canvass has produced nothing so far. No ballistics help from the slugs."

"What are we telling the locals about why there's such a big push on a routine robbery-shooting?"

"The Agency agreed that we could tell Metro that we are working this as a favor to them, as they are forbidden by law to conduct domestic investigations. Our agents on the street told their local partners that it's need-to-know, and even they were told nothing more. That's true, the street agents don't know any more than that."

"What about Waladi?"

"Nothing's changed there. He's still the prime suspect."

"Does Metro know about his connection to Faheem and our suspicion that he is behind the shooting?"

Jason Stanley shook his head. "Nothing to be gained by the locals being read into that, until we've ID'd the shooter. We'll see how things lie at that time."

The room was quiet while Monte Sheppard moved to refill each cup and returned the coffee pot to the hotplate.

"Anything new from Faheem's Facebook page?" Delilah asked, and sipped her coffee.

Jason Stanley looked up from his folder. "She posted a short note to Naz on Wednesday, with the time of the funeral. And another one Friday saying that it was over."

He looked at Delilah. "Her only personal comment concerned how impressed she was with the State Department buildings."

"As far as we know," Delilah said, "Faheem has had no communication with Waladi since the shooting."

A slight nod from Stanley confirmed her statement.

Delilah continued. "Even if he's not responsible for Cerise's murder, he's got to know she's dead. It was all over the news and anybody could easily have picked it up from Facebook. I can't imagine he won't continue the pressure to get Faheem out of that house."

"We must keep in mind that he would also know about you moving into the house," Stanley said. "She posted that tidbit as well. Another obstacle for him to hurdle. We can't delay this much longer."

"I would like a few more days to see if she won't give us a clue about what she is thinking."

Stanley shook his head. "I don't know ..."

"We need at least a hint of how she'll react when I have to brace her about Waladi."

"You have to do it in such a way that your cover is not blown. We can't trust her with that information."

Delilah nodded. "I know ..."

Will Kelly spoke out. "Why not do it so Dee doesn't say a word about it, and we can all see Faheem's reaction before going any deeper."

"What are you thinking, Will?" Stanley asked.

"Am I right that Faheem has not been interviewed by any homicide investigators?"

Stanley nodded, beginning to see where Kelly was headed.

"Have a team come to the house for a routine interview of both Faheem and Dee," Kelly nodded at Delilah. "Anyone she had any problems with? Do they know anyone who would want to hurt Cerise? The usual drill.

"They somehow work Waladi's name into the questioning, but not as a suspect. They can figure something that won't alarm Faheem. After they are gone, Dee and the girl can discuss it openly. No need then to pussyfoot around the issue."

Stanley looked at Delilah. "I like it."

"Me too."

"Monte, pick your best homicide team and schedule an interview for Monday morning."

Monte picked up a pen. "Waladi's name will be out with the locals," he cautioned.

"Can't be helped," Stanley replied, then turned toward Delilah. "Keep an eye out for that bastard!"

35

Monday, July 19, 2010
Bethesda, Maryland

Delilah rolled over and glared at the luminous numbers on the bedside clock-radio—2:10 a.m.

"Jesus H. Christ!" she muttered. She would have sworn that at least an hour had elapsed since her last look, not the mere twelve minutes shown by the clock. Despite the air conditioning, her nightgown clung, adding to her discomfort.

She hated it when the job seized control of her mind, playing scenes over and over in her head, like a continual loop recording. Shutting out any hope of sleep.

She agonized about her interview by the homicide team in eight hours. Neither the FBI agent nor the Metro detective will be aware of her undercover role, meaning that they will question her as they would any unknown entity. Lurking in the back of their minds will be the notion that she will be a possible murder suspect.

Delilah labored to anticipate any question they could pose to trip her up. If her cover story became suspect, they could spend hours chasing false leads, until someone at HQ decided to put a stop to it. Her cover would be blown, resulting in professional embarrassment for her.

Delilah was reviewing every detail of how she and Cerise had met, when she heard a faint click—a door closing, or was it the air conditioning?

It was now 2:23 a.m.

She rolled over to escape those glowing numbers when she heard another sound. Someone, or something, bumping a wall.

Delilah's bedroom was the first room at the top of the stairs. She could reach Faheem's room was through a connecting bath. Across the hall, the master suite sat empty.

Every night at bedtime Delilah ritualistically placed her Beretta Nano and cellphone side by side on the bedside table.

Now, believing she could wait no longer, she grabbed up the phone and punched in the single number connecting her to Bobby Heavens' cell. Bobby had programmed her phone with his number the first night they spoke, and she prayed that he was sleeping over the garage tonight.

"Yeah?"

"Someone is in the house!"

"Go to the panic room. I'll be right there."

Delilah set the cellphone on the table, grabbed up the Beretta and racked a round into the chamber. The cellphone again in her left hand, she ran, barefoot and soundless through the connecting bathroom into Faheem's room.

In the dim glow of a night-light, Delilah bent low over the girl and whispered, "Faheem! Quickly! Make no sound and follow me."

"Oh! You have a gun."

Faheem was quickly on her feet. Without further comment she followed Delilah across the hall and into a large bathroom that had been refitted as a refuge against a threat, whether from man or nature.

On Delilah's first tour of the house, Faheem spent several minutes detailing the room's virtues.

"See, the door is very heavy and cannot be opened from out there once it is locked."

She pointed to the telephone on the wall. "It is not the same one that we have downstairs. And see, we have some snacks and bottles of water if we need to stay in here for some hours."

Now, just inside the room, Delilah turned and whispered in Faheem's ear.

"Take my phone and lock yourself in,"

"The room has a phone."

"Please! You must hurry."

Her voice tight, Faheem whispered, "You must come with me into the room that is safe."

Gently, Delilah pushed her along. "Lock the door," she insisted, closing the door between them.

Delilah hesitated until she heard the lock click, then, pistol raised, she stepped into the hall. Staring the few feet to the top of the stairs, she heard nothing moving and began to doubt herself. Should she go down and check the first-floor rooms?

Bobby will be here any second—better to wait for him. We can search it together... I should put on a robe.

She heard a faint creaking on the stairs.

The bastard is coming!

Delilah, pistol held in front of her, lowered herself onto the carpet, in what the firearms instructors at Quantico had called the prone position.

By laying flat on her stomach, she expected to see him before he spotted her. Arms stretched in front of her, Delilah gripped the Beretta in her right fist, using her other hand to steady the shaking. And waited.

Where the hell is Bobby?

The blood thundered in her ears.

Oh shit! He's at the top of the stairs!

A thin ray of light flashed along the wall, hesitating at the door to Delilah's bedroom.

If Waladi sent him, he would have strict instructions that Faheem not be harmed. He's here for me.

"I'm over here," she growled.

The penlight swung in her direction, and she squeezed the trigger three times before the beam of light fell silently to the carpet, quickly covered by the groaning shadow collapsing on top of it.

Delilah rolled to one side, groaning with pain.

Oh, my God! I must have shattered my eardrums.

She scrambled to her feet, shaking her head as she reached for the light switch.

Delilah approached the figure, her eyes fixed on the motionless form's gun hand, her own weapon trained on his head.

"Delilah!" Bobby Heavens shouted from the floor below.

"Up here," she called. "We're all right. He's down."

Bobby Heavens pounded up the stairs, barefoot and shirtless, a Sig Sauer .40-caliber pistol aimed at the body on the floor. He knelt beside the figure, removed the gun from the limp hand, and nodded, confirming to Delilah that the intruder was dead.

"It's a Ruger .22" he said. "He was Cerise's killer."

Delilah felt Faheem standing next to her, sucking in her breath. Before she could shield the child's eyes from the bloody scene, Faheem pointed to the figure sprawled on the floor.

"That is Wazir. I saw him at Imam Waladi's house, for Quran studies."

WALADI

36

Tuesday, July 20, 2010
Montgomery County, Maryland

Waladi boarded the Red Line train at Cleveland Park and quickly found a seat in a nearly empty car. He gave no thought to being followed, fully intent as he was on what lay ahead.

Waladi left the train at White Flint Mall and proceeded directly to his favorite lunch spot, Dave & Buster's restaurant on Level Three.

Not finding Colonel bin Hassani, his contact within the Pakistani Embassy, waiting, Waladi claimed a table and waited anxiously for someone to take his order.

Nearby, children shrieked and laughed as they darted among the video games.

After a couple of meetings at the Nature Center in Rock Creek Park, Waladi and bin Hassani had agreed to "meet in a somewhat more civilized location."

Waladi had said, "When in America. We should do as they do, discuss our mischief while enjoying lunch. At the embassy's expense, of course."

Waladi had become hooked on Dave & Buster's buffalo wings and dipping fries, accompanied by an icy Dr Pepper. On their first visit, Colonel bin Hassani had balked at the restaurant's entrance.

"Are you mad?" He growled in Pashto. "There is nothing here that I will eat. And all of those squalling children." He glared at Waladi. "Is this your idea of civilization?"

Waladi, anticipating the colonel's reaction, was prepared.

"Think about it. This is the ideal place for our discussions. The children are engrossed in the games and their parents are busy watching them. No one will pay any attention to us. Anyway, with all of the noise, no one can hear what we are discussing."

"Neither can we, I say."

"If we go to a quiet place, where the customers are bored, eating in silence, they are likely to pay more attention to us."

When bin Hassani failed to reply, Waladi pressed his advantage.

"The American intelligence services would never think of finding us in such a place."

"What would I eat?"

"Come in. They have a varied menu. Many things. chicken quesadillas, a very nice spinach, and melted cheese for dipping, steamed edamames..."

"Well, I am hungry."

Bin Hassani settled for an order of the chicken quesadillas, and they finished their meal sharing an order of "hot sugary donut bites."

Waladi smirked to himself when bin Hassani ordered more bites to take with him.

Today a waitress approached the table. "Are you expecting another?" She asked, clutching a stack of menus.

"Yes." Waladi held up one hand. "I require only one of those, for my friend. And I am ready to order."

Waladi recited his order and bided his time, waiting for the colonel, by casting discreet glances at the young Mothers with bare legs and arms chasing after their children. Though he would admit this to no one, even himself, these sights tempted him.

They deserve the punishment they are soon to receive. Praise Allah.

As bin Hassani approached the table, Waladi noticed that the other man's eyes also strayed.

Though a colonel in the Pakistani air force, bin Hassani avoided wearing a military uniform away from the embassy grounds.

Likewise, for these meetings, Waladi set aside the garb which identified him as a Muslim imam.

Today each man was outfitted in the Western attire they had purchased on-line explicitly for such meetings; khaki trousers, sport shirts and loafers with no socks.

Waladi's order arrived first, so bin Hassani talked while the imam hungrily attacked his food.

"The Pilot is scheduled to arrive on August 2nd."

No one at a nearby table appeared to notice a strange tongue being spoken in their presence.

"You will need to spend more time at the farm preparing for their arrival."

Waladi dipped a French fry, while the colonel smiled at a busty teenager, who wore a bulging T-shirt. She reacted to his attention by quickly looking away.

Waladi nodded. "I noticed that one, too. Disgraceful."

Turning back to the colonel, he said, "I expect to stock the old house with provisions for their arrival. The landing strip must be kept mowed and the interior of the barn arranged to make space for the airplane you are buying. "

Colonel bin Hassani hesitated while the waiter placed his food in front of him, then chewed on several steamed edamames before responding.

"Please keep in mind that the Pilot's arrival will be quickly followed by the munitions we require. They will take up much space in the barn."

"I have planned well for that. The four horse stalls will accommodate much of the gear."

"This will require much of your time away from your home. What do you tell your wife you are doing?"

Waladi hesitated, a French fry poised at his lips. "Colonel, I tell her nothing. I do not discuss my activities with anyone. She is the wife of an imam, that is all that she needs to know.

"Now, let us speak of more pleasant matters."

Waladi rubbed a thumb and finger together as he spoke. "Being responsible for the purchase of an airplane and housing of this weaponry is expensive. It seems that such expenses would provide an opportunity for us to share more *baksheesh*."

"My dear, Waladi, I have travelled extensively, and it is my experience that *baksheesh* is always involved in large business transactions. In this case, the purchase price of the airplane can be inflated to include an ample amount of *baksheesh* for the buyer's agents."

Bin Hassani waved a hand between them, confirming that they were indeed the "buyer's agents" of whom he spoke.

"It will be a 'bonus' for our faithful service as middlemen."

Waladi broke into a broad smile. "How will this work?"

"In the case of the airplane, we will shop online for a used single-engine plane. It will need to be large enough to carry the necessary warriors and their weapons. Once we have found the aircraft, the sale price will be negotiated face to face. The only record of the final sale price is the price we submit with our expenses."

Waladi stared at a bank of video games and said nothing.

"My dear imam, if you are worried about the *baksheesh*, don't be. A little bonus is to be expected and will not be a problem, as long as we don't get greedy."

37

Tuesday, July 20, 2010
Washington D.C.

Imam Waladi made no effort to conceal his anger when Faheem was not with Qader upon his arrival for the Tuesday evening Quran study session.

"Where is my beautiful Faheem?" he snarled.

"He did not appear at the Metro station."

"Did you message him, as I instructed, that he was to attend tonight's study or risk my wrath?"

"Yes, Sahib. There was no reply."

Waladi bid Qader and Bakht to enter, and the three of them joined Amir in the study room. They exchanged the ritual greetings and, after Waladi was seated, the three young men situated themselves at his feet.

Wazir's absence weighed heavily in the room as the three supplicants watched the imam's face, waiting for him to speak.

Waladi fixed his gaze at a spot on the far wall, above their heads, and remained silent.

It was Qader who spoke. "Sahib, may we speak of Wazir?"

"No."

"May we utter a prayer for him?"

"No."

"May we know why he is not to be honored?"

Waladi lowered his gaze and looked directly at each of them in turn.

"Wazir's acts were unrighteous. Any prayers for the unrighteous are not accepted by God."

Bakht opened his mouth to protest.

"No more!"

When they rose to leave after the study session, Waladi beckoned Qader to remain.

When they were alone, Waladi gripped the boy's shoulder, a thumb applying intense pressure on the collarbone beneath it.

Qader winced. "Please, Sahib."

"If Faheem is not with you next Tuesday, you can expect far worse."

38

Wednesday, July 21, 2010
Bethesda, MD

Faheem finally located Delilah, on her knees, trowel in hand, digging weeds out of Cerise's flower bed alongside the house.

"I have found you."

"It is too nice a day to stay inside."

Faheem envied Delilah's freedom to wear shorts and a sleeveless top in such hot weather. She regretted being unable to allow herself that luxury. Maybe someday, if she were fortunate enough to stay in America, it would happen. But if she returned to Afghanistan, regardless of whether she presented herself as a boy or girl, such a display of one's self would always be forbidden.

"I'm sorry," Faheem said, "I must talk about something. It is most important."

Delilah stood and wiped the dirt from her knees with a gloved hand.

"Thank you."

"Why do you thank me?"

"For giving me an excuse stop working. Let's go inside and have some cold tea. It is much too hot out here."

Faheem laughed. "You would not do well in my country."

Delilah sponged the beads of perspiration from her neck and arms while Faheem poured two glasses of iced tea.

Once they were seated on the sun porch, Delilah drank some tea and reveled in the cold blast of the air conditioning.

Faheem began, "I'm sorry to bother you with this, but I wish to tell someone and there is no one else. Is it okay?"

Delilah set her glass of tea on the table next to her chair.

"Dear Faheem, God, or Mohammed, or fate, whatever you want to call it, has brought us together in a most unusual way."

She swept an arm in front of her. "Neither of us could have imagined being in this circumstance in our wildest dreams."

Delilah hesitated, and Faheem nodded her understanding.

"I'm sure you have wondered what would happen to you if you woke up tomorrow and I was gone." She did not wait for confirmation. "You do not have to worry about that. I will be here as long as you wish. That's my promise to you."

Faheem stood and quickly crossed the space between their chairs, bent down and hugged Delilah.

"Oh, Miss Delilah, thank you very much for saying that. I have been afraid to dream of anything in the future."

When they separated, both of them had tears in their eyes.

Faheem returned to her chair and wiped a hand over her eyes before sitting down. "Now I feel is the proper time to ask about some things, but I don't know if you would know the answers to them."

Delilah braced herself. This was a moment that everyone involved with Trapdoor had wanted: an opportunity to explore Faheem's thoughts and feelings without having them filtered through Cerise Bevard.

But it was crucial that Delilah keep separate what she knew as an FBI agent from what she would have known as Cerise's friend. Delilah, the college student.

She smiled. "There's only one way to find out. If I don't know the answer, I will do my very best to help you find out what you want to know."

Faheem nodded. "First, I must ask this: Who was it that shot Wazir on Monday night? Was it you or Mister Bobby?"

"Does it matter?"

"I am curious about why a woman keeps a gun, and how does she learn how to shoot it so well, if she is only a college student?"

Delilah had prepared herself to face this question.

"In this country it is legal for citizens to own a gun for their own protection. It is written down in our Constitution. Many women buy a gun and go to a local shooting range to learn how to shoot. If you would like to learn to shoot a gun, I would be happy to take you to a range."

"It was you who shot Wazir."

"It was. After what happened to Cerise, I was worried for you and decided to keep my gun by the bed. Do you understand why I had to shoot him?"

Faheem nodded vigorously. "Oh, yes. It must have been him who killed our good friend, and he was in this house to kill me. How could anyone know that he was so very bad? But I still wonder this: Why did he do these things? Why would he hate either one of us so much?"

"I'm certain that the police want to know the answer to that. It is very likely that they will soon come here to ask us questions."

Faheem paled and put a hand over her mouth to keep from crying out.

"Faheem, what is the matter?"

"I am frightened that they might believe I helped Wazir. We are not from the same country, but we are both Muslims, and both of us went to the same mosque. It is even more bad that we both were at Imam Waladi's house for Quran studies." She balled both hands into tight fists and began to pound her thighs.

"Please, don't let them take me! I would never hurt Mother Cerise— never, never, never! Good Muslims do not kill good people. I am a good Muslim, I did not know it, but Wazir must have been a very bad one."

"Oh, Faheem, do not be frightened. No one believes that you would ever do something like that. If they come to ask you questions, you will answer each one with the truth, because you have done nothing wrong."

"Will you stay beside me?"

"Yes, of course."

"Then I will be all right."

"There was more that you wanted to talk about?"

Faheem nodded and drank some tea.

"Whenever you are ready."

"I am not certain what you were told about me. Where should I start?"

"I know about the explosion that killed your father and brought you to this country. Nothing more."

"If you may remember, the first time we met, at lunch, I told you about Imam Waladi at the Islamic Center Mosque?"

"Oh, yes."

"I was very happy to find such a wonderful mosque, and I have been going to *Jumu'ah* prayers each Friday until Mother Cerise was murdered. After that, I was very sad and did not feel like being with all of those people.

"A few weeks ago, I was invited to the imam's house on Tuesday nights to study the Quran with only a few others—that's where I saw Wazir. After a few nights of study, Imam Waladi took me aside and said that he would name me as his assistant imam. It was a great honor and made me very proud.

"I hope you did not know all of these things. It would be quite tiresome to hear it all once over."

Delilah shook her head. "Go on," she said.

"As I said to you, I was very proud of this honor, until some weeks ago when Imam Waladi called Mother Cerise an infidel, and said I must not live in the same house with her. God would not want me to live in such a place, and I must go to live with him, if I wanted to become an imam."

Faheem rubbed her shoulder where Waladi had gripped her when he spoke of this.

"What did Cerise think about you going to live with him?"

"I had not told her, so we never spoke of it."

"What do you want to do?"

"The last time I was at the mosque, Imam Waladi was angry that I had not left this house. He grabbed my shoulder until it hurt and demanded that I leave soon."

"He must think much of you, or he wouldn't have named you an imam."

"That is why I came to you today. I have a Facebook message from Qader. Imam Waladi was angry that Qader did not bring me to Quran study last night. The imam told him that if he does not bring me next Tuesday, he will be very sorry."

"And you are not sure what to do?"

Faheem nodded. "I don't know what the imam will say to me, but I do not want Qader to get into trouble because of me."

"We have a few days. Let me think about it and we will talk again. Is there anything else you want to tell me?"

Faheem sighed and looked out at the lush lawn, dotted with verdant maple, elm and flowering dogwood trees.

"This is very hard, but I must tell you ... I am not a boy named Faheem, I am a girl with the name Faheema."

Delilah, uncertain how shocked she should appear, had prepared what she hoped was a suitable response.

"I have studied about the *bacha posh* of Afghanistan in my college classes. I must say you certainly play the part very convincingly. I had no idea."

Faheem was perplexed. "You know the reasons for the *bacha posh*?"

Delilah smiled. "I am studying sociology and, by coincidence, I wrote a paper on that subject."

"I am so pleased. You will understand what it has meant to my family. And you may understand how much it hurts me to say that I hope not to return to that country. I wish to become an American citizen."

Delilah was not prepared for this revelation, and she struggled with it in stunned silence. When she recovered, she asked, "Did Cerise know that you did not want to return home?"

"We talked about it. She knew I was thinking about it, but I had not decided until only before she is dead."

"You have given this a lot of thought, haven't you?"

Faheem nodded. "There are so many things. Since Mother Cerise brought me here, I have learned so much about this county. But I had started to wonder about America when I worked for the soldiers, at Base Ripley near my house. They helped me and my family so much. Giving me extra food and money to take home. They would smile at all of us who worked there. They had their own name for me—they called me 'Sarge'.

"It made me wonder what a country was like that grew such friendly people. So different than the Afghani or Pakistani soldiers—they never smiled or said anything nice to anyone.

"Since I have been in this house I have watched your TV shows and swam the internet."

Delilah concealed her smile with a question. "Do you have a favorite TV show?"

"Oh, yes! I very much like two shows. 'Dancing with the Stars' and 'America's Next Top Model'. Oh, and 'Glee'. How could I forget 'Glee'? The women in all of these shows are so beautiful, but most of all—they are having fun."

Faheem hung her head. "I should not tell this, but sometimes, when I am alone, I pretend I am a dancer—which I could not do at home. Here, the music is wonderful."

Delilah said nothing, waiting for the girl to finish her reverie.

Faheem sighed deeply. "I know if I went back to Afghanistan, I would, all the time, dream of America. I could not see any of my best TV shows or hear any of the wonderful music. It makes me cry to think what would happen to me, if someone saw me dancing in my bedroom."

She looked at Delilah. "All I want is to be what I really am— a teenage girl, not a pretend man. Is it awful to want only that?"

Delilah shook her head.

"Besides," Faheem added, "I could never be cruel enough to be a man."

"What do you think your Mother will say about this?"

"I will not tell her until I know that I will be allowed to stay here. Then I would work very hard to bring her over here, if she wanted to come. But I don't think she would like to be living in a different country, even a country as great as America."

Delilah rose to her feet, but before she took a step, Faheem said, "There is one more thing I would like to say, if it is all right." Delilah nodded and sat down.

"One of the last things Mother Cerise said was, that if I decided I wanted to stay in this country, she might know of a way to make it happen. Do you know what she was saying?"

"No. The only thing I can think of is that you should ask the FBI about that. They should be able to find out ... Say, FBI agents are coming out to talk to us about Cerise. You could ask them."

Faheem came to Delilah's chair and hugged her again. "Oh Miss Delilah thank you so for being my very good friend. I feel so better."

Delilah hugged her, then stood and walked directly to her bedroom, where she locked the door and punched a direct-dial number on her cellphone.

"Hello."

"She's ready."

39

Bethesda, Maryland
Thursday, July 22, 2010

Faheem's identification of the gunman Wazir as a Tuesday night regular at Imam Waladi's house drastically altered the course of the FBI's joint investigation with the Metropolitan Police Department into the murder of Cerise Bevard.

The Bureau would dispense with the integrated teams of agents and detectives and, henceforth, the interviews of certain individuals were to be conducted solely by teams of FBI agents.

Delilah Bone answered the front door chimes and admitted FBI Special Agents Jason Stanley and Monte Sheppard into the entryway.

"Are you Delilah Bone?" Sheppard asked.

"Yes."

"Is this the home of an Afghan boy named Faheem?"

"Yes. Is this about the Cerise Bevard shooting?"

Sheppard, following the script they had worked out, answered, "Yes. We're sorry to disturb you at this time, but we need to ask you both some questions."

"Of course. Please follow me."

Squad supervisors in the FBI do not accompany field agents on routine interviews in routine cases. Supervisory Special Agent Jason Stanley's presence indicated that the Bureau did not view today's talk with Faheem, nor its related investigation, as routine. Far from it.

Since the meeting at CIA Headquarters, all reports from Stanley's squad relating to Trapdoor had been marked "eyes only" and routed through the inner sanctum of FBI headquarters officials en route to the director's office.

The latest report from the CIA had mentioned a possible attack at an unspecified location in the Washington, D.C., area. Though vague, the report served to heighten the tension surrounding Trapdoor and the investigation of Cerise Bevard's murder.

Delilah Bone's shooting of Wazir in Cerise's house had confirmed the FBI's growing suspicion of Waladi, as the force behind the killing of Cerise Bevard.

Little doubt remained that Waladi coveted Faheem, and the Bureau had orchestrated a plan designed to secure her collaboration against him.

In a conference call with headquarters, just before he and Sheppard left the field office, it was made clear to Jason Stanley how vital this meeting was to the security of the nation.

"Do whatever is necessary to secure the girl's cooperation," Martin Lemon had ordered before terminating the call.

Delilah Bone left the agents in the sun porch, while she went off to retrieve Faheem.

Returning with the girl, she said, "These are the FBI men that we talked about. They're here to ask us some questions about our friend, Cerise."

When the introductions were complete and the four of them seated, Supervisory Special Agent Stanley began.

"Let me start by saying that we apologize for intruding on your grief. While it is true that we believe the man Wazir who was shot while invading this house, was the person who killed Ms. Bevard, we are just as certain he was not acting alone—there was someone else involved. So it is important that we get answers to some questions in order to learn the whole truth about Ms. Bevard's killing."

Faheem and Delilah nodded their understanding.

Agent Monte Sheppard paused as if to remind himself of Delilah's name before saying, "Ah, Ms. Bone, do you acknowledge shooting the man Wazir on Monday of this week, in this house?"

"Of course."

"Did you know Wazir before that date?"

"No. Never saw him before."

Sheppard shifted his focus to Faheem. "Faheem, may I ask how old you are?"

"Yes. I am fourteen years."

"Did you know the intruder Wazir before Monday night?"

Faheem glanced at Delilah Bone, who nodded. Returning her gaze to the agents, Faheem said, "Yes. I saw him at *Jumua'h* Friday prayers and on Tuesday nights."

"You are a Muslim?"

Faheem nodded.

"So you saw him at a mosque."

She nodded again.

"Anywhere else?"

Faheem flicked a look at Delilah before saying, "For some few Tuesday nights I have gone with a boy named Qader to the home of Imam Waladi for the reason to study the Quran. Wazir was also there."

"Did Wazir or any of the others at these meetings know Ms. Bevard?"

Faheem shook her head vigorously.

"If he did not know her, then why would he shoot her down like he did?"

Faheem hung her head and said nothing.

Agent Stanley joined the questioning. "Do you think that Wazir did not shoot her?"

Faheem gripped her knees so tight her knuckles turned white. She feared that they were about to accuse her of taking part in the crime. Did they suspect her of being part of some twisted plan by local Muslims to kill Cerise?

Faheem wanted to scream at them—*I could not shoot Mother Cerise!*—but, the FBI men had not accused her...yet.

"I am not saying he did not do it. I am saying to you that I do not know who did this awful thing."

Agent Sheppard said. "Please, name the others who attended these Tuesday night study sessions with Wazir."

Faheem relaxed the grip on her knees and recited the names. *Maybe they think it is one of them,* she thought. *But why would any of them do this terrible thing?"*

The agents quickly dismissed the other names and focused their attention on Imam Waladi.

"How can you be so certain that the imam and Ms. Bevard had never met?" Sheppard asked.

Faheem considered the question before saying, "Whenever we spoke of Imam Waladi, she said things...well, things that...make me sure she would have told me if she had ever talked to him."

Agent Stanley, continuing to follow the scenario Delilah Bone had prepared for this meeting, turned his attention to her.

"Ms. Bone, I understand that you and Ms. Bevard were friends for some time."

"Yes. We went way back."

"Did she ever confide in you about this Imam Waladi?"

"No. And I, too, think that she would have mentioned it if they had met."

"How about her killer, Wazir?"

"Nothing."

The agents thumbed through their notes, searching for a question to ask.

Sheppard shifted in his seat and said, "We know that it was Wazir who killed Ms. Bevard before breaking in to this house and trying to kill one of you."

Looking directly at Faheem he added, "We have established that Ms. Bevard had never met either Waladi or Wazir. Did either of them ever say anything about her. Especially anything—denigrating?"

Faheem looked to Delilah.

"He means, did one of them say anything bad about her...go ahead and tell him what Waladi said to you."

Faheem sighed. "Very soon ago, Imam Waladi told me that I was doing very well with my Quran studies and he would soon name me as an imam, to assist him at the mosque on *Jumu'ah* Friday. I was very proud, but Mother Cerise did not seem happy when I told her of my great honor."

Faheem unconsciously rubbed her shoulder, adding, "Some days ago, after *Jumu'ah* Friday prayers, the imam held me apart from the others and said that Mother Cerise was an infidel. And that God would be angry if I served as an imam while I lived in the home of an infidel. He got mad and grabbed my shoulder as he spoke of this, saying that I must leave her house and live with him or I could not be an imam."

The two agents exchanged glances, as if hearing this news for the first time.

Stanley nodded at Sheppard, who asked, "Did you tell the imam that you would come to his house?"

"I said nothing to him. I could not tell him that I was afraid to talk about that to Mother Cerise."

"And you never spoke of this to her?"

Faheem shook her head.

Agent Stanley asked, "Do you think this boy, Wazir, would do whatever Waladi asked him to?"

Faheem chose her words carefully. "A Muslim would be expected to do what an imam asks without question."

Agent Sheppard spoke up, "He wasn't asking you about just any Muslim, only Wazir and Waladi."

"I cannot tell you what is in another's heart. Only what is in my own."

Sheppard turned to Jason Stanley. "It would seem that Wazir had no reason to shoot Ms. Brevard on his own, or to try and kill Faheem. He must have been acting on someone's orders. The only one we can connect to Wazir, Bevard and Faheem is...Waladi."

"But why," Faheem moaned, "would the imam want Mother Cerise to die? I can't believe he would want to hurt me."

Stanley answered, "It seems clear. Waladi decided she was an infidel who was interfering with God's will. It is very easy for men like him to justify anything when they believe they are doing God's bidding. If he believed it, how hard would it be for him to convince a devout follower like Wazir to do what God had ordered?"

Faheem hugged her knees and rocked back and forth, her eyes tightly closed. "Praise be to Allah," she moaned. "Praise be to Allah."

Stanley continued, "As for Wazir, he was not here to kill you, Faheem, he was here for Miss Bone."

Stanley shifted toward Delilah. "Waladi must have feared that you would be a roadblock in his efforts to persuade Faheem to move out of here and labeled you an infidel who also must die."

For a moment Faheem's soft moaning was the only sound in the room, and then Agent Stanley said, "There is little doubt that Waladi gave the order to kill Ms. Bevard and Ms. Bone. Our problem is, I don't see any way we can prove it. I doubt that he or Wazir confided in anyone else."

He shifted his attention back to Faheem.

"What about the others you named in the Tuesday night study group? Would Wazir have bragged to any of them about the important mission he was going on for the imam?"

Faheem shook her head. "I think not, but cannot be certain. Wazir spoke little to any of us in the group. Every Tuesday night I came with Qader and Bakht, and Wazir was always sitting there, on the floor, when we came. We would exchange the proper greeting of Muslim men and he would say nothing the rest of the night."

"If we had someone close to Waladi..." Sheppard mused aloud. He referred to his notebook before directing a question to Faheem. "Do you think one of these boys, Qader or Bakht, would be willing to help us?"

Faheem's answer was a slow shake of her head. "If I was not here to see Wazir lying dead," she pointed up with an index finger, "on that floor, and heard what you said here, today, I would not believe that the imam could be a murderer. I'm still not sure what I believe. Besides, Qader and Bakht would be too much afraid to go against a man of God."

Agent Sheppard flashed a look at Delilah and, getting no sign of dissent, posed the question of Faheem. "What about you, Faheem? Do you think that you would be able to help us, if it meant telling us what Waladi said or did?"

Faheem spun around, looking at Delilah as if to say *What do you think of that?*

Delilah leaned forward and took Faheem's hand. "Remember, you told me that Cerise had said that there might be a quick and certain way for you to become an American citizen?"

Faheem squeezed Delilah's hand very hard and nodded.

"I think," Delilah continued, "that this is what she was talking about. If there was some way for you to help the U.S. government, then, in return, you could become a U.S. citizen. But you would need to be a very big help. Perhaps it would be to help the FBI name Waladi as Cerise's killer, something no one else but *you* could do."

Faheem flashed Sheppard a look which clearly asked, *Is that what you meant?*

"I, uh, I..." Sheppard stammered and looked to his supervisor.

Stanley leaned toward Faheem. "Are you asking—if you help us arrest Waladi—would the U.S. government grant citizenship to you?"

Faheem glanced toward Delilah who returned a quick nod. "Yes, sir. That is a question I would like to know the answer of."

Agent Stanley motioned between Sheppard and himself. "As FBI agents, we cannot give you an answer here, today. The final answer has to come from the U.S. Immigration Service. It is a different part of the government than the FBI."

Faheem hung her head, her shoulders sagged and she gazed at the carpet.

Stanley went on, "Faheem, look at me."

She slowly raised her head and fixed Stanley with a gaze.

"This is not an unusual question and there is a set procedure that we follow.

After someone like yourself has helped us arrest very bad people, a high FBI official goes to the immigration service and gives them the facts of the case. Then that department issues the citizenship papers in your name."

Faheem's gaze bounced around the room, avoiding eye contact with the agents.

Stanley asked, "Faheem, is this something you would like us to do for you?"

She studied her hands, her fingers laced together. Without looking up she said, "Many people will hear of what I am doing to help you. Maybe Imam Waladi will hear, then what will happen to me?"

Stanley shook his head. "The FBI will keep your name very secret. Only a few of us will know how you are helping until Waladi has been put where he can't hurt anyone."

"You will kill him?"

"Only if he forces us to. It will be his decision."

Faheem raised her head to look into Agent Stanley's face before saying,

"To get this citizenship, Would I have to go from here to live in Imam Waladi's house?"

"That is a possibility."

Faheem was again silent. Jason Stanley said, "It usually takes years to earn the honor of being a citizen. It is earned by living here as a good person, by showing that you will make this an even better country than it would be if you did not live here. That process can be speeded up only when a person does something to help this country that is so important the government would say, 'Faheem has already made this a better country, we do not have to wait.'

"Do you know of anything that you could do, besides helping us arrest Cerise's killer, that would be so important?"

Faheem shook her head. "No."

"Is there another way to help us learn of Waladi's activities, if you do not move to his house?"

Faheem, again downcast, shook her head in silence.

Stanley's voice was soft. "This is a big decision for you to make. You can wait a few days, and then tell Ms. Bone what you would like to do, and she will pass it on to us."

When Faheem raised her head, her fists were clenched in her lap, her jaw tightly set. She looked directly at Stanley. "You are saying that I am the only person who can show all people what a bad man is Imam Waladi."

"Yes, We can see no other way."

"And, if I don't give you this help, he will be able to remain in this country, but I might have to return to Afghanistan?"

"Yes. That could happen."

"It was really him who killed Mother Cerise, not Wazir. And he was the real cause of Wazir being killed," she indicated Delilah Bone, "and not her."

"Yes. That is also true."

Faheem stood suddenly, marched to Stanley's chair and thrust out her hand. After shaking hands with the two agents, she ran to Delilah and hugged her.

Back at his desk in the Washington, D.C., field office, Supervisory Special Agent Stanley was finishing a telephone report to Martin Lemon at FBI Headquarters.

Lemon was saying, "Bone will monitor the girl's activities."

"Just as we drew it up."

"Kudos to you and Bone."

"...And to Monte Sheppard."

"Yes, of course."

While Faheem is very intelligent, Stanley thought, after talking to Martin Lemon, *the saving grace is that the life she has been forced to live has aged her well beyond her years. The role of a* bacha posh *has conditioned her to present herself as someone she is not. Being exposed to violent death on the battleground that is Afghanistan and surviving the wounds suffered as she watched her father disintegrate in front of her has prepared her for the role she has agreed to play.*

.

40

Friday, July 23, 2010
Washington, D.C.

As *Jumu'ah* Friday prayers ended, Imam Waladi stepped down from the *minbar* and pressed through the knots of worshippers, brushing aside those craving a moment of his time. He had fixed his eyes on Faheem, determined that the boy not elude him this day.

"Do not leave, Faheem," he called out, assured that any of the men within hearing would serve as if a herald of his royal message.

A din swept across the prayer hall, "Do not leave, Faheem. The imam is coming."

Yesterday, the FBI agents had stayed at the house into the late afternoon, preparing Faheem for this moment. They did not leave until confident that she would be able to play out her role as they had tutored her.

The first minutes of her reunion with the imam would be crucial, they told her.

The agents supplied her with reasons to give Waladi, for not moving into his house.

Stanley, not wanting Faheem to know that the FBI had been monitoring her conversation through her cellphone, had secured her permission to wire the device so that they could eavesdrop on her talks with Waladi.

"You will have your cellphone back before you go to the mosque tomorrow. Under no condition will you let him bully you into moving into his house," Agent Stanley had cautioned her.

"We will be listening and will not let him do anything to hurt you."

Faheem answered with a solemn nod.

"We believe, Sheppard had told her, "that he will decide for himself that it is better to delay any move. If he does, you will be in control...for now."

Faheem, her prayer rug rolled up under one arm, forced a smile as Waladi approached.

"Faheem, my child, we have been most worried about you. I am very pleased to see you here for *Jumu'ah* Friday prayers, which is necessary for you to earn God's protection. I know that you are sad for that Cerise woman, but you should not be surprised that she was struck down. She was an infidel and did not deserve God's protection."

The agents had instructed her how to respond if Waladi spoke of the killings. If he failed to bring them up, Faheem was to question Waladi about God's reason for these tragic events.

"But why did Wazir die? Was he also an infidel...without God's protection?"

Imam Waladi summoned his most benevolent look and, speaking softly, said, "Dear Faheem, I see that we must have a long discussion about the ways of God. Tonight, after you have moved into my house, we will have a nice talk. I will answer all of your questions about God's work."

"I don't know. I'm so upset."

"You..."

Faheem shuddered. "Sahib, why did Wazir come to my house to try and kill me?" She looked up. "Can you tell me?"

Waladi touched Faheem's arm and guided her to a quiet corner, apart from the milling congregation.

"I can think of no reason for Wazir to want to harm you. I am greatly distressed by his death. Perhaps he knew of this Bevard woman's killing and came there looking for jewels. She must have been quite wealthy."

Faheem sighed heavily. "I'm sorry to be the one to tell you, Sahib, but the American FBI believes Wazir was also the shooter of Mother Cerise."

She had been alerted what to expect from Waladi when she revealed the FBI's suspicion that Wazir had also killed Bevard.

The imam grew pale, his eyes narrowed to mere slits and beads of sweat formed on his upper lip. He swallowed hard before saying, "Uh, what...how could you know what the FBI believes?"

Faheem glanced around and, seemingly satisfied that no one else could hear their conversation, motioned the imam closer. Voice quavering, she murmured, "They came to my house to question me."

Waladi drew away. "Question you? What about?"

"They think that I helped Wazir in the killing of Mother Cerise and told him where to find her jewels and that's why he was in our house."

"Perhaps, once you had let him in the house, he decided to kill you and keep the jewels for himself."

"That is what they think," Faheem whispered. "One of them said that I had turned off the alarm, so that he could enter."

Faheem brightened. "Miss Delilah stood up and yelled at them. She told them that someone from outside of the house broke the alarm with their computer so that Wazir could sneak in. I don't know if someone could really do that but the FBI men didn't say anymore about it. Do you think someone far away could break the alarm in our house with their computer?"

Waladi, shrugged. "I doubt it," was all he could say.

Faheem flared, anew. "They are wrong, there are no jewels and I was not helping Wazir. I was shocked to see him lying dead in the hallway. So, I still must find out why he had come there to kill me."

"I can be of much assistance to you. I know friends of Wazir, I will speak to them."

"I am very sorry that I will not be able to move in with you, Sahib. The FBI said I must not leave that house until they know if I helped Wazir."

"Did you tell the FBI about me? That Wazir was present at our Tuesday meetings?"

Faheem shook her head. "They did not give me a chance. They were mostly mean, and yelled and cursed at me. It was very awful for me."

She planted both feet and, hands on her hips, spat out, "And I will never tell those infidels anything!"

"They are not our friends. Tell me, Faheem, it was not you who killed Wazir. Who was it then who shot him?"

"There is a man, Mister Bobby, who lives on top of the garage. He saw Wazir going in the house and ran over with a gun. Poor Wazir had no time to save himself."

"And Wazir died at once? He said nothing to anyone?"

Faheem dropped her gaze. "If he did, I do not know what words he spoke."

Waladi allowed himself a hasty smile and said, "It pleases me that the infidels have allowed you to visit the mosque. But for the present, it is better that you don't appear at our Tuesday night session."

"I think they will not stop me. When I said I was coming to *Jumu'ah* Friday prayers, they whispered about religious freedom and said nothing."

"Dear naive, Faheem. What about this woman who has moved in with you? Did the infidels question her?"

"Yes, but she spoke very few words and threatened to get a lawyer. They did not curse her as they did me. They seem quite nervous after she spoke of the lawyer. Do we have Muslim lawyers in America?"

"I will advise you about the law. Though I am not an attorney, because Muslim law is a religious law, they are not allowed to question you about our conversations. Do you agree that I am to act as a lawyer for you?"

"Oh, yes, Sahib. Thank you, so very much."

"Then you must agree to be of service to me."

"Of course! How may I serve you?"

"I am very distressed by the death of my good friend, Wazir. You ask if he was an infidel. He was not, but he was murdered by one, and I will seek revenge for him. Would you like to help me avenge Wazir?"

"Oh, yes!"

Waladi patted her shoulder. "Good, very good. They are probably watching you, so we must not be seen together. They are not allowed in any mosque, still, we should not be seen talking like this. There are spies ... and we don't want to give them the wrong message."

"How will I be able to help?"

"We will send messages on the internet. On the Facebook."

Waladi smiled and moved away, being heartily received into a nearby cluster of worshippers.

41

Saturday, July 24, 2010
Hume, Virginia

    Imam Waladi had timed his departure from Cleveland Avenue, in the District, so that, with no traffic problems, he would reach exit 27 on Interstate 66 just after sunset.

    At exit 27, he left the interstate and turned south at Virginia Route 647, which took him under the I-66 overpass, where he pulled to the side and sat until two cars had passed him. He then continued south on Route 647 toward his destination, near the crossroads town of Hume, Virginia.

    Waladi paid frequent visits to the "horse farm," as the acreage was known to the few aware of its existence, and his reasons for arriving in the area after sunset were basic tradecraft: Any trailing headlights were easily spotted on the unlit country roads he followed toward the winding dirt lane leading into the farm.

    It was July, and the country roads were vaulted for miles with mature maple and box elder trees, greatly impeding any airborne surveillance.

    The entire farm, with its acres of cleared land, was surrounded by dense woodland. Arriving after dark prevented any neighbors from identifying his Buick traveling the dirt lane back to the farmhouse.

    Waladi stopped at the front steps of the house, where he unloaded a small suitcase and several cartons of provisions on the front porch.

    Back in the car, he continued about 200 yards beyond the house, stopping at the hulking double doors to the barn.

    He got out, opened the padlock, shouldered open the bulky doors and, returning to the car, drove into the barn. After relocking the big doors he made his way on foot back to the house.

Waladi and Colonel Muhammad bin Hassani had spent months searching for a property that would meet all of their security requirements. Primarily, it must be located beyond the special flight rules area encircling the nation's capital.

The location needed sufficient clear acreage to land a single-engine aircraft and have a barn large enough to hide the plane.

This particular farm had, in years past, boasted a 2,000-foot turf runway. Though now overgrown, once mowed, it would easily accommodate the late-model STOL aircraft bin Hassani was shopping for. One thousand feet is all the runway needed for the Short Take Off Landing aircraft.

It was not unknown for a foreign government to take title to residential properties in this country. During the Cold War years, Soviet Russia openly owned a waterfront estate on Maryland's Eastern Shore of the Chesapeake Bay.

Once the purchase of the horse farm was complete, bin Hassani had registered the purchase in the embassy's name.

Now, anyone searching Fauquier County land records would only learn that the government of Pakistan was the property's listed owner.

Colonel bin Hassani had insisted that having the property registered in the name of the Embassy of Pakistan, would discourage any meddlers from further prying into the property's land records.

Bin Hassani and Waladi had been frugal with their spending on fixing up the old house. This meant ignoring the large patches of chipped plaster and strips of dangling wallpaper in the living room, and leaving the scarred pine floor as they found it.

They expected to pocket the difference when they submitted inflated charges for reimbursement. A portion of their *baksheesh.*

Waladi entered the house and just ahead, on his left, was the open doorway to the tiny farm kitchen. Though the house boasted running water from a deep well, a hand pump connected to a shallow, hand-dug well sat on the kitchen counter, a vestige of another time.

The imam, fearing that any well could be poisoned by an enemy, had insisted on having a new refrigerator to chill various beverages, including commercially bottled water.

Now he headed toward a small bedroom which, primarily because it offered an attached bathroom, he had claimed for himself. The bed chamber was furnished with a single bed; a 22-inch flat-screen TV had been mounted on the wall at the foot of his bed. The floor space beneath the TV was occupied by a cheap TV stand of stained composite wood with a roll-down door, which concealed numerous pornographic videos.

Approaching his room, he passed an open stairway leading to the second floor, where four bedrooms and a bathroom in various states of disrepair were to be found.

Waladi had decided that the second floor was to be occupied by the men who would soon be arriving. The Pilot and the others; men Waladi called "*mer yawa*" —Dead Ones.

On each visit to the farm, Waladi brought with him provisions with which to stock the house. There was not a *halal* Islamic market between Hume and Washington, D.C. In any event, a Muslim man shopping in the vicinity of Hume, Virginia, would generate intense curiosity among the locals.

His earlier days at the farm had been occupied by trudging through the woods, and scouring the house, barn and other outbuildings. He had identified obscure hiding places inside the buildings and escape routes through the woods in the event of a raid by the FBI.

He recorded copious measurements of the barn, doorways and floor area in anticipation of the arrival of the STOL aircraft and the various other pieces of equipment vital to their mission.

During one of his earliest visits, Waladi had discovered a derelict Massey-Harris 50-horsepower tractor moldering behind a straw pile in a dark corner of the barn. At the rear of the tractor, under a moldy tarp, sat a 60-inch rotary mower.

Waladi spent endless hours, over several months, determined to return both pieces of equipment to working condition. Finally, on a sunny day in April, he pushed back both barn doors, climbed onto the newly burnished tractor and drove it out of the barn, the mower blades flinging out chunks of grass as the tractor chugged up and down the weed-choked runway.

A smile crossed Waladi's face as he yearned for someone to admire what he had done, and to listen to him while he boasted of this great achievement.

He was surprised to learn that, for the first time he could recall, he was actually proud of something he had accomplished and secretly regretted that no one he cared about was there to share the moment with him.

It occurred to him that there was no one that he really cared about, not his wife Masooma, not his two daughters. Thus, it was very likely that there was no one who cared about him. The smile faded from his face.

That morning, as with everything else that he did, Waladi had not informed Masooma what he was doing, where he was going, or when he might return. And she dare not ask. She was always alerted that he was leaving town when he brought home more food and necessities than usual from the *halal* market.

From experience, the number of bags he carried in allowed her to closely estimate the days he would be gone from the house.

In his home, Waladi strictly enforced religious laws and would not permit his wife and daughters to go out of their home unless accompanied by a male relative. As Waladi was their only male relative in America, Masooma and her daughters were confined inside their home for the duration of his travels.

The women risked incurring his wrath if he received reports that any of them had been seen outside of the house. Merely being visible in an exterior doorway earned the sinner a severe cursing, which was often punctuated with a hard slap on the side of the head.

Waladi insisted on the harsh rules to prevent his women from mixing with Christians and becoming used to Western ways. No Western males would gaze upon them.

Tomorrow, Waladi's day would be full, beginning early, before the heat grew stifling. He would mow the weeds on the runway, from the barn to the edge of the woods.

Tonight, he prepared a gratifying evening meal of steak and eggs, one he assured himself he richly deserved.

Later, Waladi poured a generous portion of the fine Scotch whiskey he kept into a tall glass of ice cubes. He then took the bottle and glass into his bedroom and set them on a bedside table, next to an oscillating fan which seemed to merely blow heavy warm air around the small room.

Among his cache of pornography, were two videos of *bacha bazi,* Afghanistan's "dancing boys," which he had brought with him from Pakistan.

Waladi selected one of these, which he inserted into the DVD player. Finally, he undressed and lay on top of the blanket, sipping the scotch and humming along with the music of the dancing boys.

Soon, the *Dead Ones* would begin arriving. There was much to do.

42

Monday, July 26, 2010
Washington, D.C.

Delilah Bone sat in the tiny kitchen of the FBI off-site apartment on Prospect Street, enjoying her first cup of the day. Agents Jason Stanley and Monte Sheppard were fixing their own cups at the coffee bar.

Bone smiled as she watched Stanley pouring cream, his back toward her. It amused her to see him not wearing a suit and tie, though it was Monday, a workday. Today he wore khaki slacks, boasting knife-sharp creases, and a long-sleeve shirt of blue cotton, somewhat dated by a button-down collar.

Had someone said something, or had Stanley figured out for himself how dorky he appeared, wearing a business suit to an off-site in mid-July?

When they sat, Stanley opened by asking Delilah about Faheem.

"Are you getting any bad vibes after her encounter with Waladi on Friday?"

"Nothing bad. Faheem reads people pretty well. She went to the mosque expecting Waladi to demand that she move to his house, which is the way it started."

Delilah indicated Monte Sheppard with a nod. "You told Faheem that if Waladi was behind Cerise's killing, he would dump her in a New York minute if he believed that she was a suspect.

"While she was somewhat perplexed by the term 'New York minute'; she understood the meaning. And she saw that he was figuring out how to use her to keep him informed about the investigation, yet not get so close to her that he, too, would become a suspect."

Delilah looked from Sheppard to Stanley. "She was very impressed how you two could predict what Waladi would do, without ever having met him."

"Don't mention that we were profiling," Sheppard said. "We might get censured."

Bone smiled, and ended her discussion of Faheem by saying, "If she had any doubts about Waladi, they evaporated on Friday. She said some of the American soldiers called their officers 'bastards', but as far as she knows, Waladi is the first bastard she had ever met. She is ready to do whatever she can to help catch him."

Sheppard nodded, but Stanley said, "It sounds good, but we have to be careful."

"About?" asked Delilah.

"Any false info we give Faheem to feed to Waladi. Nothing is out of bounds to him—he will do anything to divert suspicion from himself. If he decides that we need a nudge to charge Faheem with Bevard's murder, I can see him coming up with a plan to have Dee killed and frame Faheem for it."

Stanley turned to Delilah. "By the way, where is Faheem while you are here?"

"Bobby Heavens said he would stay around until I get back. I thought we agreed that Waladi is no longer a threat to her. Am I wrong?"

Stanley shook his head. "I don't think she's in imminent danger from him. But, we have to be very careful around that demented sonofabitch."

The apartment door opened and Special Agent Will Kelly, the surveillance squad coordinator, walked in, accompanied by a man unknown to Delilah.

This man was 3 or 4 inches taller than she, and wiry, wearing cargo pants and a black muscle shirt. To Delilah, however, a shaved head was his most compelling feature. His bronze scalp, gleamed— from the aviator sunglasses he wore to the nape of his neck.

He was undoubtedly former military, certainly not someone who now spent his days behind a desk.

Monte Sheppard spoke up. "Will, how did you get the Count to come out while the sun is up?"

"I promised him a good cup of coffee."

Sheppard held out his coffee cup. "Sorry, Count, but he lied. This tastes more like weak yur ine than coffee."

"Count," Jason Stanley said, "thanks for coming out so early."

He nodded to Delilah, sitting next to him. "Meet Delilah Bone. The Count is one of the Pilots for Nightstalker, our surveillance plane. We seldom see him during daylight, hence his nickname, short for Count Dracula."

Delilah raised her cup. "Hey, Count."

Now at the coffee bar, he turned and nodded. "Hey, Miss D."

With coffee cups filled and everyone in a chair, Jason Stanley looked to Will Kelley, "How about a recap on your activities over the weekend?"

Kelly opened his notebook. "Waladi left home about 7:30 Saturday evening. We kept with him through town. When he got on 66, pointed west, I turned him over to Nightstalker and hung back, planning to close in on him once he left the interstate. Count had him to exit 27, and then he vanished."

Stanley motioned to the pilot. "What happened?"

The Count rubbed a palm across his head, hard, as if burnishing his gleaming scalp.

"Traffic was light so we were trailing him up at 3k. Had no problem keeping an eyeball on him, but by the time we got to exit 27 it was pretty dark. I think he had timed it that way.

"The Buick left the interstate and disappeared beneath the overpass. I called for the ground units to close while I circled back as quick as I could. We followed the first headlights we saw heading south." The Count shrugged and looked at Will Kelly. "It wasn't him."

Kelly resumed the narration. "By the time we got there, he was gone. We spread out and spent about an hour searching the vicinity with no luck. And it would have taken a lot of luck to find him. That's real rural area. Dirt lanes disappearing off of dark roads. Roads that are mostly hidden under big leafy trees.

"Nowhere for us to even check out, like a mall or restaurant parking lot.

"We went back Sunday and scouted miles of back roads. Mostly big farms and small towns. I mean real small. Nothing. The only thing we were sure of, is that Buick wasn't going to be sitting in any church parking lot."

Stanley was shaking his head. "Sounds like he's a pro at this."

Kelly nodded.

"Then we have to crank it up. We got another heads-up from the agency. Again, very sketchy. Their source reports that some suicide bombers have finished their training and will soon be shipping out."

"For?"

Stanley shook his head. "No destination given. Forcing us to play it as if they are headed here."

Will Kelly erupted. "What bullshit!" He shook a finger in the direction of the Commonwealth of Virginia, lying just across the 14th Street Bridge .

"I have no doubt that our cousins across the river are not giving up everything. They spoon-feed us just enough so they can't be accused of not cooperating. They scare the crap out of everyone with intel about an attack being imminent, but no specifics. We wind up chasing ghosts and, as usual, the FBI will be the scapegoat if Trapdoor turns to caca."

"You're saying that the Agency would risk a major terrorist attack in this country by holding back intel? Just to make the FBI look bad?" Delilah asked.

Jason Stanley spoke out, "Basically, it's a guessing game. One we all play."

Delilah turned her palms up by way of saying *I don't get it.*

"Okay," Stanley said. "Let us suppose that the intel we are acting on is good and originates from a well-placed human source in the Pakistani government, and is not a total fabrication from some low-level source who is dreaming up things to sell to his CIA handler.

"Our intel item lands on a desk at Langley among reams of similar reports, and someone has to decide how to disseminate it. The guessing game begins. Is it certified intel gold, i.e. a valid threat? Or just a rumor that the humint source overheard in a hookah bar? Or is it merely someone's pipe dream?

"Keep in mind that it is a very real possibility that the whole thing is mis-information by the Paks. Say they suspect three officials of spying for the Agency. They slowly feed out a different scenario to each one, then sit back and wait for one of these stories to surface.

"If it's intel gold, and it's imminent, we may not know that it is good until after the attack has occurred.

"And if it is gold originating with a single, highly-placed source, any intel agency will go to great lengths to conceal that source."

Delilah gave Will Kelly a questioning glance.

Stanley continued, "What Will is referring to is the Agency holds back info while they fully assess what they have been told. If it's from a high placed source they have to decide how to disguise that, before they will disseminate."

"Like now," Kelly growled.

"Maybe, maybe not," said Monte Sheppard. "We have to take what they give us and work it hard, until ..."

Jason Stanley turned to the Count. "Did you have a forward-looking infrared camera with you?"

The Count smiled. "Up to about an hour before take-off. That's when I got a call from some Bureau supervisor, telling me he was sending a clerk out for my FLIR. They don't have enough equipment for every office and, apparently, somebody decided a Detroit op needed it worse that we did."

Stanley nodded and jotted a reminder in his notebook. Looking up he said, "Will, where is Waladi? Has he come home? Do we have any clue where he might have been going? I'll take anything."

"He wasn't back as of this morning." Will glanced at the Count. "The area where we last saw him is mostly farms and horse ranches, and we were thinking that, if he is planning an attack—similar to 9/11—he could've been headed for a farm where they could stash a small aircraft. Maybe a helicopter—"

The Count added, "For what it's worth, that area is just beyond the D.C. Special Flight Rules Area. The routine operation of a civilian aircraft out there wouldn't attract any official notice."

Stanley turned back to Will Kelly. "Where are we on installing the tracking device on his car? The clock is ticking on the court order."

Kelly shook his head in disgust. "We've had no chance. When he goes home the Buick goes in the garage and the door is shut and locked. Anyplace he goes during the day, the mosque or a shopping center, is too public."

Stanley turned his attention to Delilah. "According to our computer section, Faheem hasn't corresponded with anyone since she wrote to Naz, telling her about Cerise. I think we should send an anxious reply from Naz—very concerned about her friend's welfare in America. See how Faheem responds."

Delilah nodded.

"Also, be thinking whether we should have her contact Waladi and, if she does, what she should say. Something that might help us figure out where he goes in Virginia."

Stanley directed his next statement to everyone at the table. "It is very likely that we are running out of time. Headquarters expects to hear something positive from us—an action plan. Don't dismiss any idea, no matter how bizarre it sounds in your head. If that sounds desperate, that's because it is. We can't walk out of here without something positive."

They fell silent, each one striving toward a solution to a terrorist threat poised to destroy a segment of the nation's citizens.

The Count glanced at his watch and stood, holding his coffee cup. "You were right about the coffee, Monte." He rinsed his cup in the sink and retrieved a bottle of water from the refrigerator.

Returning to his chair, he said, to no one in particular, "Sorry but I'm having trouble keeping my eyes open."

The others took turns filling their coffee cups. After returning to the table, Will Kelly spoke up.

"I went back over our surveillance logs and nothing jumps out, but, there's one," —he held up a thumb and forefinger barely parted— "very tiny item."

He looked at Jason Stanley. "But we are desperate, right?"

Stanley nodded.

"We have seen Waladi do the family shopping every couple of days. He's always alone and no one has ever seen the guy's mysterious wife and daughters. Assuming they are still alive, they never leave the house.

"This past Friday we were watching the Buick while he was in a supermarket. Brady had the eyeball, and he was so bored that he commented over the air how Waladi was loading up on groceries. More than usual."

Sheppard snorted. "Maybe he got a raise."

"That's what Brady said."

"What's the point?" asked Stanley.

The Count chimed in, "There isn't any."

"It may not be much," Kelly replied, "but I haven't heard anything else."

"Go ahead, Will."

"On Friday, he loads up with groceries then heads home The next day he disappears out 66 and hasn't been seen since. Being a Muslim, he is not going to want his wife or daughters appearing in public unaccompanied by a male relative, especially if he is as radical as we think. So, is it possible that he stocks up the kitchen on Cleveland Avenue the day before he is going to be away for a few days?"

"I think I see what Will is getting at," Stanley almost shouted. "The next time he loads up, we can expect he will be heading out 66 the next evening..."

The Count straightened up in his chair. "...And we'll be waiting for him at exit 27."

Stanley said, "Let's hope he has to go out there at least once more, before..."

"It's not much," Will agreed.

"But, it *is* something."

43

Thursday, July, 29, 2010
Potomac, Maryland

Imam Waladi gazed at the tumultuous Potomac River roiling beneath the Olmsted Island bridge. The bridge, spanning the Potomac from Great Falls, Maryland to Olmsted Island, halfway to the Virginia shoreline, proved to be an ideal meeting place.

Waladi was certain that no one had followed him into Great Falls Park and, once situated in the middle of the span, he was positioned to observe anyone that might be trailing Colonel Muhammad bin Hassani as he approached.

Once they were together, the roar of the turbulent water thwarted anyone among the throng of passing sightseers from eavesdropping on their conversation.

To Waladi, the wide Potomac, churning amid rocky outcroppings, suggested an inferior imitation of the Kunhar River in Northern Pakistan's Khyber Pakhtunkhiva Province.

These ignorant peasants, chasing to and fro, taking frenzied photographs of this miserable sham of a river, as if it were some formidable thing. It is puny and weak, as are they, when compared to the Kunhar, a truly mighty force.

Colonel bin Hassani appeared at the Maryland shore and began shouldering through a throng of excited vacationers. Waladi, peering from under the bill of the Washington Nationals baseball cap he wore, had no difficulty in following bin Hassani's wake as he crossed the span. The colonel was easily tracked as his white straw fedora with the black leather band bobbed along above the knots of vacationers.

Bin Hassani, extremely proud of the hat, which he had recently purchased online, sported it at every opportunity.

Colonel bin Hassani joined the imam at the bridge rail with the customary greeting, "*As-Salamu Alaykum*".

Waladi responded with, "*Wa'alaykumu s-salam.*"

Both men rested their forearms on the rail and, for a moment, gazed upriver, mesmerized by the frothing water churning beneath their feet.

Speaking in Urdu, bin Hassani asked, "Will you miss it?"

"The Potomac River?" Waladi answered.

Neither man took his eyes from the seething water.

Bin Hassani shook his head. "Does it bother you that when this is done you will never be able to return to America?"

"We are doing God's work and therefore we cannot fail. When we are victorious, there will be nothing worth coming back to."

The imam turned his head, "Is that the answer you were seeking?"

"My dear Waladi, I was not testing you. Making small talk. Nothing more. Now to business."

The imam turned his face again toward the river and listened intently.

"On 2 August, the Pilot will cross the border with Canada. It will take two or three days for him to make his way here. He must be cautious.

"The others will be arriving about the same date. They are coming from points across the country. I am told that their necessary materials will be coming by diplomatic pouch and should be arriving shortly.

"I have found a suitable aircraft at a small airport in Virginia, near the border with the province of Tennessee. One of your first duties will be to drive the Pilot to that place so that he can complete the purchase and fly it back to our farm."

Waladi smirked as he was reminded of the *baksheesh* awaiting them from the airplane transaction. "It will be my pleasure."

"Is the farm ready for their arrival?"

"For the Dead Ones? All will be right when they arrive."

"I wish you wouldn't call these men, Dead Ones. They will be heroes."

"Maybe so, but dead heroes nevertheless."

Bin Hassani turned back to the river.

Waladi smiled. "I'm not all bad," he said. "I am preparing a very pleasant evening for them. On their final night."

A puzzled bin Hassani faced the imam.

"Colonel, are you familiar with what Americans call a 'barn dance'?"

Bin Hassani shook his head.

"People who live away from the city, on farms, invite their neighbors to a party. For some reason they don't let the neighbors into their home. Instead, everyone goes to the farmer's barn, where there is food and drink and dancing to music.

Waladi paused, however, bin Hassani had no comment.

"As you know, Colonel, our farm has a very large barn. On the eve of their mission, we will honor the *mer yawa* with a barn dance—Pakistani style."

"Do you mean—?"

"Yes. You will have the *bacha bazi* dancers I have promised. The 'dancing boys' will be the feature of a memorable evening for these heroes."

Bin Hassani glared. "What are you thinking? You can't bring *anyone* to the farm. Even trusted Muslim boys. We dare not take such a risk to the security of our mission."

"Colonel, I would never jeopardize our mission. I will personally drive the dancers directly into the barn, where they will remain, without the possibility of any contact with the outside world.

" Following the festival, each of the Dead Ones will select one of the dancers to spend his last night with. Any dancer still alive when the airplane takes off the next morning will be martyred."

44

Friday, July 31, 2010
Washington, D.C.

Bakht approached Faheem as she collected her prayer rug after *Jumu'ah* Friday prayers.

"Faheem, Imam Waladi is waiting for you at the *mihrab*. Do not keep him waiting."

Every mosque, no matter where it is in the world, has a *mihrab*. It is an ornate alcove built into the wall of the mosque which faces Mecca. The *mihrab* serves as a guide for all worshippers by indicating the proper direction to face, toward Mecca, during prayer.

Faheem had attended services in only a few mosques, but she could not imagine one with a more beautiful *mihrab* than the one in this Islamic Center. It was lined with vivid glazed tiles reminiscent of the Ottoman Empire, a gift from the government of Turkey.

Faheem failed to notice Waladi until she was directly in front of the *mihrab*. The imam had flattened himself into the deepest angle of the recess, barely visible unless one was standing directly in front of the alcove.

"Why are you hiding, Effendi?"

Waladi ignored her question. "I only have a moment, Faheem, and I wanted to inquire about you. Is the American government still hounding you about the death of the Bevard woman?"

"I have heard nothing more from them, but I am certain that I have seen them sitting in their autos watching the house."

"Is that other woman still living in your house?"

Faheem nodded. "Ms. Bone? Yes, I think she may try to steal Mother Cerise's property for herself."

"Yes! Yes! Western women can be quite troublesome. Here women beset us, while the Muslim way of dealing with them proves to be the path to a much happier outcome."

Faheem waited anxiously for him to speak about the real purpose behind this strange meeting.

"Now, Faheem, you must swear to Allah that you will never speak of what I am about to reveal, to anyone. Do you swear?"

"Yes, Effendi."

"You are swearing to Allah!"

"Yes, Effendi."

Waladi peered out of the alcove and pulled Faheem closer to him.

"Would you like to continue your Quran studies toward becoming a true imam?"

"Oh! More than anything. Yes."

"I have been very worried about you. About the torture that the American FBI can make you suffer. I have spoken to someone in the embassy and it is all arranged."

"What is it that has been arranged?"

"My friend in the embassy, will be notified when the FBI is preparing to arrest you..."

Faheem staggered back."Arrest! Praise be to Allah! Do you think they will put me in a jail?"

Waladi was solemn. "I am told that it will happen...soon. I do not wish to alarm you, child, but I am told that the prison here in the American capital is a hell-hole. Even worse than the Adiala jail in Islamabad."

Faheem's eyes bulged and she clamped a hand hard over her mouth.

Waladi reached out and pulled her closer. "Quiet! Say nothing more. Just listen to me. Our friend has contacts in the American government. He is told things."

Waladi patted Faheem's arm and whispered. "Do not be afraid, little one. I will let nothing happen to you. There are little-known international treaties which require a nation that is going to arrest a citizen of another nation, to furnish notice of at least 24 hours to the other nation. My friend has connections at the Afghani Embassy and he assures me that the Afghanis have received no notice of any such arrest.

"Our friend will be told when your embassy receives the notice, he will warn me at once and you will be granted asylum in the Pakistani Embassy. Once you are behind those walls, you will be safe. The Americans cannot touch you there."

Tears welled in Faheem's eyes. "Are you certain that your friend can be trusted? Who would be willing to anger America over the life of one child when their bombs have killed so many of us?"

It was the first time Faheem had seen Waladi smile.

"Faheem. You are not just a child, you are going to be an imam. I have often spoken of you to my friend. He knows better than to fail me."

With one hand, Waladi gently tilted her head up. "This is very important, little one; you must be ready to flee at any time. When you receive my message, go immediately to the Zoo Metro station near my house. I will come there for you."

Faheem flung herself toward Waladi, embracing him with both arms.

"Don't let them take me! I will do anything you ask!"

Waladi's smile grew broader.

45

Sunday, August 1, 2010
Washington D.C.

As Imam Waladi moved to answer the ringing telephone, he harshly ordered his wife and daughters from the living room. He listened to the voice on the other end of the line without comment and, after hanging up, pocketed his car keys and left the house.

It was almost 5:30 p.m. when he returned home and drove into the garage. When the garage door was closed and Waladi was certain that no males could espy his women, he called his wife and daughters out to the garage to unload the Buick.

Masooma was barely able to contain her delight at the sight of so many bags of *halal* items. Certainly he would be out of their lives for a number of days. Where he might be going, and for what reasons, she did not care. It only mattered to her that he would not be in the house.

The two girls made a game out of their unloading chores and, if Waladi took notice of the women's good spirits, he said nothing.

When the front and back seats were empty, Masooma dared not ask about the items she was certain remained in the locked trunk.

Waladi herded the three women inside the house and directed that they sit quietly in the living room until he was gone.

He walked down the hall and descended into the basement, where he proceeded to open the padlock of a door to the small utility room. He reached inside for a leather travel bag which he kept packed and stored in one corner.

After relocking the utility room door, he returned to the main floor and on into the garage.

Once in the Buick, he headed out Cleveland Avenue, toward the Theodore Roosevelt Memorial Bridge and Interstate 66.

Before Waladi reached the TR Bridge, Masooma had reconnected the cable hookup and joined the girls in giggling at reruns of *The Simpsons*.

As Waladi approached exit 27 on Interstate 66, jagged streaks of lightening darted among the stacks of rolling black clouds pushing in from the west. Very soon, the highway was coated by sheets of torrential rain and traffic edged its way to the side of the road.

For a moment, Waladi considered leaving the interstate at exit 27, as he had the last time he travelled to the farm, and then waiting out the storm in the shelter of the overpass. He quickly dismissed that notion as a breach of tradecraft. To travel the same route on consecutive visits would be repetitive—in violation of his training.

Waladi slowed to about 35 mph and continued on to exit 18, where he left the interstate in favor of state Route 688 south, in the direction of Hume.

By the time Waladi reached the dirt lane leading back to the farm, the rain had abated substantially, allowing him to negotiate the path with only his parking lights illuminated. He bypassed the house and drove directly to the barn. Once inside he parked the Buick beside Colonel Muhammad bin Hassani's Ford Taurus.

On the other side of the Taurus sat an old parcel van, roughly used and recently painted with a thin coat of watery white enamel.

Waladi left the barn and, after relocking the heavy doors, dodged the raindrops back to the house.

Colonel bin Hassani and a man of obvious Arab descent were seated at the folding card table in the front room. Each man held a water glass filled with red table wine. On the table, next to an open wine bottle were two cardboard boxes from California Pizza Kitchen.

Bin Hassani lifted the cardboard lid on one of the pizza boxes.

"Imam," he called, "You are just in time—we saved a couple of pieces for you. Pepperoni and anchovies, just from the microwave."

Waladi studied the other man. *This must be the famed Pilot.*

His first mindset was intense dislike, verging on hatred. But, of course, there was still time for that.

His face is clean-shaven, which is immediately sinful. He is also too handsome and sits there with a smirk on his face. He has already decided not to show me the respect I deserve; he will merely endure me.

"Imam," the colonel said, "This is the Pilot. You will be working closely together for the time being."

Waladi, following the Muslim custom that the one arriving should offer the first greeting, said, "Peace be upon you."

The Pilot's reply was to raise his wineglass and, speaking English, said, "Grab a chair and dig in."

Waladi's complexion darkened as heat seared his face and neck.

This man speaks like a heretic. Can he be trusted to fulfill our mission?

Colonel bin Hassani smiled grimly and pointed to the empty folding chair. Speaking Urdu, he said, "Imam, please. As our guest wishes."

Waladi was able to control his anger only by recalling that, though this man was the Pilot , he was also another *mer yawa*—a Dead One.

The imam returned bin Hassani's cold smile.

"Certainly, Colonel." He sat, and after filling his glass with red wine, selected a pizza slice. "May I ask what the ancient lorry in the barn holds?"

"Treasures, imam! Treasures. Words can't describe what your eyes will behold in the light of day." The colonel lifted his glass. "Until then..."

The rain stopped during the night, the clouds lifted and by 8 o'clock the sky was aglow behind the treeline to the east.

Waladi stepped from the front porch and led the other two men along the sodden path leading from the house to the barn, where the colonel assisted him in opening the large doors.

As his eyes adjusted to the barn's dim interior, the imam made out the faint shape of a United Parcel Service logo faintly visible through the filmy white paint he had seen the night before.

Using the truck key, the Pilot opened the van's two rear doors revealing a cargo bed stacked to the roof with wooden crates and other containers of varying size.

Without comment, bin Hassani removed the first container from the truck bed and handed it to the Pilot, who passed it on to the imam for storage in the first of three horse stalls along the barn wall. This process was repeated until the van was emptied to the midway point.

Waladi was not surprised that several of these containers were stenciled *KHATAR*, Pashto for "danger," in vivid red lettering. These boxes would house the various materials from which the explosive devices would be assembled.

He walked back to the van, expecting to be handed yet another container, instead he found a smirking colonel, and the Pilot standing beside the open van doors.

Colonel bin Hassani gestured toward the remaining cargo with a sweep of his right arm.

"Imam. Behold the treasures I promised to you last night. Are you ready to be astounded?"

Waladi, irked at being the one not in on the secret, remained passive.

Bin Hassani and the Pilot tugged the first of four identical crates to the open doors. As the crate was lowered to the barn floor, Waladi saw two words, which he knew to be German stenciled along the side in thick black letters.

"Sorry, colonel, but I do not speak German. What are these words, then?"

Bin Hassani hesitated momentarily, for affect, before saying, "It means these four cartons contain...attack gliders."

He studied the imam's face for a reaction. Disappointed, he shrugged, grabbed up a small pry bar, and, determined to generate a reaction from Waladi, began to wrench apart the sides of the wooden crate, splintering the wood in the process.

"Wait until you see—."

With pieces of the crate lying scattered about the floor, the Pilot aided bin Hassani to proudly display their secret weapon.

Between them they held a molded jet wing flying suit.

"Pilot," bin Hassani said, "Please, now is the time to explain our secret weapon to the imam."

The colonel used both hands to steady the device, while the Pilot positioned himself in front of the suit, between the wings.

With both hands, the Pilot grabbed a harness device molded to the wing suit, which he fastened across his chest, strapping himself onto the weapon.

He said, "The glider is molded of a dark carbon fiber, weighing 13 and a half kilos, with a wingspan of 1.8 meters.

"As you can see, while it is similar in shape to the costume of the comic super-hero Batman, it also bears a resemblance to the wings of a small jet fighter plane."

Bin Hassani shifted his feet to steady the assault glider.

"The glider," continued the Pilot, "has a built-in compartment which carries a payload of 45 kilograms. That much plastic explosive can do immeasurable damage.

"Each wing is equipped with a micro-turbine engine. When an attacker leaps from the airplane strapped to one of these, he is capable of speeds up to 217 kilometers per hour and a glide range of 77 kilometers.

"You should also know that this glider is virtually invisible from the ground and, on radar, appears as a small bird.

"As you can see, imam, with this weapon our enemies will not be aware of an attack until it is over."

Imam Waladi was unable to contain his glee.

46

Monday, August 2, 2010
Hume, Virginia

It was an early morning for Waladi and the Pilot, who were on the road at 7:30.

In the imam's Buick, they headed south on Interstate 81 toward a small airport a few miles above the Tennessee line. Outside, thick air was quickly heated by a piercing sun; inside the car, Waladi had the air conditioner on high.

The day before, Waladi had worked alongside the Pilot and bin Hassani into the early evening, unpacking each container and storing its contents safely about the barn.

The four wing-suit attack gliders were secured in upright positions, filling one of the stalls. Each suit included a carbon fiber helmet with a built-in oxygen supply and a digital heads-up display.

Colonel bin Hassani had insisted that each item be inventoried and catalogued.

"It will not do to wait until the final day to find that we are without a critical piece of equipment."

As they left the barn, Waladi had quietly marveled at the sum of money represented by this weapons arsenal. *And this is merely a farthing compared to the billions being spent worldwide for our cause. Surely, they cannot be concerned by the trifling amount of* baksheesh *taken by the colonel and myself for our services.*

Back inside the house, the colonel had issued detailed instructions for the retrieval of the used airplane he had purchased.

Then bin Hassani, citing his need to tend to his duties as air attaché, left for Washington before dinner.

Waladi thawed two steaks and cooked them on the stove. He and the Pilot ate the steaks and shared a bottle of red wine, in silence.

After supper, though dreading tomorrow's four-hour drive together, Waladi issued the Pilot a curt invitation to join him in watching *The Long Goodbye*, a porn flick. The other man declined with a smile and headed upstairs to his room.

Following a quick breakfast, the two men drove from the farm in a heavy morning mist.

Now, ninety minutes into their trip, Waladi pulled off of I-81into a Sheetz gas station for fuel.

Back in the car, with each man balancing a glazed donut and large cup of milky white coffee, they regained the interstate and continued south.

Waladi, who had spent the drive in silence, fantasizing about the stash of weapons in his barn, broke the silence.

"Pilot, I have no choice but to admire you and your comrades for the mission you have undertaken."

"Very kind of you, imam."

"I must confess, I was put off by your lack of respect for the ways of Islam."

The Pilot shrugged, "I did not intend an offense."

"I see—still..."

"This discussion will serve no purpose. May we speak of something else?"

Waladi sipped some coffee before saying, "As you wish. I am very interested in your experience with the wingsuit—the assault glider. You have actually worn one?"

His passenger finished chewing a section of his donut before replying. "Of course. My team trained for many weeks."

"Is your entire team coming here to help with the war against the Great Satan?"

The Pilot put a finger across his lips and shook his head. "I am not told those things and, even if I was...We all trained on flight simulators of cities such as Paris and London as well as New York. We did not know we were headed here until we were well on our way."

"So, our target will be New York City?"

"This I cannot say."

"Because..."

"Imam, I am certain that you will be told the intended targets at the last hour, as will all of us."

Waladi drank his coffee while working up the courage to ask, "Would it be possible for me to test fly an assault glider, before the last day?"

"Are you volunteering for this mission?"

"No. Of course not. As much as I envy all of you, I have other, very important responsibilities."

"How many hours of BASE jumping do you have?"

"Why...I...none."

"I'm sorry. What you ask is not possible."

The Pilot, hoping to take some of the sting out of his reply, said, "I walked the landing strip in front of the barn yesterday. You have it in excellent shape for our aircraft. I am told that you spent many hours readying it for today."

"I am pleased that you appreciate my efforts. That is only one of my many responsibilities. All of which I take very seriously. I cannot equal the sacrifices that you and your team are making. Still, I do what I can.

"Tell me, Pilot, have you flown this STOL aircraft?"

"I have many hours in jet fighters—the Chinese JF17 Thunder and the French Dassault Mirage 5, however, I have recently trained in the STOL. A matter of familiarization."

The two men lapsed into silence for several miles until Waladi asked, "How soon may we expect your team members?"

"Soon. Their arrivals are staggered and they will be entering through various cities."

47

Friday, August 6, 2010
Washington, D.C.

Supervisory Special Agent Jason Stanley had called the case agent for Trapdoor, Monte Sheppard, and Agent Will Kelly, coordinator for the office surveillance squad, to an urgent meeting at the FBI off-site apartment on Prospect Street.

Stanley, seated at the kitchen table, coffee cup in hand, seemingly oblivious to the humidity outside, was again wearing a long-sleeve dress shirt. A suit jacket draped over his chair back.

Across the table, Agents Sheppard and Kelly were unable to ignore the maroon silk bow tie, dotted with grey polka-dots, bobbing at Stanley's throat as he spoke.

Neither of them could recall having ever seen an FBI agent wearing a bow tie.

I wonder what J. Edgar would say about that? Will Kelly mused.

"The Bureau is going ape-shit over the fact that we still haven't found the place out I-66 where Waladi goes."

"For what it's worth," Kelly said, "he turned up at home about 7:30 last night."

Monte Sheppard nodded, "He was gone for five days. If I recall, that's the longest he's been away."

Kelly scanned his notes, relieved that the act require him to look away from the bobbing bow tie. "Five days. Yup," he agreed.

Sheppard continued, "Either they are getting close to D-Day or the imam has a girlfriend."

Without looking up, Kelly said, "Do imams do that?"

Stanley dismissed the question with a wave of his hand. "The Bureau wants a detailed account of how we lost him on his last trip out I-66."

Will Kelly, well known for his anti-Bureau outbursts, erupted, "Jesus H. Christ ... !"

Stanley countered with, "Enough, Will! That's not helping. The B is always the B, we all know that. Help us figure something out. This is nothing compared to what we are in for if there is a terrorist attack the next time we lose him."

Kelly, no longer amused by his supervisor's bow tie, mumbled, "Okay—but they're still assholes ... "

Will Kelly looked from Stanley to Sheppard and began to detail the circumstances involved in the disappearance of Imam Waladi the previous Sunday.

"It was a hot Sunday afternoon and he hadn't moved all day. The Buick emerges from the garage and he heads for the *halal* market where he proceeds to spend a month's salary. Fills the trunk and the front and back seat. To be safe I sent two units bust-ass out to exit 17. Doesn't matter if he goes north or south from there—we got him covered.

"He leaves the city by the T.R. bridge and heads west on 66. It's a clear day, so we let Nightstalker take the lead and we lay back until we are needed close-in. A few miles before exit 17 the sky filled with black clouds, flashes of lightning and suddenly rain poured down like a tropical storm. For him, it was the perfect storm. Nightstalker had to climb above it and we couldn't close on him in time."

Kelly shrugged. "All we know for sure is that he didn't get off at 17. The units waiting there would have seen him."

Stanley swigged at his coffee, made a face and moved to the sink where he dumped the rest. Over his shoulder he said, "Any ideas?"

Monte Sheppard said, "I think it's time we started following that Pakistani colonel he has met with."

Kelly nodded a vigorous agreement.

Stanley returned to the table with a fresh cup of coffee. "I agree. And, Will, you'll be surprised to know that HQ agrees. But State is blocking us."

Kelly opened his mouth to mount a protest, glanced at Stanley and slumped back in his chair. "I know. Preaching to the choir. What is State's reason?"

"Same old. Pakistan is a partner in our war on terror. There would be an international incident of epic proportions if it became known that our government was treating a high-ranking member of their diplomatic delegation like a common criminal—even worse, a suspected terrorist—without any real basis. A couple of meetings with a countryman—who, by the way, we don't have any real evidence of committing a crime, is no evidence of anything. And, above all, the colonel has diplomatic immunity, so it would be a big waste of time."

Stanley, relieved that there was no outburst from Will Kelly, asked, "Anything, Will?"

Kelly doodled in his notebook before returning Stanley's gaze. "Would you say that we are approaching—desperate?"

"I'm afraid we have passed desperate and are nearing panic. The Agency sent us another alert from Pakistan. More movement west. Probably headed here, but, as usual, nothing specific."

Monte Sheppard sagged in his chair at the news. Will Kelly stiffened.

"Well, Jesus, we've got to act," he almost shouted. "Do we agree that the colonel, all wrapped up in his immunity, likely doesn't worry about surveillance?"

Monte nodded. Jason Stanley replied, "Unless he's a trained intelligence officer. Then he's watching even when he drives to the store. Force of habit."

"If he is a terrorist, " Sheppard offered, "it doesn't require that he be an intel officer."

Kelly's voice was strong. "Look, even if he is an intel officer—so what? We are good at what we do—very damn good. We have surveilled Russian, Chinese and Syrian agents—even Mossad." He glanced at his associates for any reaction.

"Screw State," he added, "their asses aren't on the line if shit strikes. Mine is. All we need bin Hassani for is to find the location out 66 where he meets Waladi. Once we find that, it will be wham, bam and over. We won't need the colonel after that. He takes his chances with the rest of them."

Jason Stanley closed his notebook, signaling an end to the meeting.

"Do not get caught."

48

Friday, August 7, 2010
Washington, D.C.

Imam Waladi was distracted as he intoned the prayers to the *Jumu'ah* Friday worshippers prostrated on their prayer rugs behind him.

Last evening, on the return drive from Hume, Waladi was near-frenzied with the notion of having to leave his farm in the hands of the Pilot.

The STOL aircraft was secure in the barn and the Pilot would be occupied assigning the explosives and other *materiale* to each of the Dead Ones as they arrived.

Once at the farm, each man would need time to organize the weaponry required for his particular mission. Maybe two or three days.

During the unloading process, Waladi had become curious about the need for such a variety of weapons. He observed containers of TNT and C4 and PETN, which he knew was a form of nitroglycerin. Combined with other ingredients which, though unfamiliar, nevertheless caused him great concern for the security of his barn.

These birdmen better know what the hell they are doing.

The Pilot, having read Waladi's expression, set one of the containers at his feet and kicked it viciously.

"Do not be concerned, imam—they are quite safe in their present state. When we begin playing around with them, that is another matter."

"Of course," Waladi mumbled and, as evidence of his indifference, hefted a container marked PETN on his shoulder.

When the unloading was complete, Waladi, curious at not having seen any firearms—not even sidearms—had commented on this to the Pilot.

The Pilot shrugged. "What use are such weapons to dead men?"

Having completed the *Jumu'ah* Friday prayer, Imam Waladi turned to face the rows of worshippers, searching the faces for Faheem. He needed to also speak with Qader and Bakht, but he could rely on them to approach him. With Faheem, he was uncertain.

Waladi positioned himself in the narrow passage through which worshippers were moving toward the room where they stored their prayer rugs. If Faheem had attended prayers this Friday, the child would pass in front of him.

As Faheem approached, Waladi motioned her to follow him around the corner, out of the streaming crush of worshippers.

"Peace be upon you."

"And upon you, peace."

"It is so good to see you, once again Faheem."

"And you, Effendi."

Waladi quickly scanned the worshippers for anyone who appeared interested in their conversation. Satisfied that no one was eavesdropping, he spoke.

"How goes it with you?"

"Peaceful."

"Is the FBI still hounding you?"

"I have heard nothing from them for some time now."

"Do you yet see them watching your house?"

Faheem shook her head.

Waladi offered a curt smile. "Excellent news. Did you tell me whether they had asked you about me? If you did, I dismissed it as being of no importance."

"They did not say anything about you, sir."

"And you made no mention of me."

"To what purpose? You have nothing to do with these terrible killings. If your name was ever spoken of, I would strongly tell them that you, a man of God, had nothing to do with these most awful events."

Waladi sniffled and wiped an imaginary tear from his eye.

"There were others, but I chose well in selecting you to be an imam. You are a remarkable young man, and no one has shown me greater loyalty."

"So it gives me great pride to be able to tell you that we will soon resume your training to be a true imam."

"Oh, Effendi, that *is* so wonderful. I have been studying and my prayers to Allah are truly answered. May I know when this will happen?"

"I am not able to say a day, but it will be soon, very soon." Waladi held up a hand in warning. "You should know that I may decide to change the day of our meetings. If you don't get an internet message before, I should have good news by the next Friday prayers. You will be there?"

"Oh, yes!"

"Until then, read the Quran and recite your prayers."

"Oh, Effendi, you have made me most happy."

Waladi made his way to a small office he maintained at the end of a long hallway toward the rear of the mosque. There he used a deskphone to place a call to Colonel bin Hassani at the Pakistani Embassy.

"Peace," he said when the phone was answered.

"And to you," bin Hassani replied, completing their familiarized Islamic greeting.

"I am most anxious to return to the farm," Waladi began. "I will ask a favor of you so that I may leave directly, from the mosque."

"Is there a problem? I thought you intended to spend the weekend days with your family."

Waladi snorted. "Our mission is of the utmost import. Certainly of more concern than the women who live in my house."

"Still ... has something occurred to cause you to worry about our recent guest? I had hoped your long drive together might have eased your concern."

Waladi, unwilling to admit being spurred to action by feelings of jealousy toward the Pilot, replied, "Nothing like that. There is still much to be done and he asked that I return as soon as possible ..."

When the colonel did not press him on his lie, Waladi added, "Perhaps, if I knew more..."

197

"Enough of that! What is it you wish me to do?"

"Very well. Select a trusted member of your staff to visit my *halal* market and purchase as many items as he can carry in his auto and deliver them to my house."

Colonel Hassani mulled the request before replying, "That can be done, but how will he know what items to select at the store?"

"Instruct him to meet me inside the *Halal* Market on Connecticut Avenue. Do you know it?"

"Of course. We all know it."

"I must point out to him some items that are *haram* not to ever be inside my home. I will furnish him with a list and money with which to make the purchases which are *halal*. These items I will allow in my home.

"From the market, I will go directly to the farm."

"Is that all?"

"No. He is to take the purchases to Cleveland Avenue. He will park in front of my house and call you ..."

"Me?"

"Please listen. Following his call to you, you will please telephone my home number and hang up after one ring. That will tell my wife to operate the garage door opener. When the boy sees the door open he is to drive in and unload the bags. When he is finished, he will drive away, the door will be closed and only then will my women be permitted to enter the garage and carry the packages into the house."

"Is all of this really necessary? The boy will have a cellphone. Why can't he call your home directly?"

"I do not want some lusty boy calling my home. Anything might happen. This procedure will protect my women from violating *ikhtilat.* The illegal mixing of men and women, even if by accident, can demean the value of a woman when negotiating her marriage. For two daughters, that could cost me a great deal of money."

After a silence, bin Hassani said, "He will meet you in 30 minutes at the market," and hung up.

Waladi stood, hands on his hips, at the end of the produce aisle, gazing through the front window of the *Halal* Market onto Connecticut Avenue.

H*alal* means "allowed" in the Islamic world, and Waladi had become quite angry when he identified several items which he deemed *haram*, or forbidden for sale in these aisles.

Initially enraged by the sacrilege he had uncovered, Waladi intended to lash out at the first store employee he encountered. This turned out to be Ruby, the cashier. who, obviously not a Muslim, fixed her gaze on the items the imam had strewn along the counter, as he pointed to each one and ranted about heretics and infidels.

When Waladi's tirade ended, Ruby looked up. "So, you want these or no?" She asked.

Strangling with fury, Waladi had stalked out the door.

He returned to the same *Halal* market within a week after determining that it stocked the fewest *haram* items in the area. He further rationalized his change of mind, by concluding that all markets selling Islamic goods had been depraved by the influence of a satanic Western culture.

Within minutes, a small, silver-colored auto appeared and proceeded slowly along the curb lane. Directly in front of Waladi's position, the car stopped and the driver, seeing the imam through the market window, waved vigorously before being prodded along from behind by a blaring auto horn.

Soon after the car disappeared down Connecticut Avenue, a young Pakistani man walked through the front door and approached Waladi.

"Ah, Sahib," he said, smiling, "It is I, Abdul Ali, from the Embassy of Pakistan. How may I serve you?"

Waladi wanted to slap him across the face, so hard that he could never forget the pain. Instead, he stifled his rage and spoke through grinding teeth.

"Is that your auto?"

"Oh, yes, Sahib. It is a fine..."

"...It looks like a small turd, a silver turd. Do you know what is a turd?"

The boy, his face crimson with humiliation, cast his eyes to the floor. Unable to guess at the extent of his sin, he had no way of knowing what response was expected of him.

Waladi grabbed the boy by one arm and jerked him to the side, out of the aisle.

"Perhaps this is your idea of a sick American joke, Abdul Ali."

Unable to stammer an answer, tears welled in Ali's eyes.

"What do you think Colonel bin Hassani will do when he is forced to come out here and atone for your sins?"

"But...but...Sahib...I was told only to meet you here and assist you, nothing more. What have I done wrong?"

Waladi grunted and, yanking the boy by one arm, dragged him toward the back of the store. "I have been called away on a secret mission for our government and can waste no more time on this outrage. My Buick is parked at the curb. We will exchange car keys and I will be forced to cramp my body into that turd box of yours. Because of you, I will suffer during a long drive."

He shoved a sheet of paper into Ali's trembling hand. "You will buy the items on this paper—and only these items which are *halal*, understand?"

"Yes. Yes, Sahib."

Waladi released Ali's arm and produced a wad of bills, which he crammed into the boy's shirt pocket.

"Pay with this. Now, I show you the items which are *haram.* You will purchase only the *halal,* load up my Buick and deliver them to my house. Do you understand?"

"I'm sorry, Sahib, but I don't know..."

"Call Colonel bin Hassani, he will instruct you."

Waladi grabbed Ali's shoulder in a painful grip and forced the boy's face upward. "Know that you are not to speak to, or set your eyes on, my beautiful daughters, or their Mother. To do so would violate *ikhtilat* and you would not live to see Pakistan."

It was just after 6 p.m. when Imam Waladi left Abdul Ali's silver "turd box" parked in the barn on the farm in Hume. He strode through the front door to find the Pilot sitting at the card table sharing a bottle of red wine with a stunning Pakistani woman.

A light blue *hijab* scarf only partially covered the thick, black hair brushed long to her shoulders. Black eyes, over classic cheek bones, challenged her surroundings.

Waladi was stricken by the tight-fitting blue jeans and pair of long legs crossed beneath the table. Still seething from his long ride in the cramped subcompact he erupted anew.

"What in the name of Allah are you doing, Pilot, bringing your whore to this most sacred of places? I knew you could not be trusted here alone. I was very wise to return so quickly."

Waladi stepped toward the woman, face twisted with rage, shaking a finger at her as he walked.

"This harlot must be removed at once. If you refuse to kill her, I will have no choice but to act without hesitation..."

"So nice to see you, Imam. If you have finished your welcoming speech, may I present to you a captain in the Pakistani military forces and a valued member of this attack team. Please, join us."

Waladi glared at each of the others, spun around and stalked into his room, slamming his door with a force that rattled every window on the first floor.

49

Saturday, August, 8, 2010
Hume, Virginia

Imam Waladi busied himself in the tiny kitchen, preparing an early breakfast of scrambled eggs and dry toast. He looked up to find the beautiful captain approaching the doorway.

This morning the gossamer scarf covering her hair was lemon yellow, a maroon leather vest unbuttoned over a black T-shirt, and black jeans worn tucked inside leather cowboy boots, which were identical in color and texture to her vest.

"Ah, Captain. If it is permitted, may I say that you look lovely this morning."

"Compliments are never discouraged. Thank you, imam."

Waladi hoped she would join him in pretending that last night's shameful outburst had never occurred.

"I am preparing scrambled eggs. I would be pleased to add two more, if you care to join me."

"Thank you," she said, "but I have my own food."

Waladi was aware of the scent rising from her body, as she eased past him to the refrigerator.

She said, "I prepare this yogurt from a Lebanese recipe. I take it with me wherever I travel."

"At least join me at the table in the other room. I will bring your coffee."

Waladi pushed away his empty plate and picked up his coffee mug. Glancing at the stairway he said, "Captain, I am pleased to have some time to speak to you in private."

As the Captain delicately spooned her yogurt, the imam spend a moment imagining what pleasures would be found within those black jeans.

When there was no reply, Waladi continued, "I have planned a little surprise for the Pilot and his team for the night before your mission. I very much admire what you have undertaken. Now, I would ask that you honor my request for silence to all others about what I say to you."

"If that is your wish."

"Captain, are you familiar with the term, *bacha bazi?* It means..."

"I know what it means, imam."

"Have you enjoyed the artistry of the 'dancing boys,' then?"

"You would be amazed at what I have done during the months the Pilot's team trained together."

Waladi gave a quick smile. "You were the only woman among those men?"

She returned a smirk. "What is it you wish me to know?"

"I have assembled a troupe of *bacha bazi* dancers and wish to honor the Pilot's team with a dance and feast on the eve of your mission."

Waladi dipped his head in the direction of the barn. "To be held here—a Middle Eastern 'barn dance,' if you get the meaning?"

"I know about the *bacha bazi* and I know what is a 'barn dance'. Also, the Russian dance, *kamarinskaya,* the Macarena..."

"...Of course. My apologies, I intended no offense. The question is, how am I to know when the food and dancers, are to appear? I need at least two days..."

The Captain interrupted, "Is the colonel aware of this...barn dance?"

"Of course. He much enjoys the dancers and is eager for me to arrange this."

"Then, would he not be the one to ask about the day?"

Waladi nodded. "Of course, but he has been much distracted with all of the final preparations..."

The Captain stood and collected her dishes.

The imam said, "You should know that I selected a beautiful *bacha bazi f*or each team member, without knowing that one of you was a woman. If you desire, please select one of them to accompany you to your room after the dance ..."

She stood looking at him.
Waladi added, "If you prefer a grown man, you only need ask."

50

Tuesday, August 11, 2010
Mexican-U.S. Border—Rio Grande River
Piedras Negras, Mexico—Eagle Pass, Texas

Aabir al-Saad, a lieutenant of the Pakistani Air Force, sat sweating in the rear seat of a vintage ten-passenger Cadillac limousine. The overheated motor hissed as it idled in a long line of vehicles inching toward Bridge 1, spanning the Rio Grande River between Mexico and the United States.

Several miles back, the driver, Pedro, had said something that caused the various other passengers, packed around al-Saad, to become incensed.

Though he spoke no Spanish, al-Saad assumed the driver was informing the crowd that the air conditioning, which had given out, would not be returning.

Yesterday, al-Saad had arrived in Pedras Negras carrying a Venezuelan passport bearing the name Raul Quiros, of Caracas.

At a pre-arranged meeting, the lieutenant had handed Pedro, the owner of this decaying motorcar, 5,000 U.S. dollars, which had bought him a cramped, sweltering place in this torture chamber as a family member crossing into the United States for the day to attend a niece's wedding.

Al-Saad's suffering intensified his anger at the wrongs he suffered at the hands of his comrades. Before leaving Pakistan, he was ordered to shave his elegant beard, which he prized.

"With that beard, you look too much like a terrorist. Remove it."

Sitting in this oven on wheels, he was certain that the Pilot, and his special student, the Captain, had not suffered as much on the path they had taken to enter the United States.

Very likely they travelled first class on British Airways.

The lieutenant turned his head slightly and took in his surroundings.

Fear of capture by U.S. authorities, previously at the top of his list of fears, had sunk to the bottom.

Running his tongue between his lips, al-Saad tried, unsuccessfully, to swallow. He pictured himself sitting in an icily air-conditioned room, a glass of ice water in his hand, being questioned politely by two U.S. officials.

I am a warrior, an officer in the Pakistani Air Force—soon to be martyred—I should be treated with more respect. I look too much like a terrorist? Am I no longer a military officer, merely a terrorist?

Now the line began to move and the limo crept onto the bridgespan.

Am I being martyred or merely committing ritual suicide? I cannot know, for they will not disclose our mission beforehand. Am I a fool, taking my own life, and the life of others, based solely on their word that what I am to do is a holy act, and not a political one?

I would surely hate it if I had died, and others were slain, to aid some tyrant's political agenda.

I have read, and truly believe, that God has made life sacred for human beings.

The Quran says, "And do not kill yourselves (nor kill one another) Surely. Allah is to you ever merciful."

It is a fact that many of these so-called, suicide-bombers are not good Muslims or faithful followers of any religion. They are simply madmen.

"Is that what I am, to be doing this? Merely, some madman?"

When the limo stopped at a Catholic church in downtown Eagle Pass, al-Saad, liberated himself from his backseat prison.

On the sidewalk, gawking at his surroundings, he eyed an American flag, fluttering atop a building three blocks away.

His throat scorched with thirst Al-Saad followed the flag until he stood in front of the post office on Garrison Street. The lieutenant entered the air-conditioned lobby and presented his fake passport to a security guard stationed at the entryway metal detector.

When al-Saad failed to respond to questions in two languages from the bilingual security guard, he was escorted upstairs to the office of Immigration and Customs Enforcement.

51

Wednesday, August 12, 2010
Hume, Virginia

Imam Waladi carried his breakfast to the card table to find the Pilot seated there with a cup of coffee, holding a cellphone to his ear.

Upon seeing Waladi, the Pilot smiled a greeting, picked up his cup and left the table, disappearing out the front door.

Waladi abandoned his meal and charged out of the room in pursuit. On the porch, fists clenched, face blotched with fury, he rushed after the other man.

As Waladi closed on him, the Pilot offered him the phone saying, "Ah, imam, there you are. The colonel wishes to speak to you."

Waladi snatched the phone away and immediately unleashed a tirade.

"It is a security violation for anyone except me to have direct phone contact with anyone. We agreed that once we were operational here, all contact would go through me. I will confiscate this phone and any others I..."

"Silence, Waladi! That was a condition *you* demanded but was never sanctioned. The farm is not your realm. If it belongs to anyone, it is mine. You will not interfere, in any way, with any communications..."

"I must protest. It is a serious breach of security for any of the Dead Ones to have contact with..."

"Enough! These people are in the military and take orders only from a superior officer or government official; certainly not a mere imam. I have given the Pilot an assignment which he will relate to you."

"Colonel, I must be the first one informed..."

The phone went dead, and when Waladi stopped speaking, the Pilot wrested the phone away and slipped it into a deep pocket of the cargo pants he wore.

"I would be very careful if I were you, imam. I can tell you this; my orders are to fly the plane to a small airport in North Carolina where another member of my team is waiting."

52

Wednesday, August 12, 2010
Washington D. C. field office of the FBI

FBI Supervising Agent Jason Stanley ushered Agents Sheppard and Kelly into his office and closed the door behind them. He took a few steps across the small room and closed the connecting door to the space occupied by Helen, the squad's secretary.

Stanley settled himself behind the GSA-issued metal desk as the two street agents pulled their chairs closer. Their backs were to the solid-glass office wall which commanded a view of the "bullpen," an open room with rows of identical desks assigned to the agents of squad CI-4.

At this time of the morning, only two of the desks were in use. The remainder of the squad were out on the street, following leads on their assigned cases.

"We may have caught a break on Trapdoor," Stanley said.

"About time," Kelly muttered. "We're overdue."

Stanley, reading from an FBI headquarters communication, said, "Yesterday, a Pakistani Air Force lieutenant, traveling under a Venezuelan passport in the name of Raul Quiros walked into an ICE office in Eagle Pass, Texas, and asked for asylum."

Monte Sheppard was quick to say, "The ICE office in Eagle Pass is a long way from D.C. What's the connection to Trapdoor?"

"I may have been overly optimistic about 'catching a break.' It was a guess by Marty Lemon at headquarters. It could be wrong.

"The lieutenant seems to only knows a few words of English—at least he won't speak it— and ICE needs the few Pakistani speakers they have here and in New York.

"Lemon got a call from a friend at ICE HQ and, from what they could piece together, Trapdoor sounded like the best fit. Some gibberish about a Pilot and an imam. He seems to know whatever English words he needs to get his message across.

"The guy at ICE HQ is a retired agent. He and Lemon worked together at the Bureau. Anything like this, he calls Lemon first. If the Bureau isn't interested, he passes it on to Homeland.

"Anyway, Senor Quiros has said '*no mas*' on more info until he gets a written promise of asylum."

Monte Sheppard said, "We need to get a native speaker to him."

"Sounds like you are volunteering to take one of our linguists to Eagle Pass."

"How am I getting there?"

"Nightstalker is being fueled and the Count is waiting to take off when you get to the airport."

"Who's running the show? FBI or ICE?"

"FBI. Once you are there, they will be thrilled to turn it over to us. They are terrified at the idea of eventually having to explain this to the State Department."

Sheppard smiled and made a note.

"As soon as you can make some sense out of this through the translator, fill me in and then make room for the lieutenant on Nightstalker and bring him back with you. Even if your linguist has to come back on a commercial flight."

Will Kelley asked, "Are we certain that State *doesn't* know about this? It would be like ICE to see a way to curry some favor with them, then realize they're in over their head and kiss it off to us."

Stanley shook his head. "ICE was getting ready to make the call until Lemon convinced them to wait until we know what we are dealing with. The inference being that we would be responsible for making the notification to State."

"It seems very odd that a commissioned officer in the service of one of our allies in the war on terror would want our protection from his own people. Especially after entering the country, on a phony passport, through Eagle Pass, Texas. Smells bad to me."

Monte Sheppard said, "Sounds like this lieutenant is smart enough to insist on seeing an asylum agreement in writing before he'll say any more?"

Stanley replied, "If he thinks he has the upper hand, he'd be wrong. We don't have time for the extended negotiations required for a legitimate asylum agreement.

"Instruct your linguist to explain to him that unless he tells us what he meant by the word 'terrorism,' he has no possibility of being granted asylum. If he chooses to remain silent, tomorrow he will either disappear into a cell in Guantanamo, with the other terrorists, or be returned to Islamabad and we'll let the Pakistani government deal with him. I doubt that he will choose either of those options. "

Stanley glanced at his watch. "Monte, you've got to get going, but keep this in mind: Whatever he's up to, he's not acting alone. Are the others already here? Where are they? How soon are they planning to act? We need to know."

Monte Sheppard hastened from the room and Stanley turned to Will Kelly. "I guess there is nothing new from our surveillance."

"It's driving us nuts out there. Waladi has not appeared since last Friday, when we watched that kid loading the Buick. The eyeball naturally assumed the kid was a bag boy helping Waladi load up. When the kid finishes, *he* drives away in the Buick, Waladi is long gone, and we haven't seen him since.

"His Buick shows up every day at the Pak embassy, driven by the same kid. We're guessing he is a flunky there and Waladi is driving the kid's car, whatever that is. We don't know the kid's name, so we can't get a registration for him. If we could, at least we would know what Waladi is driving."

"What about your plan to follow the colonel?"

"He goes to the embassy and back home. That's it. So we are guessing that Waladi and the colonel are communicating via landline to the embassy."

"Any other *good* news?"

"It's Thursday. Waladi is due to appear on Cleveland Avenue tonight. It's unlikely he will miss tomorrow's *Jumu'ah* Friday prayers.

"I guarantee this: Once we have him, the sonofabitch is not getting away from us again."

Kelly noticed Jason Stanley's gaze had wandered past him to the rows of empty desks in the squad room.

"Picking out your desk in case this turns completely to shit?"

"Close. I was thinking that my once-promising Bureau career, may well hinge upon the results of Sheppard's interview with Senor Quiros, a Pakistani lieutenant in Eagle Pass, Texas. If the senor is not connected to Trapdoor, or even if he is, and things still go boom, I won't be picking out one of these desks, I'll be back on the street working background investigations, alongside another GS-10."

"If Trapdoor goes boom and a bunch of citizens get killed, I'm thinking that will give you a lot more pain than being demoted a few pay grades."

53

Thursday, August 13, 2010
Hume, Virginia

The STOL had landed at dusk, with Waladi waiting beside the open barn door while the Pilot taxied inside and cut the engine.

The captain, who occupied the co-Pilot's seat, had been the first one out of the plane's cabin, followed quickly by a small dark-skinned man wearing Levi's and a black polo shirt.

Clearly uneasy with his surroundings, his small black eyes darted about the barn's interior. Upon seeing Waladi, he drew himself stiffly to attention and attempted a salute.

The captain reached out and yanked the man's arm to his side. "No, sergeant. He is a civilian."

The sergeant quavered, "Yes, Captain. My apologies."

The Pilot handed the Captain three carry-out food bags and descended from the plane. He nodded to Waladi and motioned the others to follow him to the house.

Waladi's anger at being left to secure the barn alone surged when he entered the house to find the downstairs empty. His eyes glared toward the ceiling.

They are up there, probably for the night. The Pilot did not have the courtesy to offer any of their food to me. Certainly, he will not share that whore captain with a lowly sergeant. The curse of Allah upon them.

Earlier that morning, Waladi had crept up the stairs, hoping to glimpse some part of the lovely captain's body. It had quickly become clear that she would not make herself available to him—a glimpse at her naked beauty would be all that he could hope for.

At the top of the stairs, he listened at the door to the Pilot's room, dreading the sounds of ecstasy that would reach him from within.

Hearing nothing, he moved down the hall, hesitating in front of the door to her room.

Behind him, the Pilot's door flew open. He filled the doorway, his smooth, swarthy body glistening with sweat.

"What is it, imam?"

Waladi's voice was firm. "I wondered if there was anything the captain might require to make her more comfortable."

"The captain is a military officer. Her comfort is no concern of yours. This floor is declared a military base. As such, it is restricted to military personnel and is off-limits to you. Don't let me catch you up here again. As a matter of fact, you are of no good to us here. Why don't you return to the mosque? At least there you might be of use to someone."

The Pilot slammed the door and threw the bolt.

Waladi, in a rage, stormed down the stairs.

The imam sat on his bed, clenched fists pounding the mattress. Tears of anger and humiliation stung his eyes as he listened to the sounds of the Pilot and the Captain preparing their breakfast meal through the thin wall.

I will not be dismissed from my own farm by this Dead One. I am no longer needed! Of no use here! We shall see about that! The man is an infidel.

Waladi stayed in his room until the three Dead Ones had proceeded to the barn to ready their weapons.

When they were gone, the imam picked up his smartphone and punched in the colonel's private number at the embassy.

Waladi recognized the colonel's voice at the other end of the call. "Yes. What is it that you require?"

"Colonel, this is..."

"I know who it is! What do you want?"

"There is an urgent situation out here! Your immediate presence is required."

"Three hours."

54

Thursday, August 13, 2010
Washington, D.C.

Supervisory Special Agent Jason Stanley detailed two agents to meet Nightstalker upon its return from Eagle Pass and, thereafter, the agents were to escort Monte Sheppard and Lieutenant al-Saad, along with the FBI linguist, to a secure compartmented information facility, known in the intelligence community as a SCIF. This one was deep within the J. Edgar Hoover building.

Al-Saad was first off of the plane, followed closely by Monte Sheppard and trailed by the linguist. The two escort agents, waiting on the tarmac, marched the lieutenant to the car, where they situated him in the middle of the back seat. Sheppard and one of the escort agents crowded in on either side, leaving the front passenger's seat for the linguist.

The agents found themselves in a tenuous situation. Al-Saad had agreed to come to Washington after being convinced that his presence was required in the nation's capital if his request for political asylum was to receive further consideration.

While Sheppard was on the telephone with Jason Stanley from Eagle Pass, they had agreed that al-Saad was not to be placed under arrest; rather, he was "being transported," and as such would not be handcuffed.

Al-Saad had been carefully searched for weapons at the ICE office and again before boarding Nightstalker, but he would know that a weapon was available just beneath the suit coat of each of the FBI agents beside him.

Sheppard instructed the linguist to explain to al-Saad that he was being closely watched and must keep his hands in plain sight at all times during the ride to FBI headquarters.

Al-Saad nodded his understanding.

Jason Stanley held open a secure entry door within the basement garage of FBI HQ, as the Bureau car containing Lieutenant al-Saad rolled to a stop in front of him.

As the car emptied, Stanley said, "Through here. They will be waiting for us in the SCIF."

Agent Sheppard was relieved that Stanley was there to guide them through the warren of hallways. Though an FBI agent with eleven years on the job, Sheppard had never been authorized to enter an ultra-secure SCIF and had no idea where to find this one within the labyrinth of the FBI headquarters building.

When Sheppard graduated from the FBI training academy at Quantico, Virginia, in addition to his badge and sidearm, he was granted a Top Secret security clearance.

Possessing a TS clearance does not automatically entitle its holder access to any and all information relating to national security. Ultra-sensitive data can be further categorized as Sensitive Compartmented Information (SCI) or as Special Access Program (SAP).

Due to its extremely sensitive nature, the storage, review or discussion of either of these two categories of TS data must take place in a SCIF, to prevent spying on our information systems through the inadvertent leaking of sounds, signals and even vibrations.

During the Cold War years, the U.S. learned the hard way that the walls of every embassy located in an Iron Curtain country likely contained listening devices planted by the Soviet KGB. This discovery resulted in the construction, within every embassy, of "a room within a room," where discussion of sensitive matters could be held in a secure environment.

The continuing requirement for enhanced security measures resulted in a National Security Agency program, code-named Tempest. This program listed specific requirements necessary for a SCIF to receive certification for the storage and review of sensitive compartmented information.

These specifications include a prescribed distance the SCIF must be constructed from the exterior walls of the outer building. Requirements for duct work, perimeter doors, telephone and electrical power and intrusion detection systems are only some of the myriad requirements further specified in updated intelligence community directives.

Though Monte Sheppard had never pondered the size and shape of a SCIF he was somewhat surprised to see that this particular SCIF was a windowless modular building about the size and shape of an empty semi-trailer. It stood isolated within an otherwise empty room the size of a small gymnasium.

As Sheppard and the others approached the room, two very serious-looking young men appeared beside the vault-like door and assumed the civilian equivalent of attention.

After verifying the identities of each person to be admitted to the SCIF, the serious young men, in turn, bent over key pads located on either side of the entry door and, shielding the keypad from the view of others punched in the pass code that he alone possessed.

Interesting, thought Sheppard. *Two separate passcodes possessed by two individuals are required for entry. Knowing the Bureau, it has been made very clear to these intelligence analysts that if either one divulged the pass code in his possession to another living soul, even the person holding the other code, he would be spending most of his remaining years in a federal prison.*

No wonder they are so grim-faced.

Sheppard followed Jason Stanley through the doorway and turned to find al-Saad, feet planted, had refused to enter. His face was pale and he mumbled something to the translator, who turned to Sheppard.

"He's afraid this is a prison cell where he will spend the rest of his life. If he enters, he will never leave."

"Tell him that this is a very special meeting room where high government officials are coming to speak with him." Sheppard made a circular motion with one hand. "We will all leave this room together when the meeting is over."

Al-Saad watched Sheppard's face intently as the linguist translated the agent's words.

Three well-dressed FBI officials approached the SCIF and, after confirming their identity to the two security men, walked through the doorway, eyeing Al-Saad as they passed him.

Sheppard recognized two of them. One was named Burns, the deputy assistant director of the Counterterrorism Division; the other, Martin Lemon, the section chief to whom Jason Stanley reported on Trapdoor.

Later, Sheppard would learn that the third official represented the Office of General Counsel, assigned the job of tracking the legalities of al-Saad's request for political asylum.

The arrival of the three officials was fortuitous for al-Saad, who, obviously encouraged by their presence, followed them inside the SCIF.

The three Bureau officials arranged their chairs side by side, presenting themselves to al-Saad as a panel of inquisitors. The escort agents placed him in a chair directly in front of the panel, with both agents seated directly behind him.

Sheppard settled himself in a folding chair and wished that he had brought his sunglasses with him. The ceiling of the small room was lined with fluorescent bulbs whose light glared off of the white painted walls.

As he waited for the proceedings to commence, Sheppard considered the sequence of events which led them to this secure room. Until today, no one had found it necessary to hold any conferences relating to Trapdoor in a SCIF.

Actually, it was likely that nothing about the Trapdoor investigation would be discussed in here today. This meeting focused on Lieutenant al-Saad and his future.

The important officials comprising the panel would not travel to a field office, even one as close by as the Washington, D.C., office. The agents and their catch were expected to come to them.

Therefore, this meeting was being held in FBI headquarters and it would not be helpful for word to spread around town, that a Pakistani Air Force officer was being escorted to a high-level meeting with the top brass from the FBI's Counterterrorism Division. Quickly, phones would be ringing in offices throughout the building resulting in inquiries from State, the CIA and, most probably, the Embassy of Pakistan itself.

Hence the clandestine route to this room.

The three headquarters officials were here to evaluate the lieutenant's worth to the Bureau's anti-terrorism program. If they determined that al-Saad was worth the trouble, they would return to their offices and formulate a strategy for coping with the State Department and the Pakistani government for as long as was required to make use of him.

Should they decide he was of little or no value, a Bureau minion would be tasked with the job of explaining the matter to State, who in turn would have to answer blistering questions, certain to follow, from the Pakistani government.

As the proceedings began, Jason Stanley summarized what little information had been obtained to date from al-Saad.

"On 8/11/10, Lieutenant al-Saad, an officer in the military service of Pakistan, entered the United States through Eagle Pass, Texas, in possession of a Venezuelan passport in the name of Raul Quiros.

"Al-Saad appeared, voluntarily, at the ICE office in Eagle Pass where he identified himself, and spoke the word 'terrorism' in English."

Stanley nodded toward Monte Sheppard. "On 8/12/10, Special Agent Sheppard accompanied by FBI linguist Handel, travelled to Eagle Pass to interview al-Saad."

Whenever his name was mentioned al-Saad looked up and glanced at the three FBI officials, thereafter returning his gaze to the floor.

"During his interview, the lieutenant confirmed his true identity, again mentioned terrorism and refused to speak further."

Deputy Assistant Director Burns, the ranking FBI official in the room, spoke first.

"Thank you, Agent Stanley." Turning to the linguist, he said, "Mr. Handel, please explain to Lieutenant al-Saad that the three of us are empowered to review his request to remain in this country. That can only happen if he truthfully discloses everything he knows about this terrorism of which he spoke."

Handel, unnerved by working for a high-ranking Bureau official, stammered out his first words in the Urdu language. He paled, swallowed hard and began again, this time with fluency.

Al-Saad quickly responded to the translation of the statement and Handel turned to the panel. "He says to tell your lordships that he is most happy to be of assistance and, that you can be assured that what he tells you will be the truth. 'I do not speak lies,' is a quote."

The panel huddled momentarily, before Burns, occupying the middle chair in the three-person panel, spoke. "Please ask him to describe, in as much detail as he can, what he meant when he used the word 'terrorism.' "

When al-Saad finished speaking, Handel began, "He is saying, 'I trained for weeks with a team of three other air force persons. No one told us what it was we were training for, but we followed orders, all the same.' "

The panel, sensing a major intelligence coup, listened intently.

Deputy A.D. Burns said, "Ask him to identify the others, and describe the training."

"He says: Those in his group I know only as 'Pilot,' 'Captain' and 'Sergeant.'

"Of course, the Pilot flew the plane. Three of us were given a flying suit called an attack glider. We put them on almost every day. Many days we wore them while we leaped from the tallest peaks in the Karakoram mountain range of Pakistan and steered ourselves toward a small target thousands of feet below us.

'Other days we wore the wing suits while we practiced climbing in and out of a small airplane.'

"I'm sorry, sir, but here he is using some words unfamiliar to me. I think he's speaking of a flight simulator."

Burns nodded. "Understood. Please proceed."

"He's saying that they trained by flying at moving pictures of the cities of New York, Chicago, Berlin and Rome."

"That is very disturbing. Have him describe this attack glider flying suit."

The panel held a short discussion while the linguist relayed the request.

Handel was shaking his head as he turned toward the panel. "If what he says is true, it is very scary."

"Go ahead."

"The wing suit is constructed from a carbon-fiber material with a 6-foot wing-span, but it weighs only thirty pounds. It sounds very much like a Batman costume, if you can picture that. It has a built-in compartment which can hold 100 pounds of equipment.

"Here, he is very likely saying 'equipment' instead of 'explosives' so you won't become angry at him.

"He claims to have jumped out of airplanes from as high as 10 kilometers—30,000 feet. The wing suit is equipped with on-board oxygen—and travels up to 40 kilometers at maximum speeds up to 135 mph.

"He says that it is virtually impossible to detect a soldier operating in such a suit while approaching the target. On radar, according to him, the suit shows up as the size of a bird."

The panel stiffened in amazement.

"Jesus," Burns muttered. "Handel," he continued, "You and the lieutenant can take a break, while we confer."

Burns turned to one of the intelligence analysts and waved a hand indicating Handel and al-Saad. "Please find some water for these men."

The analyst stepped to the rear of the room, opened an obscure door in the wall, and returned, handing a plastic bottle of cold water to the two men.

Al-Saad grinned and held the bottle above his head for all to see, then proceeded to drink half of the contents in one motion.

When the panel was ready to resume, it was Martin Lemon who spoke. "Mr. Handel, please inform the lieutenant that he is wrong if he thinks that, by alarming us with some science fiction tale, he is making a stronger case for his political asylum plea. We will not be persuaded by lies."

Handel was certain that al-Saad was telling the truth and was agonized by being directed to call him a liar. Still, he had no option.

Al-Saad's quick response to this edict pleased the linguist. "I'm quoting here," Handel began.

"I say the truth. You lords will be making a serious mistake not to believe me. Many of your people will be killed. What else can you do but act upon my words?"

Lemon's response was immediate. "There are a couple of points requiring some clarification. Anyone who has flown knows how important it is to track your altitude, especially if one were descending to earth at 135 mph. Could he explain how this is accomplished in this attack suit?"

Handel relayed al-Saad's answer. "The glider comes with a helmet equipped with a 'heads-up' display of air speed and altitude."

"We assume that this assault glider is equipped with handheld controls for maneuvering in flight, but we are very curious about the braking system one uses on such a device."

Following a brief exchange with al-Saad, Handel turned to the panel.

"The lieutenant apologizes for failing to mention that each wing suit comes with a parachute. When the wing suit operator descends to a certain altitude, he separates the wing from the rest of the rig and opens the parachute to complete his landing.

"Though the wing falls away, it remains attached to the rig by a strong tether and lands just ahead of the operator."

The lieutenant leaned closer and spoke quickly to Handel.

"He forgot to explain that, of course, no parachutes would be issued on the last day."

The panel nodded solemnly and Martin Lemon quickly posed another question.

"Are the other members of your team presently within our borders, and, if so, where might we find them?"

Al-Saad's response was very different from his earlier ones. Handel could tell from the body language and hesitation that the lieutenant knew his answer was not what the panel wanted to be told.

"He says that each person on the team left Pakistan from different cities within a day or two of one another. He had expected to find them already here, but now has no way of contacting them."

"Where was he headed from Eagle Pass, and how was he to get to his destination?"

When al-Saad finished his response to this question, he slumped in his seat, head bowed.

"His orders were to go to the bus station in each city he was given, there he would be contacted with instructions for the next leg. He did this in Caracas and, of course, that ended in Eagle Pass, without contact."

"If this *is* true," said Lemon, "They would already be alerted when he failed to turn up at the bus station in Eagle Pass."

Handel motioned for quiet and leaned closer to better understand what al-Saad was now saying.

"He doesn't know if this means anything, but he recalls talk among other air force officers in Islamabad, that a colonel in the Washington, D.C., area is somehow involved."

Lemon leaned forward, fixing a penetrating gaze on the lieutenant as Handel translated the next question. "What are the ultimate targets for this terrorist attack and what is the date?"

Al-Saad shook his head and mumbled a few words in response.

"He regrets that he does not have an answer. They were to receive that information after they arrived here, likely mere hours before the attack."

The Bureau officials conferred for a moment before Deputy A.D. Burns said, "Is there anything else the lieutenant wants us to know?"

Al-Saad shrugged and shook his head when the question was posed to him.

Burns nodded to the escort agents. "Please take the lieutenant into the outer room for a few minutes while we try and sort this out. Let him light a cigarette if he wants."

As the escort agents prodded al-Saad to his feet, he held his arms out in front of him, waiting for the handcuffs. One of the agents shook his head, and al-Saad grinned his appreciation.

As the lieutenant and his escorts turned to the door, Burns said, "Ask Lieutenant al-Saad what made him change his mind in Eagle Pass and seek political asylum?"

"The lieutenant says that he was compelled by a maddening thirst and the conviction that it was pointless to die in such a fashion."

55

Friday, August 13, 2010
Washington, D.C.

When the door to the SCIF was again secured, Deputy A.D. Burns turned his attention to Agents Stanley and Sheppard.

"Your thoughts on what we just heard. Do you believe him? Does any of it connect to our investigation of Trapdoor?"

Supervisor Stanley said, "I believe he is telling us what he knows of the truth. Trapdoor is predicated on two CIA reports regarding an imam being sent to the D.C. area to abet a terrorist attack.

"Surveillance has connected Imam Waladi and the Pakistani air attaché, a colonel, in a few covert meetings. Other than that, we have little to show for many hours of surveillance."

"Are we following this colonel?"

"We were on him for several days, but he never moved and we were forced to call it off. The units were needed on other matters."

Burns nodded and Stanley began a summary of the Cerise Bevard murder investigation and the shooting of the man who invaded Bevard's home.

"We have been working closely with the local police on the two killings that you know about, and it is generally agreed that Imam Waladi is connected to both of them, but we don't have enough to charge him.

"All we really have is an Agency source in Pakistan making vague references to an imam in the D.C. area. We have no real proof that Waladi is the imam being reported on to the CIA, and we have nothing to say that the Pakistani air force colonel we have seen him with is the colonel al-Saad is talking about. It is precious little, while, at the same time, too much to just ignore."

"What does your gut tell you?"

Stanley glanced at Monte Sheppard for a silent confirmation before answering. "We are convinced we have the right ones."

"On what do you base this conviction?"

"Experience. Their covert meetings. The way Waladi moves around indicates that he has had some training in covert ops. When he got off of 66 Nightstalker never saw him emerge from beneath the overpass, and by the time ground units got there, he had disappeared. All we got from that is that he was headed south into Fauquier County."

Sheppard spoke out. "What al-Saad seems to be telling us is that the Pakistani military, at least a segment of it, is preparing to launch a military-style terrorist attack against the United States.

"That may seem bizarre, yet in May, Faisal Shahzad, the Times Square bomber, turned out to be a Pakistani national, trained over there, who returned here to act basically as a lone-wolf terrorist.

"It came out that much of the planning and financing was carried out in Pakistan and was undoubtedly backed by the TTP, the Pakistani Taliban. Pakistan went so far as to arrest an army major for being involved."

Burns cut in. "If you remember, the White House threatened a retaliatory unilateral military strike, if a successful terrorist attempt were ever linked to militants based in Pakistan. Maybe that's their goal, provide the direct link that forces the president to act."

"If that is their goal," said Monte Sheppard, "they haven't been paying attention."

"What does that mean, Agent Sheppard?"

"That it is obvious that this president isn't going to attack Pakistan or anyone else."

Burns glared at Monte Sheppard, "Politics is not a consideration in this room," he snapped. "Are you aware that the president recently invited the Pakistani prime minister to visit, in hopes of sorting out their differences?"

Sheppard, knowing better than to continue a political debate with a deputy assistant director of the FBI, stayed silent.

Lemon spoke up. "If al-Saad is telling the truth, they are going to require some type of aircraft to complete their mission. That fact, coupled with the use of attack gliders and highly trained military officers, makes this a much more sophisticated attack than a lone wolf parking an old Nissan packed with a homemade bomb in Times Square."

The lawyer from the Office of General Counsel was not a sworn FBI agent and therefore was not expected to contribute to discussions involving field tactics. The current FBI director had hired her out of the Department of Justice to fill a vacancy in the Office of General Counsel. On the rare occasion that she did offer advice, her words were given due consideration.

"If I may," she said. "It would be very expensive, and extremely chancy, for any foreign government to attempt to smuggle an airplane into this country, if they are concerned that any such attempt could be linked to that government. It is doubtful that they would bring an airplane over under cover of the diplomatic pouch. And, if we are to believe the lieutenant, the airplane will only be used the once; it would make sense for their advance agents to buy one privately. They could likely find one cheap on Craigslist, and with no questions asked."

"If," Stanley added, "al-Saad has given us the entire assault team, their airplane wouldn't need to be very large a single-engine private craft that accommodated the four of them and their death suits.

"They could stash such a plane anywhere. It is doubtful that they would leave it unattended at a public airport, even a private one. There are plenty of small landing strips in Farquier County, many with a barn big enough to hide it, or just parked in a field. Not too risky, as it is only for a few days, I wouldn't think."

"Our time may have shrunk dramatically," Deputy A.D. Burns growled. "With al-Saad being a no-show, they have no choice but to assume he is talking to us and proceed with haste. At least we must act on that premise. Let's focus on potential targets, see if we can come up with anything."

"I'm a licensed Pilot," Martin Lemon offered, "and all aircraft are subject to D.C. area special flight rules and restricted zone restrictions. I doubt very much that their pilot will file a flight plan for this airplane. Normally, it would set off alarm bells if any such craft penetrated the restricted zone without permission. But, from what al-Saad told us, their plane can discharge the wing suits outside the

THE CARROLL COUNTY FARMERS MARKET
3 Great Shows for Spring

SPRING FLING - MARCH 23, 2019

8:00 a.m.- 2:00 p.m.

EASTER SHOW - APRIL 20, 2019

8:00 a.m. - 2:00 p.m. - *Free Door Prize Drawing, Discount Coupons, Easter Bunny*

MOTHER'S DAY MARKET - MAY 11, 2019

8:00 a.m. - 2:00 p.m. - **Free Plant to First 400 Mothers**

Juried Crafters, Fine Arts, Plants, Gourmet Foods, Home Baked Goods,

Fresh Eggs, Jams & Jellies, Pasture Raised Meats

4 ENCLOSED BUILDINGS

For information call Anita (410) 848-7748

For All Market Updates go to

www.carrollcountyfarmersmarket.com

"like" us on **facebook**

Follow on instagram: carrollcountyfarmersmarketmd

Permit Holder Carroll County Agricultural Center, 702 Smith Ave., Westminster, MD 21157

Carroll County Farmers Market
706 Agricultural Drive
Westminster, MD 21157

***********ALL FOR AADC 210

M.L. WILSON
OR CURRENT RESIDENT
8 CAVAN DR
LUTHERVILLE MD 21093-5401

restricted zone and they can reach their targets with very little chance of detection."

Stanley injected, "al-Saad said that the wing suits won't show up on radar, but the airplane will be on radar as soon as they take off, and if they haven't filed a ..."

Lemon interrupted. "...If he is flying VFR, visual flight rules, he's not required to file a flight-plan. He'll show-up on radar along with hundreds of other aircraft and receive no notice unless he does something crazy. Even if he does do something, by then it might be too late."

Burns responded, "I think they will attack permanent, fixed targets a la 9/11—government buildings, naval vessels. Can you think of any circumstances which would allow us to rule out targets, other than the range of their airplane?"

When the agents were unresponsive, he turned to the attorney seated next to him.

She shook her head. "Sorry."

Eventually, Burns returned to Jason Stanley. "How thoroughly have we covered the area around the 66 exit where Waladi was last seen?"

"On his first trip, ground units crisscrossed the entire county for two days, looking for his Buick. They cruised parking lots, gas stations, anyplace we could think of. Nightstalker was up a couple hours each day before sunset. Nothing."

Deputy A.D. Burns stared at the leather folder balanced on the arm of his chair. Moments later he addressed Stanley.

"When I get back to my office, I'll have the FAA alerted to the significance of any radar blip coming out of Fauquier County."

Stanley and Sheppard nodded their understanding.

"Now," Burns continued, "this is a long shot, but I believe it *is* a shot. I want you to co-opt two of the sharpest investigative specialists in WFO. Tell them to pack a bag, collect their laptops, cellphones, anything else they might possibly need, sign out a Bureau car and get themselves down to whatever town is the county seat of Fauquier County. And, do it ASAP. I want them there tonight!

"They are to scour county land records, tax records and any other records that might show us anyone of Pakistani heritage who owns or rents land in that county."

To Stanley, he said, "They are to immediately report any results to you. Make certain they understand how vital this is. If they have any doubt whether a name they discover is Pakistani, they are to get that name to you for resolution.

"If anyone says, 'Isn't this profiling?', you're to answer, 'You're goddamn right it is.'

"Oh, one more thing. If Quinn gives you any crap about the assignment of his personnel out of the division, you tell him to call me. He may be your SAC, but he will answer to me on this."

56

Friday, August 13, 2010
Hume, Virginia

It had become quiet on the second floor of the farmhouse, the area that the Pilot had proclaimed to be territory of the Pakistani air force and thus off limits to Imam Waladi.

Colonel Muhammad bin Hassani had gone directly upstairs upon his arrival, and, immediately, someone began pacing the floor in the large bedroom overhead.

Waladi was certain that he was listening to the colonel, stalking angrily back and forth, while he assailed the Pilot and his team for the manner in which they had disrespected the imam, bin Hassani's very close friend and ally.

The pacing continued for several minutes and then ceased.

Waladi expected that the Pilot, and his band of Dead Ones, would directly appear before him, shamefaced, as they begged his forgiveness.

When minutes passed and no one appeared, Waladi, deep in thought, began to stride back and forth across the room, eyes downcast. This would be his sole opportunity to administer the scolding for which they were overdue. It was no concern of his that they were the Dead Ones with merely a few hours left on this earth.

Waladi turned to begin his trek back across the living room, and found the colonel waiting for him. He had changed from a business suit to khaki pants and a blue knit polo shirt.

Waladi was somewhat perplexed by the small alligator figure embroidered on the upper left chest of the garment.

"Colonel, I..."

"Imam, let us walk. The exercise will be healthful for us both."

Waladi glanced at his wristwatch. "I am ready to leave for home, I must prepare for the *Jumu'ah* Friday prayers."

"Of course. This will only take a few minutes. Come."

With that, bin Hassani turned and stepped off briskly toward the front door.

Waladi, reacting slowly and not willing to run in the blazing August sun, did not catch up to the colonel until they stood in front of the big doors to the barn.

"Ah, imam, Help me push these doors open."

Waladi glanced toward the house before stepping up to the massive doors."Why are we here?" he grunted, as the doors slid aside. "Are the others coming?"

Inside the barn, the sultry air was strong with a lingering smell of moldy hay; still, Waladi preferred it to the stifling heat of the outdoors.

The black STOL aircraft sat just inside the double doors. Bin Hassani motioned toward two ancient wooden milk crates, sitting on end, beneath one of the wings.

When both men were seated, the colonel began, "The heroes are not coming out here. They each have assignments that will keep them in the house.

"In any event, they do not need to hear of what we speak."

"When will I hear their apology?"

Hassani shook his head. "That is not going to happen."

Waladi indicated the cramped silver auto, still sitting where he had parked it, along the far wall.

"I'm sorry, colonel but that is unacceptable. And I expected you would be good enough to drive my Buick out here and take that turd with you when you go back...Don't tell me that stupid boy has damaged my car..."

"You must stop fretting about trivial matters. There are much more urgent things to be considered than your bruised feelings."

Bin Hassani leaned forward. "I am going to tell you what you have been pleading to know, and I can promise you that when our discussion is over, none of those petty matters will be of concern you."

A resentful Waladi, his lips pursed, sat back, crossed his arms and glared at the barn wall.

"Imam, do you know what is Camp David?"

Waladi shook his head.

"It is a retreat for the American president, located in the Maryland mountains." Hassani's glance moved upward, toward the airplane wing stretched above their heads.

"It is only about an hour from here, in this."

Waladi straightened. "Praise to Allah. When?"

"The day after tomorrow. Saturday, in the very early morning."

Waladi's smile broadened at the notion of an abrupt end to the Pilot, and his acolytes as well. "Brilliant! What a coup. Well done, colonel."

"What an interesting choice of words, imam, a coup. For that is exactly what it is."

Waladi frowned.

"The prime minister of Pakistan is to be the president's guest at Camp David for the weekend."

"How can you know this?"

"One of the P.M.'s security men is on our payroll."

"What does our prime minister have to do with our mission?

Bin Hassani stared at him in silence.

"I don't understand. Do you expect our prime minister to be blamed for a terrorist attack that kills the American president?"

"No! I expect him to die in a terrorist attack that the world will blame on your friends, the Taliban."

Waladi's shoulders sagged and no words would form. He stared at bin Hassani and eventually uttered, "Die? Are you saying that our mission here is to assassinate our own prime minister?"

"My dear imam, it is much more than that. Our present government has become too sympathetic toward the Taliban. This assassination will trigger a carefully orchestrated revolution within our country, designed to replace the present government so smoothly that the Pakistani people will hardly notice the change."

"But this Camp David must be well guarded when their president is there."

Bin Hassani gestured toward the horse stalls filled with devices of destruction.

"You give us too little credit. That is why we have the wing suits. The plane will fly well west of the target, near Hagerstown, Maryland.

That is where the attack gliders will leave the airplane and descend, unnoticed, into the camp."

Waladi stood. "This is utter madness. I want no part of in it."

"Sit down! I am not through."

Waladi, stung by the bitter edge in his friend's tone, quickly dismissed the notion of a dash to the compact car, parked a few yards away.

He spoke with a quiver. "Please be brief, colonel, I must get back to the mosque," he said, and sat heavily on the crate.

Forcing a last attempt at a bravado, Waladi added, "How can you expect that the Taliban will be blamed for this outrage?"

"Blamed? Those devils will not pass up the opportunity to take credit for such a heinous act. And, if the American authorities are able to identify your remains, and then dig deep enough into your background, which they surely will, your early history with the Taliban will confirm the Taliban's claim. Even though those jackels were unaware of your involvement."

Waladi was suddenly ashen, both hands flew to his head covering his ears. "No! No! This cannot be. I believed we were plotting against the Great Satan, the sworn enemy of Islam."

"That is what we intended you to believe."

Waladi, now more desperate, cried, "Do you forget, colonel, I am a servant of Allah."

"I have doubts about that claim, as well."

"What does that mean?"

"I know that you had that woman from the State Department murdered."

"I..."

"The FBI knows it, too. You did it because you lusted after that Afghani boy, Faheem. It was your relentless pursuit of this passion that got another boy, Wazir, killed."

"That's..."

"Don't say 'That is 'absurd,' Waladi. My sources in the American State Department tell me that the FBI is only days away from arresting you."

"It is absurd!" Waladi cried. "They have no proof ..."

"They are tracing the gun which the boy was holding when he was shot on the second floor of that house. The same gun you gave him to kill the Bevard woman.

"The boy was in the group who studied the Quran each Tuesday at your house, as was Faheem who lived at the woman's house And, they have a witness who says you threatened the woman's life, just days before she was killed."

"That's..."

The colonel abruptly held up a hand, silencing Waladi.

"What sort of man of God drinks freely from bottles of whiskey which he has concealed, and enjoys himself while he watches those videos which they call 'porn' in this country?

"I personally find the *bacha bazi* dancing disgusting. Your excitement over young boys dressing up as women and dancing exotically for your enjoyment is a perversion for any man, certainly one who professes to be a servant of Allah.

"Then there is the way you bully your wife and daughters...Oh, don't look so stunned. You have twisted the teachings of Islam to satisfy your own sickness for control of women. You have no secrets from us."

Waladi's shoulders sagged under these recriminations, and he was unable to raise his eyes.

"I believe," bin Hassani, continued, "that if I were in your *kameez,* I would deem this a blessing."

Waladi's head snapped up, a look of betrayal in his eyes.

"It will be a blessing for you," the colonel continued, "because, when your fate is reported, many of your friends in the Taliban, will consider you to be a hero. Most likely, the real truths about you will never be known. That is the best you can hope for."

The imam studied the colonel, desperate for an argument that might somehow prolong his life. "But I was not trained in these wing suits. You cannot ask me to be a *mer yaw*—a Dead One."

"My dear imam, this is not a request—you do not have a choice. You were selected with this moment in mind."

Bin Hassani again motioned to the horse stalls.

"Training is not required for you to wear one of those suits. Your mission will be accomplished regardless of where you land."

"That reminds me, I understand you very recently pleaded to be allowed to wear an attack suit. A perfect example of 'Be careful what you wish for.' Wouldn't you agree?

"The captain and sergeant are trained to achieve the results we desire.

"Unfortunately one of our attackers has failed to arrive as planned. We must assume that he has been taken by the authorities and act accordingly."

Waladi was buoyed slightly. "No doubt this attacker will have revealed your plan and the Americans will be waiting for the Pilot and the other Dead Ones?"

Bin Hassani shook his head. "That is precisely the reason we do not divulge the details of our plans to underlings until the last possible moment. The lieutenant knows nothing specific, and the little that he could reveal will be of no use to them before Saturday. Our mission is secure.

"And you should know that the Pilot is not one of the Dead Ones. He will fly the airplane back here, after you and the others, have jumped, and then return to Pakistan for the next assignment. Oh no, he is much too valuable to be wasted on this one mission."

Waladi shook his head slowly back and forth. "No," he muttered. "No! No! No! This cannot be."

Bin Hassani smiled. "If you should wonder about the airplane, it will be resold. An opportunity for additional *baksheesh*, if I'm not mistaken."

Waladi hung his head, a man thoroughly defeated. Softly he said, "Will you be good enough to see that my family receives my share of our *baksheesh*?"

"*Baksheesh* is a very involved process, no one can foresee the outcome, and I do not like to make promises I cannot keep.

"I will give you my word that your Buick will be returned to your wife. That is the best I can do."

The colonel smiled. "I have no doubt that if she had a choice between getting back you or the Buick, she would choose the automobile without hesitation."

Waladi maintained his silence, and eventually Colonel bin Hassini stood and held out his right hand.

"Your keys, to the 'turd box,' please."

Waladi remained seated. "They are in my room," he replied, making no effort to stand.

Bin Hassani displayed a small automatic pistol and pointed it at Waladi's head.

"Let's understand one another. In addition to taking your keys, that 'turd box' will be disabled. It is of no use to you. The only way you will leave here is inside that airplane. Get on your feet now and accompany me back to the house, where you will be locked in your room. It should be of some comfort that you will be allowed to keep your whiskey and pornography. If we find you to be too troublesome, you will be shot," bin Hassani waved the pistol at the horse stalls.

"Then stuffed in one of those wing suits and stored in the plane until it leaves here on Saturday. As I said, it will be unimportant, especially to you, exactly where you come to earth."

Slowly, Waladi stood and glanced at the compact car he disparagingly referred to as a "turd box." Next to it was parked the tractor he rode while mowing the field that will be used as a runway for the machine that would take him to his death.

He shook his head and turned to the colonel, "I want to say goodbye to my wife and daughters."

When Colonel bin Hassani did not reply the imam said, "It would be the decent thing to do."

"That would be true, in most cases, but your family hates you with such a fury, that the news of your death will no doubt cheer them.

So, no."

57

Friday, August 13, 2010
Washington D.C.

Supervisory Special Agent Jason Stanley cradled his desk phone and called to the squad secretary through the open connecting door.

"Helen! Locate Monte and Will and get them back here ASAP."

Helen rolled her desk chair back and gave him "that look."

"Please. And then please get Deputy A.D. Burns on the phone. If he's not there, ask them, very politely, to locate him."

Helen had been the secretary for the Counterterrorism squad for eleven years, enduring three supervisors in that span. Jason Stanley had been in the adjacent office for over three years and Helen read him as good as she had any of the others.

She located Will Kelly in the field, and when he began to resist leaving a surveillance to return to the office, she replied, "He wants you! Now!" and rang off to begin her search for Monte Sheppard.

Helen found that Sheppard was signed out to the firearms range in the basement.

After speaking to her, Sheppard completed the mandatory firearms qualification round. He quickly cleaned his weapon, arriving at Stanley's office just ahead of Kelly.

"What's up?" Will asked, when he walked in.

He jerked his right thumb upward in the accepted sign for "all clear," then jammed it down to indicate trouble.

Both he and Sheppard grinned when Stanley responded with a thumbs-up.

Supervisor Stanley motioned both agents to the chairs in front of his desk and was about to begin his briefing when Helen rolled back her chair and waved the telephone at her boss. "It's him," she mouthed and disappeared.

"This is Jason Stanley."

"I understand you have some news for me."

"Yes, sir. I have agents Sheppard and Kelly with me and I was about to fill them in. Can I put you on speaker?"

"Of course."

Stanley punched a button and Deputy Assistant Director Burns said, "Good afternoon, gentlemen."

The two agents mumbled responses as Burns continued, "I'm certain your message is positive, so let's have it."

"I just received a call from the two techs I sent at your instruction to Fauquier County. They have identified a 120-acre farm near Hume, which is registered in name of the Embassy of Pakistan."

Stanley held the phone away as the deputy A.D. shouted, "Yes! Yes! Yes, that is it. Great job. Go ahead."

"They looked it up on Google satellite. It shows a large barn situated at the end of a long, clear field which could easily serve as a runway."

"I want those two techs' names. They may have saved a lot of lives. Anything else?"

"That's it for now, sir."

"Who are you sending down there?"

"I'll be going with Sheppard and Kelly's surveillance squad. For now."

"I want your SWAT team down there."

"SWAT sir?"

"This is Friday afternoon. I can't see the bad guys waiting beyond the weekend, with their lieutenant a no-show. SWAT needs to be close. I'll call Quinn."

"Yes, sir. Anything else?"

"Agent Kelly?"

"Yes, sir!"

"You're the surveillance guy, right?"

Kelly stiffened and leaned forward. "Yes, sir. That's right."

"When we are finished here, I'm going down the hall to brief the director. I'm certain he will have no trouble okaying Nightstalker for this. Around the clock, at least through Sunday."

"Understood, sir."

"When you get down there, keep in mind we need to get a look inside that barn. Set something up."

Kelly grinned. "No problem, sir."

Stanley hunched over the phone. "You talking about PC for a search warrant—right, sir."

"We are suspending probable cause for the duration of this case."

"But, sir..."

"When this is over, the occupants of that farm will either be free or dead. It will never go to court."

58

Friday-Saturday, August 13-14, 2010
Hume, Virginia

This was their third pass by the dirt lane leading to the farmhouse listed to the Embassy of Pakistan.

Monte Sheppard drove while Jason Stanley, in the passenger's seat, maintained coverage of the area through Bushnell 10x42 binoculars.

"Still nothing," Stanley muttered. "I get a glimpse of some kind of building through the trees, could be the house. They're too thick to be certain."

The Cobra handheld radio beeped a warning and Stanley retrieved it from the seat beside him. "Go ahead."

Will Kelly said, "We finally made it close enough to see activity around the target. Don't dare get closer, but from here I see at least three subjects coming in and out of the big doors. Can't see inside. No point in staying here, We'll come back after dark and try to get closer, 10-4?"

"Sounds like a plan. Let's meet up before you go back in."

"10-4."

Stanley pressed the button and, again, spoke into the handheld radio.

"Count, can you see anything from up there?"

"Not much. I'm travelling in a race track circuit, so the target is only in my view for a minute or two out of every circuit. After dark, I'll be useless unless they are airborne. Besides, there are no high-profile targets for them to hit at night. They're not going to need an airplane until daylight. "

"Understood. Still, check in every thirty minutes."

"10-4."

After another hour of watching the dirt lane leading to the farmhouse, Stanley called one of the surveillance units to replace them.

Within minutes a black Dodge pulled alongside Stanley's door. He lowered the window and nodded to the two agents in the unit.

Through the open driver's window of the other car, Neal Brady asked, "What's the drill?"

Jason Stanley grinned. "Couldn't be easier," he said and pointed at the dirt lane. "Keep an eye on that road. If it moves, shoot it. Otherwise, if a car goes in, get a description and report it. If a car comes out, call a unit to replace you and another for backup. If these people are who we believe they are, don't take any chances. Follow the vehicle until your backup shows, then stop it and ID the occupants. Depending on what we have, it's very likely they'll be detained.

"For now, we're playing this by ear. Later, I'll be in touch with the B and have a plan for overnight."

Neal Brady whooped. "Are we having fun yet?" and the Dodge backed off of the road, under a tree.

The Farmhouse

Colonel bin Hassani unlocked the door to Waladi's bedroom and peered into the dim interior.

"Come. Join us for a meal, imam," he said.

Waladi rolled on his back and, shielding his eyes from the glare flooding the doorway, replied, "If I were a follower of Jesus Christ, this would be my 'Last Supper'."

"Regardless of your faith, it is indeed your last supper. If you want something to eat, you must have it now. Soon, we will go to the barn where there is still much to be done. Your flight leaves at 3 a.m. sharp."

"Not that it matters, but what is gained by taking off so early? They will be arriving on the target while it is still dark."

The colonel scoffed. "Not only they—you, too, will be arriving in the dark.

It is the only way to be certain where the target will be. The Prime Minister is an early riser. This Camp David has several separate cottages and, thanks to our informer, we know exactly which ones to strike. If we wait until daybreak, they could be stirring and our targets on the move.

"Our attack suits are equipped with night vision devices, ensuring that the Captain and the Sergeant will hit their target. You however, are free to land wherever you like."

The colonel glanced around the room, taking in the empty wine and whiskey bottles littering the floor. "Now, please come out of this sty."

When Waladi failed to respond, bin Hassani drew the handgun from under his shirt. "You are going to the barn with the rest of us. How you go is your choice."

FBI

Agents Stanley and Sheppard were parked on the side of Hereford Lane about 50 yards south of the dirt lane they were watching. Neal Brady and his partner were located the same distance north of the lane. Each unit was shrouded from casual view of any passersby by drooping tree branches heavy with wide maple leaves.

Fortunately, there had been no traffic along Hereford Lane since just before 9:00 P.M.

Stanley shifted his weight in a vain search for a more comfortable position. Behind the steering wheel, Monte Sheppard sat with his head tilted back, his mouth agape.

Stanley was appreciative of the fact that his partner had not yet begun to snore. The luminous dial on his wristwatch showed 10:58 pm. Kelly was due to call in at 11:00.

The Cobra handheld beeped and Jason heard Will Kelly say, "Still no luck getting a look inside that barn."

Stanley's voice was strained."What's the problem?"

"There's still a lot of activity with at least 200 feet of open ground between us. It's too risky. Much as I hate to say it, Jack and I will have to sit tight until they close up and go back to the house."

"Burns will go apeshit when he hears we haven't gotten a look inside the barn. Without confirmation of al Saad's story about the wing suits, we can't move."

"It sounds like one of those 'The fate of the free world is in your hands' situations?"

"Something like that."

"Thanks."

Monte Sheppard stirred, bumping his knee on the steering wheel. "Trouble?" He grumbled, and massaged his leg.

Stanley picked up his cellphone and punched in the speed-dial number for Deputy Assistant Director Burns' phone. "Yes. And I'm about to find out just how much."

Burns answered. "What's in the barn?" He asked.

"I have two agents in the woods as close to the target as they dare get. There has been constant activity around the barn all evening, so they haven't been able to get a look inside."

Burns' response was icy. "Do I need to personally explain to those two agents how urgent this is?"

Stanley rolled his eyes, which went unseen in the dark. "No sir, I have made certain that they understand your concern."

"Concern? Jesus Christ, man, concern doesn't begin to say to it. If there is an airplane in that barn and it gets airborne with those attack gliders...

"I have alerted the D.O.D and they have flight crews standing by at Naval Air Station Oceana, in Virginia Beach, and Wright-Patterson in Ohio.

"But I can't tell them what the target is or what to look for. We're beginning to look like fools. I didn't have the balls to tell them to be on the lookout for attackers in flying Batman suits.

"The next time you call me I want you to tell me what is in that barn. Understood?"

"Yes sir. Sir?"

"What is it?"

"Is there any chance that this not the right farm?"

Burns heaved a great sigh. "My gut tells me no, But if it turns out to be the wrong barn, we will have failed. And, as a result, I'm afraid a lot of innocent people are going to die."

Burns ended the connection.

Monte Sheppard was wide awake. "I could hear that over here."

When Stanley did not comment, Sheppard continued, "Look, it's early yet. The targets will be going into the house soon, our babes in the woods will get inside the barn and, *voila,* we can wrap this up and go home."

"If you heard it, you know that D.O.D has alerted the Navy and Air Force. Crews are standing by to intercept."

Sheppard shrugged. "It's not like I could make out the words—it was more his tone. This could get hairy."

"You think?"

"What if Will gets closer and lays down in the field where he can see in when they open the big doors. He sees an airplane and we move."

"It's not that easy."

"I thought that was what we were looking for— an airplane."

"That might be enough for probable cause to search the place. But it's way beyond that now. What we see will be relayed to jet Pilots and, if this airplane gets airborne, they will have to shoot it out of the sky."

"If there's a plane in there, what else could it mean?"

Stanley sighed. "I will wager that there are several other barns with airplanes in them within this county. None of which are going to be used in an act of terrorism. Crop dusters, rich farmers who like to buzz their poorer neighbors. Could be many reasons which do not justify telling the Air Force to destroy them. No, we need to see something in addition to an airplane. Ideally, the Batman suits."

"Close your eyes," Sheppard said. "I'm awake."

"You think I can sleep after the ass-chewing I just got?"

The handheld beeped, Stanley saw that it was a couple of minutes before 1:00 a.m. and depressed the 'push-to-talk' button.

Will Kelly said, "It's 1 o'clock, do you know where your terrorists are?"

"Jesus, Will, that's not funny."

"I thought you would like to know, the gang's all here. No one has left the barn. We can't figure out what the hell is going on. An all-night poker game? Do Pakistanis play poker?

"Jack and I are agreed that something is going to happen. We figure they are going to leave real early, maybe right after sun-up. We've been racking our brains over what their target could be that early. And got zip.

Stanley said, "I'll touch base with Nightstalker."

And then added, "FYI, no one has come in or out. All the players must be there. Watch your 6 o'clock."

"Always!"

At 2:55 a.m. Stanley answered the Cobra. Kelly was yelling, "Do you hear it? Do you hear it?"

"Now I can hear something. It sounds like an engine."

"The barn doors are open and an airplane is rolling out."

Stanley turned to his partner. "Call Nightstalker and have him get over the target, ASAP."

Struggling to keep his voice calm, Stanley returned to the Cobra. "Tell me what's happening."

Kelly was shouting to be heard above the roar of the airplane engine. His distorted voice signaled that he was already plunging toward the barn.

"It's turning toward the open field...engine revving...gathering speed..."

For a moment Stanley visualized the agent, chasing down a moving airplane.

Kelly was gasping for breath as his legs churned. "...will be taking off to the east... should be airborne in a couple of minutes...it's moving ..."

Now Stanley was shouting. "Give me a description."

"...black...single-engine...wings above the cabin...we're going inside..."

Stanley dialed Deputy Assistant Director Burns number. When Burns spoke, he sounded alert, awake.

Stanley strained to control the tremor in his voice. "Sir...the plane is taking off...agents are almost inside the barn..."

"Good work! Stay on this phone, I'll alert D.O.D. by landline and be right back."

Stanley, the cellphone held to one ear and the Cobra in the other hand, turned to his partner. "Where's Nightstalker?"

"ETA, one to target."

"Will! Will!" Stanley was now yelling to be heard above the roar of the airplane lifting from the ground, through the trees just behind them. "Jesus! Talk to me!"

When there was no response he turned his attention to Nightstalker.

"Have you got the target?"

The Count responded, "I'm coming from the south there is a black shadow climbing through 700 feet up ahead. That must be him."

All was silent for more than a minute until Burns returned to Stanley's cell.

"D.O.D. launched interceptors from Wright Pat and NAS Oceana. What's happening?"

"Sir. Nightstalker has picked up a dark image moving from the direction of the farm and is staying with it.

"Haven't received a report from inside the barn."

Burns voice was tight. "We need that report. We have no idea where they are headed or how soon the attack gliders may bail from the plane. Then it will be too late to stop them."

"Yes, sir. I'll try the barn now."

"Don't hang up," Burns directed. "Leave this line open."

"Yes, sir."

Back on the Cobra, Stanley was yelling again. "Will! Will!"

Stanley grabbed the microphone for the Bureau car-to-car radio. "C-2, get down to that barn and see if they need help. Take SWAT in with you. Let me know what's happened ASAP. And watch yourselves."

"10-4."

Stanley re-contacted Nightstalker. "Where are you?"

"The target is heading west at about 2,000 feet. I'm trailing him at 3,000 feet. He is flying dark. No lights and likely he has turned off the plane's transponder and radio. That's how drug smugglers sneak through."

"He's headed west? Keep us posted."

"10-4."

Stanley took a deep breath and turned to Monte. "Let's get down to the barn and see what's up."

Once on the dirt lane, Monte followed C-2's taillights as Neal Brady bounced along the rutted path just ahead of them. Both units skirted the dim porch light of the farmhouse and raced toward the barn.

At the barn, Stanley saw three figures standing in the square of light cast by the open barn doors. Will Kelly and his partner, Jack, each held an arm of a dark- skinned man, his hands cuffed behind him.

Stanley, out of the car before it had come to a complete stop, ran to them.

Will Kelly was grinning. "Agent Stanley, meet Colonel bin Hassani, air attaché to the Embassy of Pakistan."

In his free hand, Jack held out a small-bore automatic pistol. "When we came in he drew this and waved it around. It looked like a feeble attempt at 'suicide by agent.' But, you could tell his heart wasn't in it."

He turned to the handcuffed man. "Now he is demanding political asylum."

Will Kelly spoke out, "Jack, keep track of the colonel, while I show Jason what we found." He turned and Stanley followed him, digging out his cellphone as he walked.

"This is Stanley again, sir," he said into the open-line connection.

"What do you have to tell me?" Burns asked.

"I'm inside the barn with Agent Kelly. We have a Colonel bin Hassani, the Pakistani air attaché, in custody. Displayed in a horse stall is a carbon fiber attack glider wing suit, like the one described by

Lieutenant al Saad. It does look like a Batman suit. In the adjacent stall are the remnants of assorted explosives."

Stanley heard an audible sigh as Burns said, "Great news. I'll tell D.O.D. and then get back to you. Do nothing until you hear from me."

Burns rang off and Stanley turned to find Neal Brady standing behind him. "SWAT has secured the house. Nobody inside."

Monte Sheppard rushed through the doorway and thrust the Cobra at his supervisor. "Nightstalker!"

"Stanley!"

"The target has turned due north and seems to be following I-81. Still flying totally dark. High clouds obscure the little moonlight. If not for the night vision gear I couldn't keep track of them."

Stanley turned to Will Kelly. "Take the colonel into the house and don't let him touch anything. Burns will be sending down a team to gather up all of this evidence. Let's make certain it's all here."

"Gee. And I was just imagining how that wing suit would look standing in the corner of my den."

Burns' voice was shouting at Stanley from his cellphone. "Stanley! Answer me, Goddammit!"

"I'm here, sir!"

"Tell Nightstalker that the Air Force has launched an A-10 Thunderbolt from Ohio, and the Navy, an F-18 Hornet from Oceana. They'll be with him very quickly. Tell him to make certain they can identify the target. And tell him to get the hell out of the area as soon as they signal that they are locked on."

"Yes, sir."

"Now, I'm coming down there and take personal charge of the scene, and I'm bringing an evidence crew with me. Have one of your agents call me on my cell in 30 minutes and be ready to guide us to your location."

"Yes, sir."

"If I haven't said it, I should have. Well done, lad. Well done to all of you."

"Thank you, sir."

Jason Stanley passed A.D. Director Burns' orders on to Monte Sheppard, who went off to saddle some poor bastard with the burden of directing an FBI Deputy Assistant Director to the farm with daylight still more than two hours away.

Using the Cobra handheld, Stanley again contacted the Count in Nightstalker and repeated Burns' message about the two jets that would be joining him shortly.

"An A-10 has been dispatched from Wright-Patterson and a Navy Hornet from Oceana."

The Count snorted. "Tell the A-10 to stay home. I flew an F-18—it will be done with its business and back home...

"Standby," the Count said, breaking radio contact.

In a couple of minutes, the Count re-established contact. "I'm back," he said. "The F-18 has arrived and I was told, rather curtly, to get the hell out of the area. He was not interested in the fact that I am a former Navy Pilot with many hours in an F-18.

"Hell, I would be grumpy, too, if I had orders to shoot down an unarmed civilian aircraft. I feel for him."

"Never mind that. Did you get the hell out of their way?"

"Without hesitation."

"But you still have the show in view."

"I'm not about to miss this."

"Your 10-20?"

"Approaching the West Virginia line. What is he waiting for? The wing suits could bail out anytime."

"Maybe they..."

"OH... MY... GOD!"

"What?"

"The sky lit up like it was high noon for a few seconds. The target must have been loaded with armament. There were at least three explosions after the air-to-air missile hit. The target disintegrated."

56

Saturday, August 14, 2010
Montgomery County, Maryland

Jason Stanley was two blocks from his home when he pulled to the curb and dialed a number into his cellphone.

"Hello?"

"Delilah Bone, Jason Stanley. It has been a while. How are you?"

"I'm fine."

"And Faheem?"

"She's fine. Do you have some news for us?"

"There is news, but I'm too beat to go into detail. Turn on the TV and catch the breaking story. Whenever I wake-up, I'll fill you in."

"Faheem, turn on the TV." To the phone, Delilah said, "If you will tell me if the news is good or bad, I'll be patient."

"You won't be able to tell from the news account, but all is well."

The noon news contained only one breaking story, yet Delilah was still uncertain if it could be the news story Jason had called about.

While the video repeatedly displayed aerial footage of wisps of smoke curling up from a heavily charred wooded area, a voice-over reported:

*The Drug Enforcement Administration is reporting that
shortly before dawn this morning, a private plane believed
to be smuggling a large quantity of cocaine exploded in
midair in a remote area just north of Inwood, West Virginia.
The FAA is investigating the cause of what is described as a
horrific explosion and reports that there were no survivors.*

Faheem, muted the television and looked to Delilah, "What does it mean?"

Delilah, now certain that the real story behind that news account was indeed the happy ending to the FBI case code-named Trapdoor, smiled.

"I don't know. We'll keep watching the news for more, but it is quite possible we will never learn anymore."

Faheem folded her arms and frowned at the TV.

60

Tuesday, August 17, 2010
FBI Washington Field Office

FBI linguist Handel knocked timidly on the door of Supervisory Special Agent Jason Stanley's office.

Jason looked up from his desk and waved him in. "Handel, sit down. What can I do for you?"

"Oh, uh, thank you, sir." Handel rubbed both palms against the outer leg of his suit pants and shifted his gaze away from the man behind the desk. "But I won't be long."

"Fine. What is it?"

"Well, sir, I would like to thank you for giving me the opportunity to work on," he edged toward the desk, his voice barely audible," the Trapdoor case."

Stanley smiled. "You performed admirably, and you should know that Deputy Assistant Director Burns asked me to submit your name for a meritorious award for outstanding work."

Handel's face reddened and he shuffled his feet. "Thank you, sir. Um, sir, could I ask you a question about the case?"

"Of course."

"Do you know— when will a decision be made about Lieutenant al-Saad's request for asylum?"

"Lieutenant al-Saad and Colonel bin Hassani are both back in Islamabad. They flew out yesterday on a U.S. Air Force cargo flight."

Handel paled and grabbed the arm of a wooden chair as he sunk into the seat.

Stanley said nothing as he waited for the young man to recover.

Handel quickly rubbed his eyes before looking up. "But...he helped us...we said that if he helped us..."

"He was told that we would put in a good word for him with the State Department. And we did that."

Handel sat, his eyes gazing down at the desktop.

"There was nothing that could be done. Pakistan is an ally of the United States in the war on terror. Many believe that their government could do more—nevertheless, they are an ally.

"The colonel is the one who told us, albeit after the fact, that the plane was headed for Maryland, and the target of this attack, in which Lieutenant al-Saad was to have a major role, was the attempted assassination of the Pakistani prime minister, a guest of our country at Camp David.

"If the situation were reversed, and American military personnel tried to assassinate our president during a visit to Pakistan, we would demand their return to this country for prosecution. And the Paks would damn well do it."

When Handel looked up tears brimmed in his eyes. "...They are going to execute him...aren't they?"

"I'm sorry."

Thursday, August 18, 2010

Delilah Bone answered her cell on the second ring. "Jason Stanley. It's about time. That news flash you called about produced more questions than answers."

"Sorry, been busy," he replied, and then proceeded to answer all of her questions about the mysterious airplane which exploded over West Virginia, and other queries regarding, Trapdoor.

"Are you satisfied that Waladi was responsible for Cerise's murder and the reason that I was forced to shoot that poor boy?"

"We are. While Colonel bin Hassani has no evidence, he volunteered that Waladi liked young boys, and was scheming to get Faheem away from Cerise Bevard. I wonder—had Waladi known Faheem was a girl, would Cerise still be alive?"

"That bastard!"

"I must confess to neglecting my supervisory responsibilities regarding you and Faheem. Please, bring me up to date."

"Faheem and I have talked a lot, mostly about her future. She has said that when whatever was happening was over—and I am assuming that it is now over—she wants to return home and continue to be Faheem for as long as her Mother and sisters need her to be.

"It is her dream that someday she will be able to return to being Faheema, without fear of being stoned to death. Watch the news. I expect her to become an activist for women's rights in Afghanistan.

"And you're off the hook."

"Which hook would that be? There have been several, lately."

"It was only a few days ago that you sat here and promised to help her become a legal alien, if that was her wish."

"Yes. Well, that would have been very difficult to pull off, the way things turned out. I was hoping that Cerise Bevard's good will at State would help swing it."

Delilah laughed. "Cerise bequeathed this house and grounds to State, so that should have helped."

"Really! I hadn't heard. So have you and Faheem been evicted?"

"We're not waiting for that. I have lots of leave accumulated, and, now that Trapdoor has been successfully closed, we will be booking a flight to Dubai, connecting on to Kandahar.

I'm taking her home."

CPSIA information can be obtained
at www.ICGtesting.com
Printed in the USA
BVHW04*0736160418
513283BV00001B/2/P